The Sentinels: Requital

Cassandra Davis

2021

The Sentinels: Requital

Published by: D&S Publishing, Georgetown, Texas
Text and cover copyright © 2021 by Cassandra Davis
Definition of "requital" © Merriam-Webster.com

Cover art courtesy of Jeanine Henning, https://www.
jeaninehenning.com/

For information address:
Cassandradavis.author@gmail.com

ISBN print: 979-8-9851686-1-7
ISBN Kindle: 979-8-9851686-0-0

This one's for all my St. M's crew.

Thanks for the music, the laughter,
the support,
and your love.

TABLE OF CONTENTS

Chapter One 1
Chapter Two 6
Chapter Three 13
Chapter Four 17
Chapter Five 23
Chapter Six 29
Chapter Seven 36
Chapter Eight 42
Chapter Nine 49
Chapter Ten 57
Chapter Eleven 61
Chapter Twelve 69
Chapter Thirteen 74
Chapter Fourteen 83
Chapter Fifteen 92
Chapter Sixteen 97
Chapter Seventeen 104
Chapter Eighteen 113
Chapter Nineteen 120
Chapter Twenty 127
Chapter Twenty-One 136
Chapter Twenty-Two 144
Chapter Twenty-Three 152
Chapter Twenty-Four 157
Chapter Twenty-Five 166
Chapter Twenty-Six 177
Chapter Twenty-Seven 185
Chapter Twenty-Eight 191
Chapter Twenty-Nine 199
Chapter Thirty 207
Chapter Thirty-One 215

Chapter Thirty-Two 223
Chapter Thirty-Three 231
Chapter Thirty-Four 239
Chapter Thirty-Five 248
Chapter Thirty-Six 255
Chapter Thirty-Seven 261
Chapter Thirty-Eight 267
Chapter Thirty-Nine 274
Chapter Forty 283
Chapter Forty-One 291
Chapter Forty-Two 296
Chapter Forty-Three 306
Chapter Forty-Four 311
Chapter Forty-Five 317
Chapter Forty-Six 323

About the Author 327

f

requital (n): something given in return, compensation, or retaliation

CHAPTER ONE

Vivian stepped around a pile of rain-soaked blankets on the steps of St. Simeon's Catholic Church. She reached for the decorative metal door handles then stopped. The puddles started to leak into her three-year-old boots. Those blankets probably had a person rolled into them. Someone too down on his, or her, luck to make it the remaining five feet into the sanctuary.

She leaned over to gently shake what she hoped was a shoulder outlined by the increasingly sodden fabric. The bundle screeched like an offended eagle, flung dank wool into Vivian's face, and rolled away from her. Unfortunately for the woman, or girl—it was nearly impossible to tell her age—she rolled right down the stone steps.

"Oh no, I'm so sorry! I didn't mean to startle you. I just wanted to let you know the church has warm—"

"I don't need your charity, bitch! Don't touch me! Fuck you! Fuck you! Fuck you!"

The last "u" trailed behind the woman as she ran off into the gray twilight of an October night in Seattle.

"Vivian? Vivian, child, what are you doing out here in the rain?"

Now drenched and smelling of wet wool—with a dash of human urine—Vivian ruefully turned back to the church. Father John stood framed in the doorway. His clean-shaven face, prematurely wrinkled, was like a hearth on a cold winter night: safe and exuding warmth.

"Well, I was *trying* to be merciful. Or charitable. Whichever. Certainly not punctual." She turned her ballcap covered head to watch as the homeless woman turned into an alley. "Maybe I should go after her. It's not safe out there."

The priest grunted. "She knows that as well as you do." He looked over the head of his petite parishioner. "Well, child, are you going to stand in the rain all night or would you like to come in?"

"In, definitely in." She walked through the open door, trying not to wince as her boots squelched on the tiled floor.

Father John handed her a towel. She was never really sure where he kept them, but any time a parishioner came in from the street, he had a towel ready. If she was to turn and go back to her car, he'd conjure an umbrella, for sure. Hmm, maybe conjure wasn't the right word.

"Father, is it a sin to think of you as a magician?"

He laughed as he led her down a hall toward the basement stairs. "A magician? I don't believe so. Witchcraft is... frowned upon." He gave her a wink over his shoulder. "But I do not believe the Scriptures comment on the ability to pull rabbits out of hats." The priest wanted to ask the young woman what prompted her question, but he knew from experience that her mind was a whirlwind. He didn't really have the time to hear the wild tangents she'd traipsed down to start asking him the Church's feelings on magicians.

"I'm sorry I'm late, Father. I really tried. I even took that short cut through Columbia City."

"That's not a short-cut."

"Well, I know that *now*."

Father John pushed open the fire door at the base of the stairs and motioned her through. "Never mind about the time. I put Evan to work serving meals. You know, if he serves the full shift, he can eat too. It would be a shame to waste an hour of his work."

Vivian knew where this was going. "This is where you tell me that there's always more work than willing hands, and that I can earn my meal too."

"Well," the priest said, failing to cover his chuckle, "your first attempt at charity went so well..."

Vivian's shoulders slumped, but she knew when to admit defeat. She wordlessly handed the priest her towel and went to join the soup-kitchen serving line.

By the end of the following hour, her feet were dry but sore from standing in one spot. Her face muscles felt unnaturally stretched. Between her retail work, walking the five blocks between where she'd parked and the church, and serving dinner to the two-hundred men and women taking refuge in the church basement, she was exhausted.

"Hey, Vivian, you know you can check my work any time, right? We don't ha' to do it tonight."

"We skipped tutoring last week, Evan." She rolled her shoulders and re-did her blonde hair into a ponytail. "Let's finish eating and we'll try to get thirty minutes in before I take you home."

"Ah Viv, you don't gotta do that."

"I know I don't have to, but I'm going to anyway. Did you complete that assignment on Khan Academy?"

Evan, having cleared his plate, eyed her dinner roll. She pushed her tray his way. "I swear you keep your mouth full just so you don't have to answer my questions."

"Naw," he muttered around a mouth full of bread. "I di' the Java."

"I *know* you did the Java, it's the Trig I'm worried about."

The painfully skinny, unshaven teen shrugged unabashedly. "Doug says there's no Trig on the GED."

3

"That's all well and good for Doug. Not that he'd recognize trigonometry if it slapped him in the face, so I'm not sure you should take his word for it. He failed the GED twice last year. But it doesn't matter, does it? You're not taking the GED. You're going to graduate with a diploma and take the ACT. Then you're going to BCC for two years before you transfer to UW." She pronounced it "u-dub", as all native Washingtonians did.

"Yeah right." He carried both their trays to the dish line. He might protest, but any time Vivian mentioned the University of Washington robotics program, Evan's eyes lit up. Abandoned by a heroin addicted mother, then shuffled among multiple foster homes, Evan had spent a year on the streets before Father John found him a spot in a group home for at-risk teens. He'd given up hoping—or trusting—long ago. Ever so slowly, during their twice-weekly sessions, Vivian tried to convince him that he could make a better life for himself.

Vivian knew what it was like, that feeling that the grime, mildew, and darkness of the Seattle streets would swallow her body and soul. She'd spent just two nights in a shelter before determining that her car was a far safer option. Without the timely intervention of the priest, she would be eating all her meals in the church basement and living a precarious existence without a job or even a bed to sleep in.

After thirty minutes of studying, the pair left the church. "How far away did you park this time?" Evan pulled his too-large raincoat tighter around his body.

"Just up here. I wish they'd finish the construction. I'm tired of—oof!"

Evan grabbed her arm and jerked her away from the curb. A hybrid SUV turned the corner with two wheels on the sidewalk, skewed sideways toward them, then

4

straightened and sped the wrong way down a one-way street.

Before Vivian could catch her breath, a black motorcycle turned into the street from the opposite side of the intersection. The biker turned his helmeted-head in their direction, then gunned his engine and raced down the street after the SUV.

"Idiots!"

Evan laughed. "You tell 'em, Viv." He sobered. "Actually, please don't. I don't think we want their kind of trouble."

Just as she started to respond, flashing lights blinded them. Several Seattle police cars flew past, sirens wailing.

"Next time, remind me to park closer."

"Yeah. This is why I take the bus. So much safer."

After signing Evan in to his group home, and explaining to the night-monitor why he was out past curfew, Vivian trudged back to her car, ready to fall asleep on her feet. She reached into her coat pocket for her keys. Her hand brushed the edge of a card. Knowing what it was before she pulled it out, Vivian waited until she was in the car with the doors locked before examining the prayer card.

Father John was always slipping daily devotionals into her coat. He often wrote the names of local kids who needed tutoring or mentoring. This time, though, there were two words: Reed Investments. A number with a 206 area code was written underneath. Too tired to figure out why the priest thought she had money to invest, Vivian put the card back in her pocket and forgot about it.

CHAPTER TWO

Vivian had one day off a week. That one morning was precious. She got to sleep in, ignore her work emails, and enjoy the lack of people asking her questions all day. But, she was also actively job hunting, so her phone ringer remained on. When it started playing a pirated ring tone from "Breath of the Wild" at 8:30am, she stifled a groan. The number wasn't in her contact list, but it looked vaguely familiar.

"Hello?"

"Ms. Vivian Richards?"

She sat up in bed and tried to focus. *Collection agency or job lead?* "This is she." *Was that the right use of "she?" It always sounded so weird and stuffy.*

"Ms. Richards this is Angela Ghiadello from the Human Resources department of Reed Investments. Your resume has recently come to my attention and I'm wondering if you would consider coming by for an interview?"

"It has? What? I mean, uh, what is the position?"

"We have an opening for a systems administrator in our corporate office. Are you available next Monday between 9 and 10?"

"Uh, yes. Of course. Where—"

"Excellent. We'll see you then. I'll forward the details via email. Good morning to you."

Vivian stared at the phone. "What the hell just happened?"

It wasn't until she was standing over the sink, brushing her teeth, that she remembered the devotional card in her pocket. "Ah ha!" She winced as toothpaste splattered over the mirror. Father John, known to be both a romantic and career match-maker, was at it again. She grabbed toilet paper to clean the mirror. It was Friday. She'd see him at Mass on Sunday and have a chat.

"What the hell is this mess?" Detective Joel Kwon peered at the bloodstained floor. "Where's the body?"

His younger, blond partner shrugged. "No bodies, just a lot of blood—and I do mean a lot. It dripped through the floor into the apartment downstairs. Lots of H, though." Detective Adam Suisse used his thumb to indicate the table over his shoulder. Kilos of uncut heroin sat neatly stacked on the table.

Kwon's eyebrows moved fractionally upward, a gesture of extreme emotion for him. He looked at a crime scene technician kneeling beside the blood pool. "Is there any chance that our blood donors are still alive?"

"Sure, if there were three or more of them. If it's just one..." The young woman shook her head. "I'm taking samples and we'll test them to see how many victims you should be looking for."

"No victims in this," Suisse interjected. "This is a Triad stash house. That's a lot of lives saved with these drugs off the street."

"Unless," Kwon snapped, "there were more drugs, or guns, that the perpetrators removed before we got here."

"Ah come on, you and I both know who did this."

"No, *we* don't know." The senior detective pointed at the bloody floor. "Whoever did this is just as much a criminal as the people selling those drugs." He pulled his phone out. "I'm calling the captain. That's a lot of weight and we want it inventoried correctly."

Behind his partner's back, Suisse rolled his eyes.

Vivian lit a candle for her parents while she waited for the Sunday morning crowd to file past Father John. Trailing behind the last of them, she caught his eye and cocked her eyebrow.

"Good morning, Vivian."

"Reed Investments, Father?"

"Oh good, you called."

"Father, you know very well that I didn't."

"Walk and talk, child. The Lord's work is never done." He marched briskly down the aisle, stopping to collect stray papers, stow the kneelers, or pick up lose pencils. Vivian, almost unconsciously, helped on the opposite side of the aisle. "So Angela called you, did she?"

"Yes. I have an interview tomorrow."

"Wear that blue suit. You want to look your best."

"Yes Father." She didn't quite roll her eyes, but her tone implied the action. "What am I going to do at an investment firm?"

"They need a systems analyst, or designer, or some such. I'm never entirely clear on these things."

"Yeah, because you're so ancient and all."

He straightened, holding a soft-bodied doll in his hand. "Molly Prentice will be missing this. Did Amazon or Microsoft call you?"

She winced. "No."

"Because they have thousands of entry-level applicants every year."

"Day, more like."

He tutted at her interruption. "So, go and work for Reed Investments for a year or two, get the experience you need—while also earning a living wage and health benefits—then get your dream job with the big boys."

"I see your point."

"Well of course you do. Here, hold this for me while I go see where Mrs. Lampet has gone off to. The altar boys have left the Host out again."

Vivian stood holding the doll. Sunlight flooded through the high stained glass windows. A cool draft brushed her blonde hair against one cheek. For a fleeting instant she was transported back to her childhood home. Waves lapped against the pier; the ferry horn sounded; tourist children and their parents chattered as they walked down the hill.

"Vivian?"

She started. "I'm sorry, Father John. What did you say?"

He reached out to take the doll but squeezed her hand as he did so. "It's going to be OK. You'll see."

"Thank you, for everything. I'd better go. I have the afternoon shift."

"Go in peace." He started to make the sign of the cross, but she interrupted him.

"Wait... The HR lady said she had my resume. How did she...?"

"The Lord works in mysterious ways—sometimes through word processing and email. Now go. I'll see you Wednesday night."

"Hi. Vivian Richards to see Ms. Ghiadello. I have an appointment."

The receptionist wore a dark blue suit with a white silk blouse, a necklace of tiger's eye stones interspersed with onyx beads, and a French manicure on her nails. Her smile didn't quite reach her brown eyes. "One moment please." She tapped a button her phone, repeated Vivian's name, then said, "Yes, right away." She hung up and swiveled in her chair to come around the desk. "Follow me, please, Ms. Richards."

The woman swiped a key card on a door and held it open for Vivian to precede her. Muted tan and pine green carpet lined the hallways. Standard faux wood doors were evenly, if somewhat tightly, spaced on either side. Halfway down the hall, the receptionist—she hadn't offered her name—knocked once, then opened a door.

Angela Ghiadello had steel gray hair perfectly arranged in a French twist. Her tailored suit was of obviously expensive, honey brown material. The tiniest of crow's feet delineated the corners of her eyes. Like the receptionist, her smile was polite, but did not seem entirely genuine. She held out her hand. Vivian shook it.

"Welcome to Reed Investments, Ms. Richards."

"Thank—I'm sorry, did you say "welcome"?"

Ms. Ghiadello sat down behind her desk. She held herself erect without a hint of relaxation or ease. Those searching hazel eyes belonged behind steel-rimmed glasses, Vivian decided. "I did. You come highly recommended; your resume and qualifications are exactly what we're looking for."

"*My* resume? I'm an associate at a boutique electronics store downtown, and not the one with the fruit in the name! I've never held a systems administrator job in my life! I don't even have my degree yet. I'm sorry. I think you've been misled, and I'm wasting your time. I... I'll go. I'm sorry again." Vivian picked up her worn purse with the discolored bottom and rose to her feet.

"Sit down, Ms. Richards. You *are* Vivian Richards, aren't you?"

Vivian nodded. She gnawed on her lip to keep from crying.

"You tutor under-privileged teens in mathematics, volunteer at the St. Simeon's soup kitchen, work a full-time job, and have straight As in your computer science classes at UW?"

Vivian nodded again.

"Then you are exactly as advertised. I am not easily misled, Ms. Richards. You should keep that in mind should you think of trying in the future." She flipped a paper face down, scanned the next one in the stack, took out her pen, and scratched through one line. "This is an entry-level position. I understand you will need to keep certain obligations and give proper notice at your previous employment. Will three weeks from Friday be sufficient for your first day?"

"I... Yes?"

Ghiadello's eyes narrowed slightly. "Speak up. Do you want this job? Highly recommended or not, if this isn't what you want, I can find someone else."

"Yes! Please."

"Excellent." She rotated the paper she'd just edited and pushed it across the desk to Vivian. "That will be your starting salary. We provide full medical and dental starting immediately."

Vivian swallowed. She swallowed again.

"The second number," the Human Resources director continued, placidly, "is a signing bonus. May I suggest using it for proper office attire?"

As her brain struggled to process a signing bonus that was half of what she could make in a year, Vivian winced. She was wearing her best suit. She loved her heels—they perfectly matched the shade of her slacks—

11

but her left shoe *was* badly scuffed and a tad wobbly after getting stuck in a sewer grate the previous spring.

"Ms. Richards?"

Vivian blinked. "Sorry?"

"One more thing. You will be required to sign an NDA. Anything you see, read, or hear, while working here is confidential corporate information. This is an investment firm. Our client does not wish to have his business appear in the papers—or on the Internet."

"Client, singular?"

Ghiadello almost laughed. "You don't know, do you? The "Reed" in "Reed Investments" is Nicholas Reed. He is our CEO and only client."

CHAPTER THREE

Recalling the conversation four weeks later, Vivian shook her head. Of course she knew who Nicholas Reed was. She doubted anyone with at least a modicum of online presence didn't know of the billionaire playboy. His strawberry-blond hair and green eyes, combined with a jaw line most often referred to as "chiseled", would have had him on the front of every gossip sheet even without his antics. Until the day, four years previously, when he'd wrapped his Lamborghini around a Las Vegas highway divider, Reed had been infamous for his boozy escapades.

"Usually involving three or more supermodels," Vivian muttered to herself. Then she glanced around to make sure no one had heard. Fortunately, she was alone in the server room of Reed Investments. Her "office" was little more than a desk and chair in the corner of the server room, but it was *hers*. No more working retail fixing computers and smart phones she couldn't afford; she had a company laptop, and the company paid her phone bill. Her 2009 Volkswagen Rabbit might still look like a turnip cart in the garage, surrounded as it was by high-end Volvos, BMWs, and Mercedes, but she felt less self-conscious about her wardrobe. After her first paycheck, she'd purchased three new pairs of heels and two new suits.

One thing Vivian didn't like about her job was the isolation. Ms. Ghiadello had checked on her a few times in that first month. Beyond that, she'd only met a few of the night security guards. To accommodate both her class schedule and the needs of the firm, Vivian worked the 11-8 p.m. shift. She'd quickly learned that systems maintenance during business hours wasn't well received. After 6 p.m., when the lawyers, investment bankers, and their assorted staff departed, Vivian was free to install new software updates, reboot servers, and reconfigure networks. That also meant, though, that she spent her evenings practically alone in the building.

She was supposed to be working on her semester project for class, but something in the network access logs caught her eye. Someone had been, for weeks, constantly trying to breach the company's firewall. The somewhat disorganized logs for the company's different applications created so many needless files that the attempted intrusion had gone unflagged for weeks. The hackers kept hitting one particularly port on the Reed Investments main router. Vivian had noted in her first week on the job that the port was, inexplicably, set to "open". She'd locked it down.

That foggy mid-November night, a flood of connection requests hit the network just after 7 p.m.

"Oh, you persistent bastards. Well, let's see how long you want to play tonight." She started reverse-pinging some of the requests, trying to determine their point of origin. "Where are you hiding? Mmm, nope, you saw that coming. OK. So you've got some game."

After fifteen minutes, the hackers gave up. None of Vivian's trace-routes proved successful, though. Determined that the attempted hacks would not continue unpunished, Vivian spent the rest of her evening writing up a report. She emailed it to Ms. Ghiadello, then closed down her computer. She'd have to spend a few hours at home doing the schoolwork she'd planned to do in the office.

Before leaving the building, Vivian stopped at the security office on the first floor. She looked up at a hallway camera and waved. The door buzzed, allowing her entrance.

"Leaving late tonight, Vivian?" Dave Kaskoy smiled from his seat in front of multiple computer monitors showing the security camera feeds for the building. His sandy brown hair, blue eyes, and average height meant he could blend into any crowd in Seattle. The scars on his hands and his alert gaze set him apart from the usual tech worker or college kid, though. Dave had done a tour each in Afghanistan and Iraq.

"Yeah. Since I'm already late, though, I thought I'd stop and see if you needed anything."

"You know I'm all set. Don't you have tutoring tonight?"

She smiled. "No, that's Monday and Wednesday nights, thank goodness. If those hackers had made me late for my session with Evan, I'd be *really* pissed."

Dave's easy-going demeanor instantly changed. "Hackers?"

"Yeah. Not particularly skilled ones, but they are persistent. Nothing to be worried about. I've written up a report and sent it up the chain to Ms. Ghiadello. Anyway, they kept me busy. I need to get home and work on my project before bed. You're sure you're good?"

"Better for seeing your smile. See you Thursday?"

"Count on it. Night."

He buzzed her back out of the locked room. She took the stairs back to the basement, jiggled the door to the IT department to make sure she'd locked it, then continued down the hallway to the parking garage.

Dave watched, via security cameras, Vivian walk to her car, then saw her car leave. He dropped the heavy gate over the entrance and exit of the garage. After confirming that motion detectors were set in the rest of the building, he sat back to contemplate what Reed Investments newest employee had told him. While hackers were definitely the purview of the IT department, they also presented a larger security concern. Nicholas Reed didn't need his company's data held hostage by ransomware. The twenty-eight-year-old billionaire also had more than a few personal secrets to protect. Dave typed out a quick email to Dominick Fehr, Head of Security for the Reed family and businesses.

Vivian reached her apartment building, pulled into the cramped underground garage, and walked as quickly as possible to the stairs. The garage smelled of mold, while the stairwell reeked of urine and garbage. She held her door key protruding from between her clenched fingers until reaching her fifth-floor apartment. Only once she was inside with the deadbolt thrown, two chains across the door, and her little motion-detecting camera set up in the doorway did she relax.

Less than a mile from where Vivian fitfully slept, a lean figure clad in bike leathers and Kevlar slipped down an alley. He crouched beside a dumpster surrounded by a miasma of two-day old fish. Two discarded syringes rolled underneath his left boot. Several deep breaths later, the man, certain he was alone, rose onto the balls of his feet and jumped up. He hung by his fingertips for just a moment before pulling his chin level with the window. Swinging by one hand, he taped a flat disk against the base of the grimy window. Listening device planted, the man dropped to the ground. Despite landing gracefully, he rose slowly. As he slipped away into the shadows, he limped slightly.

CHAPTER FOUR

Nicholas Reed didn't like his office at Reed Investments. It was small, furnished with heavy dark furniture that made it feel even smaller, and reminded him of his father. He could have chosen a larger office in any of the family's many buildings or worked from home. He chose to work out of his father's old office precisely because he didn't like it. It was an act of penance—one of many.

The wind was blowing a mixture of sleet and rain off the Sound. The other office workers had left two hours earlier, trying to beat the traffic snarls. Nicholas bent his head first to one side and then the other, trying to relieve the ache in his neck. Multiple medical professionals had assured him that he couldn't actually hear his repaired vertebrae grinding against each other. Multiple medical professionals had also informed him he'd never walk again. He tended to ignore all of them.

"That's the third pained sigh in thirty minutes. Let's go home, sir." Dominick Fehr, Nicholas's bodyguard and chief of security, stood from his chair in the corner of the room.

"Why is it "sir" when you're mothering me but "Mr. Reed" when I've irritated you?" Despite his grousing, Nicholas was already stacking papers and shutting down his laptop. He stopped when Dom's phone gave off a three-tone alarm. "The house?"

Dom shook his head. "Here." He tapped a few keys on the phone. "Door alarms in the basement." He removed his suit coat, leaving his shoulder holster more readily available. "I don't suppose you'll stay here if I ask you to?"

"Have I ever?"

Dom sighed but led the way out of the fourth-floor office. They took the stairs instead of the elevators. Dom glanced at his phone once more as they reached the basement. He grunted in surprise. "Someone in IT must still be working. The servers just locked down."

As they edged out the of the stairwell door, Nicholas kept watch behind them. Dominick, gun now drawn, moved toward the server room. The heavy steel-framed door was open. Shouts echoed from within the room.

"Bitch! You will unlock it now, or he dies!" A man of medium build, his head covered in a ski mask, held a gun to the kneeling form of Dave Kaskoy. The security guard's hands were bound behind him with flex-cuffs. A rivulet of blood trailed down the left side of his face. Another masked individual, shorter and thinner, held an enraged blonde woman by her elbow.

The blonde girl looked at the man threatening Dave. "No."

"No? No what, bitch?"

"No, I won't unlock the servers and no you won't kill him. If you want my help at all, you'll let him go and put those guns away." She stared up at the gunman, cool as ice. "If you could get what you wanted without me, you'd have already killed us. Good luck getting into our systems without my cooperation." Her blue eyes narrowed. "Wait... was that you, Tuesday, that tried that sloppy hack?" Her eyes flitted sideways almost imperceptibly, taking note of Dom and Nicholas sliding into the room. She snorted. "You're better off just smashing everything with a hammer!"

"Shut up!" The gunman, enraged by the petite blonde's failure to comply, stepped forward. That motion took his gun away from the side of Dave's head.

Dominick took that opportunity to step across the room in three quick strides and press his 9mm against the gunman's head. "Drop your weapon. You, let go of the lady."

Before the man holding her arm could respond to Dominick's order, the blonde whipped around, swinging her computer mouse by the cord. The mouse hit her attacker right in the ear. He yelped and staggered back, stunned by the surprise attack.

Dominick and Nicholas gaped as the woman raised her arm for another swing.

Nicholas stepped forward and used his cane to knock the legs out from under the man. "Now, both of you, get on your knees and interlock your fingers behind your head."

Dominick pulled off their masks. The smaller man looked young and had a vacant expression. The older of the two, the one who'd been pointing the gun at Vivian, had shifty eyes and a sallow complexion.

The threat contained, Nicholas took a longer look at the young woman. She still stood by her desk, holding her unplugged mouse by the cord. She was a touch too pale; it made the light scattering of freckles across her cheeks and nose stand out. Her hands trembled slightly. When he reached out a hand, she jerked backward.

"Sorry. Easy. I'm Nicholas Reed and this is my chief of security, Dominick Fehr. Are you OK?"

"I know who you are," she snapped. "And, no! I am most definitely not OK! I don't like guns and I don't like having them pointed at me by incompetent assholes!"

Nicholas briefly wondered if *competent* crooks pointing guns at her head were somehow acceptable.

He didn't get a chance to voice the question because the little blonde surged forward. She looked... fierce.

"Miss, I can't let you kick them. They're in custody.

We'll have to wait for the police." There was just a hint of amusement underneath Mr. Fehr's professional tone.

"Well, the police won't let me kick them either!"

Nicholas couldn't help himself. He laughed.

She whirled on him, but the sudden movement must not have agreed with her. She turned even paler.

"Miss, you're going to want to sit down now."

"No, I think... Oh no." Vivian just barely made it to the wastebasket before she vomited.

Nicholas looked flummoxed. Dom cleared his throat. "Restroom's two doors down. Grab a few damp paper towels?" Once his boss was out the door, Dom turned his attention to the young woman. "You're Vivian Richards, right? You started last month?"

Sitting on her knees on the tiled floor, having just yakked into a trashcan, Vivian looked up at the tall, deeply tanned man. His black hair and beard were neatly trimmed. The expensive slacks and dress-shirt he wore did not make him appear any less threatening.

"Yes." She took a few deep breaths then leaned to the side to see her friend. "Dave, are you all right? Do you need a doctor?"

"I'm fine, Vivian."

She wrinkled her nose at the smell from the trashcan. "So much for making a good first impression on the boss."

"Oh, I don't know. That was fast thinking, locking down the servers."

"Did she really hit him with a *corded* mouse? Who even uses those?" Dave moved, gingerly, to one of the spare office chairs in the room. "Maybe I imagined that part. My head really hurts."

Vivian snorted. "So much for being 'fine'. Yes, I use a corded mouse. I haven't had a chance to upgrade peripherals."

"Arguing with someone who has a gun pointed at you is not very bright." Nicholas came back into the room, leaning a bit more heavily on his cane. He handed Vivian the paper towels. After she wiped her mouth and hands and deposited the used towels in the trash, Nicholas held out a hand. He pulled her to her feet but didn't instantly release her hand.

"Thank you for saving my company's data, Miss Richards, but please know that your life is far more valuable to me than anything else in this building."

She blinked up at him. He towered over her by at least a foot. "Oh. Um, thank you. Thank you for coming to my rescue."

"My pleasure. Would you like to wait in my office until the police arrive? Dom, I assume you've called them?"

Dominick gave him an offended look.

"I... Thank you for your offer but I think I'd better stay here. Oh!" Her exclamation startled the five men in the room. "Should I unlock everything? Will the police need to do a forensic analysis of the servers? There's proprietary data that will need to be quarantined. Not that we, I mean, you, I mean your company, have anything to hide, but I'm not sure I trust the SPD to be poking around through *all* the files. In fact, I should probably just provide them with security logs and..." To the bemusement of both Nicholas and Dom, she spun around, plopped down in her chair, and began typing at lightning speed.

Nicholas leaned toward Dominick. "What just happened?"

"I really have no idea."

CHAPTER FIVE

The Seattle Police Department's response time was even longer than usual. Dominick had both assailants bound and under guard. Dave, seated in a chair at a nearby workstation, pressed gauze against the cut at his brow-line. Nicholas paced back and forth, his cane clicking unevenly on the floor. After his fifth or six pass, Vivian wordlessly pulled a chair from the desk beside hers. She pointed at it, not pausing in her scrolling. Nicholas caught Dom's eye and raised an eyebrow. Dom and Dave both grinned and shrugged. Nicholas took a seat. His hip *was* bugging him.

When the patrol officers arrived and took the two men into custody, they informed Vivian, Nicholas, and Dominick that they'd have to wait to give their statements to the detectives. Ordered to go with the paramedics to have his head wound checked out, Dave's statement would be taken later. Already flagging before any of the excitement, Nicholas grumbled in frustration. He wanted to go home and sleep.

"I can call Johann, have him take you home."

Nicholas glared at his bodyguard. "I'm not leaving my employees alone to deal with this mess."

Vivian, who hadn't said much in the previous half-hour, tilted her head to one side. She looked like an inquisitive cartoon owl. Her blue eyes swept over the tall, suit-clad executive. He wore his facial hair in a perpetual two-day scruff. The ginger hairs almost succeeded in hiding the scars along the right side of his jaw. "Why? Mr. Fehr seems very competent. I think we're both more than capable of giving an accurate accounting of what happened. Is there something you're afraid we'll leave out? Or something we'll say that we shouldn't?"

"What?" Nicholas, more shocked and baffled than angry, nearly shouted the question.

Her head tilted another degree. "I don't understand what part was unclear. You should go home, Mr. Reed. I will have a full reporting of any potential security breaches on your desk by tomorrow morning. I don't know of anything that would reflect badly on you or your company, so I can hardly reveal some corporate secret."

Anger deepening his voice, Nicholas replied in clipped words. "Your life was endangered on my property, while you are in my employ. This is my responsibility."

"Well that's paternalistic."

Sensing an imminent explosion from one or both of them, Dominick opened his mouth to intercede. Two detectives from the SPD walked in, interrupting any further argument.

"I'm Detective Kwon; this is my partner, Detective Suisse." Kwon had short-cut, graying hair, was clean-shaven, and of average height. His partner was a white man with wavy white-blond hair and blue eyes so pale they looked almost gray. Frowning at Mr. Fehr, Detective Kwon asked, "Do you have a permit for that firearm?"

The security chief, whose weapon was holstered, reached into his wallet and pulled out two cards. "I'm former FBI. I also have a Washington concealed pistol license."

Kwon looked over the cards before handing them back. "Playboy's bodyguard is kind of a step down from the Bureau." Although the insult was delivered in the blandest of tones, it was obvious to everyone in the room that the detective said it to gauge Dom's reaction.

Dom shrugged. "Yeah, but the pay's way better."

Detective Suisse hadn't said a word since entering the room. His full, unwavering, attention was focused on Vivian. He flipped open his notebook and approached.

"You are?"

"Vivian Richards. I'm the systems administrator for Reed Investments."

"And you live in Seattle... now?"

"Uh, yeah. For the last four years. Have we met?"

"I don't believe so. Please tell me what occurred here tonight."

"I work later than the rest of the staff because I have to fix stuff when it's not in use. Dave, one of the night security guards here, usually stops by on his rounds. Tonight, right after he came into the room, those men pushed their way in with guns and hit him in the head. I locked the company systems down, which triggers an alarm. The gunmen wanted access to our files. I refused. Then Mr. Fehr and Mr. Reed showed up and disarmed them."

Vivian felt Nicholas watching her as she gave her statement. The one time she dared to glance over at him, his green eyes stared back. She didn't know what emotion his expression denoted. He made her uneasy, but she couldn't put her finger on why.

"Wait. A guy with a gun to your head asked for access to a bunch of computers and you said "No"?" Detective Kwon asked the question, having walked over to hear her version of events. "Why would you do something so stupid?"

"I didn't put that much thought into it. I guess... I guess he pissed me off."

This time Nicholas managed to contain his chuckle. This spunky IT girl confused, irritated, and definitely amused him.

The detective faced Nicholas. "Mr. Reed, do you have any idea why someone would wish to access your servers? I mean, a reason that would drive someone to use physical force. Cyber-crime rarely involves armed assault."

"I have no—"

Vivian interrupted, "They weren't very good hackers. I'm ninety percent certain this is the same group that recently tried a brute force intrusion. I mean, in coding terms it was brute force. When that failed, they probably thought they could just walk in here and carry out a hard drive. Too much TV."

Looking back and forth between her and Nicholas, the detective asked him again, "So, any ideas?"

"Beyond what Miss Richards already said? Nope. I didn't know anything about a previous hack. I assume because it wasn't a serious threat."

"I wrote a damn report," Vivian muttered—just barely—under her breath.

"We cannot condone bravado or vigilante actions when faced with armed gunmen."

Sounding on edge, Vivian asked, "What about armless gunmen?"

Dominick averted his face so that no one but Nicholas could see his grin. Once he'd stilled his features to a more professional set, he asked the detectives if they had any further questions.

"No, but we would recommend greater security for the company and Mr. Reed until the motive for these attacks has been determined."

"And Miss Richards?"

The older detective glanced at her. "She wasn't the target of the attack. I would think that she is as safe as any of your employees." There was a certain bite to his words. It was Vivian's turn to look confused.

"I am concerned with the safety of *all* of my employees, Detective Kwon."

"Ms. Richards, would you like a ride home?" The junior detective, Suisse, smiled kindly at her.

"That won't be necessary," both Vivian and Nicholas said. Nicholas continued, talking over her protests, "We'll see that Miss Richards is safely returned home."

"Detectives, I'll see you out." Dominick motioned toward the door. The detectives filed out, leaving Vivian and Nicholas in a staring match.

"I'm perfectly capable of driving myself home."

"No one said you weren't."

"I still have work to do."

"You can finish it tomorrow."

Vivian bristled. She didn't want to admit it, but she was exhausted. The adrenaline high that had kept her upright and focused for the past two hours was definitely gone. She really just wanted to curl up under her quilted comforter and not come out for two weeks. She needed the job, though. What would a professional server administrator do? *What would a professional do after having a gun shoved at her head?* That ridiculous question elicited a hysterical giggle. She saw Mr. Reed's sharp glance. "Fine. I need to write an email to the staff, letting everyone know why systems are locked down until we can initiate a forensic audit."

"Can you do the audit on your own?"

"I guess we'll find out."

Nicholas shrugged on his suit jacket and held out her purse to her. "I'll get someone to help you."

"Do you... *we*... have other IT staff?"

"Surely. It's not really something I've considered, to be honest."

"Oh, of course. Good point, really. Why would a billionaire CEO know every support staffer in every company he owns? I mean, that'd take a super-human level of focus, wouldn't it? I suppose you wouldn't have met me if those idiots hadn't broken in here."

Nicholas paused, wondering if there might be an insult buried in there somewhere. Then he decided he was too tired to care. "Mmm. Let's get you home, Miss Richards."

"This really isn't necessary. My apartment is really out of the way and—"

"Miss Richards, I am exhausted. Can this disagreement wait, please? Mr. Fehr will follow you home."

When they reached the executive level of the parking garage, Nicholas held out his hand. "I regret the circumstances, but it was a pleasure meeting you. I look forward to working with you."

Vivian shook his hand but didn't quite process what he'd said until he was walking away. She looked up at Dominick. "Wait, why would he be looking forward to that?"

"Because you're one of two people in the building who's said no to him in the past two years?" The tall head of security held open her car door as she climbed in.

"Oh. Really? Who's the other?"

Dominick smiled down at her. "Me... but I certainly didn't do it the first time I met him."

CHAPTER SIX

Vivian woke up the next morning with a screaming tension headache and the nagging feeling that she'd forgotten something. Only after her second cup of coffee did she remember a meeting with her faculty adviser. A glance at her phone confirmed that a quick shower was all she had time for. Her adviser didn't tolerate tardiness. In fact, she often retaliated by making late students wait for an hour outside her office rather than re-schedule. Vivian certainly couldn't afford to be late to work after the previous night's excitement.

Since she'd overslept, then rushed to campus, Vivian didn't check her email until she sat down—five minutes early—outside the adviser's office. A terse two-sentence email from Reed Investments Security department informed her that a car service would pick her up at her apartment, take her to the office, then take her home at the end of her workday.

"Seriously?!"

A student across the narrow hallway jumped at her exclamation.

"Sorry," she mumbled. Her first instinct was to reply with an expletive-laden rant. That, upon reflection, seemed a tad unprofessional. She had barely enough time to type out a (hopefully) polite response informing the security staff that the car service would be pointless as she wouldn't be at her apartment at the appointed time.

After a thoroughly worthless advising session, Vivian made it to the office only an hour later than usual. She parked in her customary spot—in the far back corner of the garage under a huge pipe that occasionally leaked condensation onto her car's hood—and swiped her key card for building access. She'd just made it to her desk when Ms. Ghiadello came around the corner.

"Good afternoon, Vivian. As soon as you've had a moment to drop off your things, Mr. Fehr wants to see you in his office and Mr. Reed wants a full report on that recent hack attempt. Oh, and we need that forensic audit finished by Monday. We can't have the office shut down for too long."

"Good afternoon, Ms. Ghiadello. I did send you that report on the brute-force intrusion attempt. Would you like me to re-send it—"

"No, no, that's quite all right. I'm sure I have it." The older woman paused. Her lips, covered in a red-brown shade of lipstick, thinned. "I feel it necessary to remind you that you signed an NDA when you started with us. That document covers *anything* that occurs within this building."

Unsure how to respond to that warning, Vivian nodded mutely.

"Very well. Don't keep Mr. Fehr waiting."

Mr. Fehr's office, it turned out, was right beside Mr. Reed's office. There wasn't a desk for an executive assistant outside either of their doors. Vivian hesitated, then knocked on Fehr's door. No sound came from the other side. She knocked again. She heard a male voice in Mr. Reed's office say something. Tired and anxious, she didn't stop to think. Without knocking, she turned the knob and walked into the office of CEO Nicholas Reed.

She didn't know what she was expecting, but the darkly furnished small room was not it. There was only one window, covered in thick blinds. In front of that window, looking down at the street, was a tall man with slightly curly, strawberry-blond hair.

"Look, Mr. Reed, I need this job. You don't need to worry that I'll go blabbing to the media. I also don't need your charity, or a driver. Please find a different way to assuage your over-protective security needs."

The man at the window turned, but the dim afternoon light didn't immediately illuminate his features. "O...kay?"

It was the voice that finally clued her in. By the time he stepped into the light, Vivian realized she wasn't talking to Nicholas Reed. The man had to be a relation, though.

"Lee Reed. Not the CEO, definitely not your boss, but can totally commiserate on the over-protectiveness of my brother's commands." He thrust out a hand.

"Vivian Richards. I was looking for..."

"My brother. I know. Story of my life, really. Always the second-best son." There was just a touch of irritation in his jovial tone. Maybe an inch shorter than his brother, Lee still retained some of the gangling frame of a teenager. He had the same gold-tinted red hair, a few more freckles, and eyes a paler shade of green. There were no scars on his face or hands, and no accompanying cane. Vivian tried to remember everything she'd read about Lee Reed.

"Aren't you the good son?"

He laughed. "Oh, I like you. Stay, please. As you can see, my brother isn't here. I'm left to wait on him too."

"I was actually looking for Mr. Fehr."

"They'll be together. I think Dom was included in my brother's hip replacement." He looked at her expectantly. "Because they're joined at the hip? No? See, even my jokes are second-best."

"I can't compare, as I am unaware of Mr. Reed making jokes. It was nice to meet you, Mr. Reed—"

"Lee, please!"

31

"—Lee, then. I'll just wait on Mr. Fehr out there." Vivian turned to go, but Lee followed her.

"So, a car? Why's that irritating you? I like it, having someone fight the traffic while I scroll on my phone in the back seat. Saves gas money too!"

"Have you ever had to actually buy gas, Lee?" Vivian looked down the hall, hoping to see the head of security on his way.

Lee clutched his chest. "She shoots and scores a mortal blow! But wait, no, our hero refuses to be dismissed." He leaned against the wall with his hands in his pockets. "Come on, tell me what my poor, cursed, brother has done to earn your ire."

With no way out of the conversation in sight, Vivian sighed. "I don't need to be rescued. I just want to do my job, finish school, and meet my responsibilities. I certainly don't need a car service wasting their time and energy to drive me all over the city."

Lee shrugged again—it seemed to be a habit. "Fighting him on something little like this won't help. He'll just dig in his heels. Trust me. He's decided he has to make amends or take care of you for some reason, and there's nothing in this world that will stop him. It's *so* tiresome."

"I find a firm "no" works wonders."

Lee laughed. "No one tells my brother "no". Not our father, may he rest in peace, or my mother, and certainly not my sister or me. Well, mostly Jess just ignores him and does what she wants."

The elevator dinged halfway through Lee's recitation of family members bullied by Nicholas Reed. Vivian tensed, physically willing Nicholas not to be with Mr. Fehr. For once, she caught a break. Fehr was alone.

"Mr. Reed." His deep voice had just a touch of a Middle Eastern accent. Vivian hadn't noted it before.

"Your brother is briefly detained with one of the lawyers. You're welcome to wait in his office. Miss Richards, please join me." Fehr motioned toward his office.

"Farewell, brave lady! When you think of me, please do so with a smile!" Lee waved as he backed into his brother's office.

"He wasn't bothering you, was he?" Fehr patted the back of a chair as he passed it. He settled behind his desk, watching her.

"No. He seems harmless." She immediately blushed. "I mean, I really just met him and certainly have no opinion of Mr. Reed's brother..."

Fehr smiled as he raised his hand. "Please, no need to apologize. Lee really *is* harmless. Also, slightly clueless. I understand from my staff that you refused the car service Mr. Reed ordered for you?"

She took a deep breath, ready to launch into battle. "I just really don't see the need and it's a wasteful expense that—"

He interrupted her by raising his hand again. Small crow's feet, finely etched in the acorn-brown skin around his eyes, crinkled together as he smiled. His teeth, surrounded by his dark beard, shone. "I don't disagree. Can we compromise on a panic button for you and your car? Just until we're sure this isn't something more... serious?"

For this first time since the intruder had pulled the gun out of his waistband the previous evening, Vivian felt a twinge of fear. "Is there any reason to think it's serious?"

"Not that I can see, but you know tech far better than I do. Just a week, with the panic button but no other intrusive security measures. Until you're finished with your audit?"

"I... I can live with that. But... What good will a panic button do? It's a long drive from Medina to my apartment. I think calling 911 would be much faster."

"We don't all live in Mr. Reed's family home. As it happens, Johann, one of my trusted security consultants, lives not far from you. I assure you, he can get to you *much* faster than SPD."

"How is Dave?"

"He needed a few butterfly strips on that gash and has a mild concussion, but otherwise he's fine."

"So, I'm not in danger of being fired?"

He laughed. "Fired? Why would you... oh, Angela reminded you of the NDA, didn't she? Well, that was unnecessary. You don't strike me as someone stupid enough to talk about a break-in at your workplace." He leaned forward slightly. His smile reassured the young woman. "I want to ensure you're aware that our company health benefits cover any counseling you might need, and that you have plenty of time off, if you need it. Mr. Reed cares about the mental health of his staff. No, really." He responded to her snort. "He understands about trauma better than most of us."

Vivian winced at her own callousness. "Sorry."

"Again, no need to apologize. I'll have Johann stop by to introduce himself and go over the panic procedures with you. Do me a favor, Miss Richards? Take it easy on the guy."

"Uh...?"

"You're rather intimidating, and he's shy." He said it with a wink.

After watching the woman get on the elevator, Dominick Fehr turned and entered Nicholas Reed's office without knocking. Nicholas looked up from his laptop screen. "How'd that go?"

"As I predicted. She'll take the panic button."

34

"So you won her over." Nicholas leaned back in his chair, thinking.

"It's only you who sets her off, apparently."

"I doubt that. There's a tracker on her car and in the panic button?"

"Of course. I still think there's only a five percent chance she's involved."

Nicholas rolled his eyes. "When did you become the trusting one?"

"About the time you became all cynical and brooding. What did Lee want?"

"What does Lee always want? Money. He asked about her—about Richards."

"They were talking in the hall. I gather he initiated the meeting."

Nicholas didn't immediately respond. He stared off into space, trying to determine what kind of threat Vivian Richards presented. "Run a full search on her, please."

CHAPTER SEVEN

Vivian kept her head down, completed her work as efficiently—and quietly—as possible, and generally tried to forget the event now called "the break-in" by the other office staff. She carried the panic button for the week that Dominick Fehr requested. She even took the offered extra vacation days. She couldn't afford a flight out to Boulder to see her family, so she spent Thanksgiving at St. Simeon's soup kitchen with Evan and several other boys from the group home. After cleaning the rectory and the kitchen, they all sacked out on the floor watching movies and throwing popcorn at each other. That Sunday she slept in, attended the later Mass, then helped prepare for the annual *Hanging of the Greens*. By the time her evening shift in the kitchen rolled around, Vivian looked forward to returning to her usual schedule of work and classes.

She saw Evan come slouching into the basement, but lost sight of him as Sister Martha needed help carrying a big soup pot. Finally able to take a break, Vivian snatched a roll from the rack and went in search of her recalcitrant math student.

"Viv! Hey Viv, over here." Evan waved one long arm in the air. He was sitting with another man whose back was turned to her. She slowed. The man with Evan was as tall as the teen, and had curly, reddish-gold hair. "Viv! You never told me you knew Lee Reed!"

Vivian sincerely hoped her relief didn't show on her face. The younger Reed brother would surely take it as some sort of slight. "I'm so sorry I didn't update you on every person I've met in the past month." She under-hand lobbed the roll at Evan. He easily caught it. "Your turn to help." She watched Evan until he reached the serving line. He wasn't above ducking out of work if he thought she wasn't watching.

"So." She swung her jean clad legs over the bench seat of the cafeteria table. "Lee Reed. To what does St. Simeon's owe the honor of your august presence?"

He held up his hands in mocking surrender. "Easy with the vocabulary words, college girl."

"Aren't you a "college boy"?"

"In name only, thankfully. Jess, my twin, got all the brains. I got all the looks, obviously."

"Obviously." She couldn't help but smile. "But really, what are you doing here?"

He suddenly looked ashamed. "Um, this is gonna sound weird and pervy, but it's really not. I, um, asked about you and found out you help out here. I tracked you down."

While her brain frantically ran through all her Reed Investments contacts who might have known she volunteered at St. Simeon's, Vivian quipped, "Yeah, pretty stalker-y of you."

"Don't call the cops just yet. I need your help with something."

"College Algebra?"

"Eeew, no. Besides, I actually passed that already."

"Oh?" Vivian looked skeptical.

"Well, ok, Jess dragged me through it, and I survived with a D... minus. But that's passing." He looked around. "Got any more of those rolls? I'm starving."

"This is a soup kitchen for the homeless and needy."

"Well, can we go somewhere to talk and eat?"

She wanted to turn him down, but she was hungry too. "I have about 45 minutes before Evan's tutoring session. There's a Chinese place around the corner."

"Perfect!"

After checking with Father John—and assuring Evan that she'd be back in time to tutor him and get him back to his group home—Vivian joined Lee on the sidewalk outside the church.

"Which way?"

Vivian pointed to their left. As they walked, she asked "So what do you need my help with?"

"Well, you work with the company computers, right?"

"Yes..."

"How good are you at, um, slightly shady stuff?"

Vivian stopped walking. "I'm not hacking anything for you. Goodbye, Mister Reed."

"Wait! Stop, please." He reached out to grab her arm. Vivian recoiled as if burned. "I'm sorry, please, just hear me out. Please?"

I should walk away. But he looks so young, and helpless, and... Snap out of it, Vivian! He's not helpless. But he is your employer's brother...

"Turn here. You have until I finish eating my dinner."

"Deal." He held the door open for her.

They ordered, with Lee insisting upon paying for her meal. As they sat waiting for their food, he leaned slightly closer. The nearest patrons were on the other side of the dining room, so Vivian wasn't sure why he felt the need to whisper.

"Um, so, Evan was telling me a bit about your parents." Seeing her face cloud, Lee rushed to say, "And I get it. My dad was murdered and my brother nearly killed."

"Your brother wrecked his car while driving way too fast, probably under the influence."

"Except, he didn't." Lee leaned close again. "His blood alcohol was zero. He hadn't been drinking at all.

There was cell phone footage of the wreck and his car exploded before it hit the divider. I'm not talking like wheels flying off. I mean fireball, whoosh, car flipping."

Vivian stared at him. He looked so normal and sane...

"I know, I sound crazy. I can't show you the footage because it's gone. The guy who uploaded it pulled it after just six hours. All the sites that shared the footage, all the social media copies, they were all scrubbed within forty-eight hours. It was there, I saw it, and then it was gone."

"You realize that makes you sound *more* crazy."

Lee leaned back in his seat. For a supposedly starving man, he'd barely touched his food. "Then my dad dies in a mugging."

"Not an unheard-of occurrence, unfortunately."

"Do you know how many fatal muggings there have been in Seattle in the past five years?"

"Actually, no."

"One. My dad."

Vivian's chopsticks hovered an inch below her mouth. "Seriously?"

"Yeah. Also, what kind of mugger takes the cash out of the wallet, then throws it back on the body with the credit cards still inside?"

She couldn't help herself; she was too naturally curious. "But the police ruled it a mugging."

"They did. They also never caught the guy who shot him, even though there are at least four cameras pointed at the spot where my dad died."

"Were the cameras there when he died or were they installed after?"

"Before."

"What does Mr. Fehr say about all of this?"

"Fehr came home from the rehab facility with my brother. He never worked for my dad. Also, why did Nicholas suddenly rate world-class security after a car accident? And where did he find Dom? All we really know about the guy is that he's former special ops—which is kind of a vague category—and former FBI."

Vivian shook her head. "Look, you seem really emotionally invested in this. I can kind of see your point about some of these things. But, how do I fit in?"

"I thought you could help me look through the old security footage, or maybe even track down that cell phone video of Nick's wreck."

"I already told you: I don't hack. I'm not signing on to something that's going to land me in Federal prison for five to ten years."

"I just thought…"

She snapped, "Yeah, well, Evan needs to keep his mouth shut. Yes, my parents died. It sucks. I'm sorry about your dad. At least you still have your siblings close by and a mom who's alive."

"No one believes you, that your parents were murdered." He stated it as a fact in an almost toneless voice. His pale green eyes held plenty of emotion, though.

"I suppose you're going to tell me that you believe me? Don't be an idiot."

"How could I? I haven't heard the story, yet. But you do know how it feels to have no one believe you."

"Thank you for dinner, Lee." Vivian stood up and turned to go, then turned back to the table. "Say I change my mind. How do I contact you?"

He scribbled his cell number on a napkin. "Thanks."

"You OK to get home?"

"What? Oh, yeah. I'll call an Uber or something. Goodnight."

She left him sitting there, staring morosely into his Kung Pao chicken.

CHAPTER EIGHT

Vivian tugged her new brown herringbone skirt into place, then flopped down on the side of her bed to pull on her boot socks. She would have preferred to wear her chunky brown heels, but the rain of the previous three days showed no signs of letting up. Her phone intermittently beeped with weather alerts warning of increased landslide danger in Western Washington due to the super-saturated soils. So, her new boots would have to do. As she reached for her raincoat, her eye fell on the napkin Lee Reed had handed her two days earlier. She frowned. At the end of Winter quarter, when she turned in her final project for CSE 564, Vivian just needed a capstone course to complete her bachelor's degree in computer engineering. She wished she had the time, and money, to enroll in the dual Master's program, but wishing didn't make dreams come true. Maybe after a few years at Reed Investments, they would pay for her to go back to school.

Still, she did have a *bit* of free time around the holidays. Maybe she could find the time to help Lee out...

Focus, Vivian, she chided herself.

Hand on the doorknob, Vivian stopped and dropped her chin onto her chest. She sighed, turned around, and grabbed the napkin.

Work finished, but with several hours until she could leave, Vivian pulled the napkin from her purse. It felt flimsy in her hand. She should, she thought, at least put the number in her phone's contact list. What if the napkin got wet, or she lost it? After typing in the new contact information, Vivian stared down at her phone.

"Oh hell," she muttered.

He picked up on the first ring. "Hello?"

"This is Vivian Richards. From Ree—"

"Vivian! Oh thank you, thank you, thank you, so much for calling. You are calling about helping me out, right?"

Her cheek curved against the phone as she smiled. "Yes, Lee. I don't suppose you have any free time—"

He cut her off again. "I can be there in ten minutes."

"Uh, what? I didn't mean..." Vivian stared down at her phone. He'd already hung up on her. "Weird kid," she muttered.

It was closer to fifteen minutes before Lee practically bounced through the door. "Sorry!" He juggled a coffee cup in one hand and an expensive laptop in the other. "You're, uh, sure we're alone?"

Vivian took the laptop from him before he dropped it. "In the building? No. In here, though, yeah. Everyone else has gone home."

"Do you always work this late?"

His question so closely echoed his brother's that Vivian blinked a few times before answering. "Yes. What's that for?" She pointed at the laptop.

"Well, I wanted to show you what I had tried. I thought it might help."

"There's no way I'm letting you connect that thing to our company networks. I have no idea where it's been."

"Fine." He slumped in the chair he'd pulled up to her desk. His Henley shirt, a soft gray, complemented his coloring. As casual and disheveled as he tried to appear, his jeans were from an expensive designer label and his hiking boots were spotless. Vivian doubted he'd ever actually been hiking. She suddenly had an overwhelming urge to ruffle his curly hair.

Mentally shaking herself, Vivian tried to focus. She pulled her hair up into a ponytail and peered at her computer screens. "Right. What date, exactly, are we looking for?"

Lee rattled off the date and time of his father's murder, wincing as he did.

Vivian typed for a few seconds, then scrolled through the database of stored footage. "Hmm, that date's not here."

"I know. I did try that, you know." He sounded petulant.

She ignored him. "So, that far back, almost four years now, isn't here at all." She nibbled on her lip for a minute before nodding once and standing. "Come with me."

Lee followed her back into the server room, past the main company servers to where another stack stood in one corner. A solitary light blinked blue.

"What's that?"

"On-site storage. We transfer copies of information here in case the main system gets corrupted. Don't get your hopes up, though. Most data is stored at an off-site location. There's little chance that four-year-old security files will still be on this machine."

He shrugged. "Worth a try, anyway." Glancing around and not finding anywhere to sit, he stretched out on the floor at her feet. He watched her work in silence for a few minutes. "Thanks for doing this."

She smiled at him. "Well, looking for old files isn't hacking. In fact, making sure our company data is securely stored is part of my job, so this is totally work-related."

"Well... maybe don't write a report for my brother, though?"

"Trust me, Lee, your brother neither knows, nor cares, what I do."

He snorted in response.

"Damn." Vivian put both hands on her hips and glared at the small terminal screen as if giving it her best angry-teacher impression would somehow help.

Lee sat up. "What?"

"The files aren't here either."

"Deleted?"

"No, moved." She patted around her ponytail tie before realizing that she hadn't stored a pen there as she sometimes did. Flummoxed, she looked at Lee. "Got a pen?"

"Eh? Why would I have a pen?"

She rolled her eyes. "Go fetch one off my desk, would you? Bring a notepad, too," she called after him.

"You really need to meet my sister, Jess." He groused as he handed her the requested items.

"I think the less I have to do with my employer's family, the better."

"Even me?" He might have been trying for a flirtatious grin, but it didn't move Vivian at all.

"Especially you." She softened the rejoinder with a smile. "So, the files you want to see aren't here, but there is a record of them being moved. Well, that month of security files has been moved. There's no guarantee that the actual video still exists, OK?"

"So... you're saying there's a chance?"

Vivian rolled her eyes again. "Technically. Come on, let me see if I can determine where the files were moved to."

She sat back at her desk and typed in the GUID address of the device the files had been transferred to.

"You're kind of scary when you frown like that."

"Thanks. The files weren't uploaded to a cloud storage. They were transferred to an external hard-drive." She saw his shoulders slump. "Don't lose hope yet. We do that sometimes with really secure data that we don't want to put on any open network. It seems a little odd that someone would go through the trouble to move months of video feed—they actually took almost six months—via physical storage." Sensing his next question, Vivian nodded at Lee. "The device used to move the files is registered to Reed Investments Corporate Security Department." She typed a few more keys. "Unfortunately, there's no way to tell where the device is now. It could be here, but even on the off-chance that it is, there's no way the data you want would still be sitting on it. These files were moved years ago."

Lee's eyes narrowed. "How many years?"

"Uh—" She hit a few keys. "—two and a half."

"Figures." His tone and expression said that there was a lot more than just defeat behind his words. "Well, thanks for trying."

"Hold on. There's one other thing I can try. This specific device might not have ever been attached to our network from outside the building, but there's a good bet that something registered to the security department has been. How many off-site storage centers can one company have?"

He cut her a glance. "You really have no idea how paranoid my brother is, do you?"

If Vivian heard him, she gave no indication. She scrolled through a list of devices associated with Security and checked their network connections.

"Ah ha!" She shouted so loudly, Lee jumped.

He looked nervously around. "Uh, yea?"

"I have the same IP address associated with several Security department laptops and two flash drives. Let's see if I can find a physical address." She typed again, still grinning. "Uh... does this address ring a bell?" Her tone indicated it might. She swiveled her monitor so that Lee could better see.

"Oh, yeah. That makes sense. That's my—our— house. I'd imagine all the security guys log on from our house at one time or another."

"Yes, but this here—" She pointed at what looked to Lee like a random string of numbers and letters. "— that is a server, registered at that physical address and purchased two years and six months ago by the—"

"Security department!" Lee's grin matched hers.

Then her face fell. Rubbing her arms as if suddenly chilled, Vivian reached behind her and slid her arms into her cardigan. "I have no reason to visit security and go poking around in their servers. Sorry, Lee, but I think this is where my help ends."

He sat, staring at her, but seemed to have not heard her words.

"Lee?"

"You know... you're quite pretty."

"Uh, thanks?"

"And you're not that much older than me."

A sudden premonition that she would not like where this was going washed over Vivian.

"Do you, by chance, own an evening gown?"

"Are you drunk?" She leaned closer to peer at him.

He laughed and hurriedly explained. "My mother throws this ridiculous black-tie Christmas gala. I haven't attended in two years. OK," he admitted, upon seeing Vivian's skeptical expression, "I was asked to not attend unless I brought better company."

"Crashed the party with your frat brothers, did you?"

"And some girls," he muttered. Then he brightened. "But you are definitely better company. I bet you clean up really well. If I can get you to the house, can you get into the server?"

Vivian, already shaking her head, held up both hands as if to ward him off. "Do you not remember the part where I said I like my job? That I *need* my job? Or the part about how I wanted as little to do with your family as possible?"

"We're so bad?"

"You're not bad, Lee. You're just... really, really, rich. And your brother is my employer."

"And you like your job. But I have fifteen percent shares in the company. So aren't I technically your employer too?"

She didn't bother replying. She simply handed him his laptop. "Goodnight, Lee."

He looked so crestfallen that she nearly relented. Then her inner voice of reason chimed in: *This does not help find Mom and Dad's killers, Vivian. Get the degree, get the job experience, find work with a security firm so you can research, or hack, the police files. Or, make enough money to hire a private investigator. You do not have time for Reed family drama.*

CHAPTER NINE

"So, are we going to arrest that security guard at Reed Investments?"

Suisse's question interrupted his partner's thoughts. Detective Kwon clenched his teeth before answering. They were walking from the King County Adult Detention Center back to the Seattle Police headquarters where they'd parked their car.

"Why would we? We have nothing to hold him on. The DA will not charge him on hearsay evidence, and we don't even have that."

"Come on. We know it had to be an inside job. That place has better security than the courthouse. The only way those thieves got in there is if they had help."

"Yes, but the Reeds are all tied up with the Triads. Why would common thieves risk angering both the Reed family and the Triads?"

"You only *think* the Reeds are still helping the Triads. If you had proof that Nicholas was following in his old man's footsteps, you'd have busted him by now."

Kwon didn't break stride, or even turn his head, when he asked his next question. He kept his tone level. "You have history with the Triads, don't you?"

"You know I do. That was my big bust."

"In Friday Harbor on San Juan Island, right?"

Sensing a trap, Suisse cut his eyes sideways, trying to discern what his partner was insinuating.

"Where Vivian Richards is from."

"Yes. Your point?"

"Isn't it possible that the inside man is actually an inside woman?"

Suisse mulled that over. "I doubt it. Just because she comes from the same town where I busted a major drug ring a few years ago doesn't mean she's a criminal."

"No, of course not."

They rode in silence back to the West Precinct, each replaying the details of the investigation in his head.

"Well, we should at least re-question that guard. I really don't buy the Triad connection, though."

Kwon grunted. "The Triads are not a centralized organization. There could be factional fighting going on. Reed might have angered a powerful man."

"Those two we have in custody won't tell us anything."

"Neither will any employee of Reed Investments. They have lawyers on retainer and iron-clad NDAs."

"So, we wait for them to screw up?"

"Yes." Kwon moved the folders on his desk. "Let's discuss that case we picked up last week. The bloody stash-house."

Suisse groaned. "We have even less on that than we do on Reed. Can't we focus on Reed and break at least one case?"

"Don't be obsessive. Keep an open mind and look at all the angles. Did that blood analysis come in?"

Face pinched in irritation—which made him look like an albino ferret—Suisse picked up the wafer-thin file. "Yes." He whistled. "The crime scene techs found five blood types. Still waiting on DNA to see if we have any known offenders. The blood pools were all intermingled, so they can't be sure if we should look for a body." He continued reading for a minute. "This is interesting. The door was reinforced, but the door jamb and hinges were bent like someone tore the door itself outward."

"Who could do that?"

"No one I want to meet in a dark hallway, that's for sure."

Nicholas watched his head of security lock the door and flip a switch to turn on anti-eavesdropping devices embedded within the walls of his office. "You have a report on the two who broke in here? Triad?"

"If they're talking to Seattle Police, we haven't heard about it. Those two detectives, though, they've been making several not-very-discreet inquiries. Kwon seems more focused on you and the company. Johann— he's the guy I have shadowing Miss Richards—reports that Detective Suisse watched her apartment building on two different occasions and took pictures at one point. I gave Johann permission to make his presence known on that second night. He hasn't seen Suisse skulking around since."

"I assume we've run the prints of the two we apprehended?"

"Yes. They aren't known Triad associates. The Hong Kong office is due to call later with confirmation. Determining what they wanted might help us identify them."

The CEO of Reed Investments rubbed the back of his neck. "This report from Richards—on the attempted hack—do the details check out?"

Dom nodded. "I sent the report and our logs over to a former colleague. He verified that what she says happened is exactly what occurred."

"Do we know how the thieves got in here?"

"We have no footage of them entering the building. We have no footage of them at all until they jumped Dave Kaskoy as he was making his rounds."

"You will get to the bottom of why that is?"

"I will. Any idea why your brother would be in the building last night? Specifically, the IT department?"

Nicholas raised an eyebrow. "Until just now, I wasn't aware Lee knew where the IT department was located. What did he do?"

"That's just it. He didn't so much as log on to the network. As far as I can tell, Miss Richards didn't access anything she shouldn't have. They sat and talked, walked into the back of the room, then came back to her desk. They seem to have had a disagreement about something and Lee left. Miss Richards finished her shift, logged off, and went straight home."

One of Nicholas's auburn brows arched. "You still have a tracker on her car?"

Dom shrugged half-heartedly. "I haven't had a chance to pull it off."

Nicholas didn't bother reacting to that obvious lie. "So, you don't think she helped Lee with his quest?"

"I can't be sure, but I'd say no. In fact, he may have just been there to flirt. Or maybe he had laptop trouble."

Dom pulled a file from under his arm and dropped it on his employer's desk. "Speaking of Vivian Richards, I finally have something to report. She's an orphan. Her parents supposedly died in a house fire."

"Supposedly?" Nicholas started flipping through the file.

"Yeah. Four years ago, October. October first, to be precise." Dom waited for effect. When Nicholas raised his head, the bodyguard nodded. "Two weeks before your accident, her childhood home—which was also the family business—burned to the ground. Her younger brother was in the house. She managed to get him out. He swore to investigators that he heard screaming and gunshots. Miss Richards told the police she saw blood around her parents' bodies. The corpses were so badly charred that manner of death was ruled "fire-related". The place this all happened was..."

"Friday Harbor," Nicholas whispered in horror. "Oh God." He reflexively crossed himself. "Is there any chance this wasn't related to my father's drug smuggling?"

Dom frowned at him. "You know it's not."

"Why didn't any of this come up in the background check?"

"Because Ghiadello thought she was hiring an entry-level systems admin. The recommendation came from your uncle; Ghiadello checked employment and credit records—which, by the way, were abysmal. The property and all of the family savings were seized under asset forfeiture. San Juan sheriff's office justified the seizure claiming her father was involved with drug smuggling. The girl ended up on the streets. I'd assume that she came to your Uncle's attention via the shelter he runs. Some of this information was...unusually... hard to come by."

"The little brother?"

"It's in the file. He lives with an aunt and uncle in Colorado. She hasn't seen him in at least two years."

Nicholas's fair skin paled even further. "Any chance she knows about...

"Highly unlikely. That's knowledge that only five, living, people have. No, I think this is just a nasty coincidence."

"You're forgetting my uncle's involvement."

"I am not. Your uncle suspects certain details, but he does not *know*. I doubt he knows enough to have put even half the puzzle pieces together. You've always told me that he wishes to remain ignorant about your family's past activities. Do you want me to increase the surveillance of Miss Richards? I'd pulled back after our last conversation."

Nicholas shook his head. "No." He rose and glanced at his watch. "I think it's time I consulted with my uncle." He rubbed one hand over his hip. Frowning more fiercely, he grabbed his cane from the corner. "I'll see you tonight?"

"Not if that hip is still bothering you."

Nicholas Reed's eyes narrowed. "I will see you tonight," he stated coldly. He stared at his bodyguard for a few moments before the man relented with a nod.

That evening, Vivian scrolled through her emails, then checked the data backups for the week. Doing so made her think of Lee's visit. She didn't know why she'd decided to erase the record of her access of the security files, equipment logs, and backup machine. Vivian still felt vaguely uneasy about it, as if she was lying to... someone.

She rolled her eyes at her own paranoia. But, when she checked the backup process, she noted the folder size of the data the security department had scheduled to be archived. Her mind immediately recalled the size of the files Lee sought. They were three times the size of the current to-be-archived files.

Nope, I'm not getting sucked into this. She shook her head, then rose and stretched. But the thought nagged, rolling through her thoughts. Pacing back and forth in the small corridor formed between her desk at the fourth server tower didn't help. A firm conversation with herself, including several reminders that this was not her mystery to solve, didn't help either. The nagging questions remained.

Why were those six months of video files moved in that manner, but everything else was transferred in the usual way?

Why did the date of their move mean so much to Lee? *Did* it mean something?

What was moved besides security videos?

That last question really troubled her. There was just too much. The total data transfer was well over what six months of video files should be. Not that video files were small, of course. Maybe they were in higher definition, or compressed differently? Well, she should be able to answer that question easily enough. She marched back to the on-site backup server. A few keystrokes, combined with a few more minutes scrolling, confirmed that the video file sizes prior to Nicholas Reed taking over the company had been much smaller. Newer security cameras installed in the months following Nicholas's return—presumably at the behest of his new security chief, Dominick Fehr—were much higher quality and, consequently, significantly larger.

Vivian stared at the date. The files Lee wished to see had been moved two years and six months prior. When she'd told him that, he'd reacted as if the date was not a surprise. Now, as Vivian stood in the dark and stared at the screen, she realized that the data transfer occurred two weeks after Nicholas Reed's return from rehab. Why? Did Mr. Fehr's more professional approach to corporate security demand it, or was there something on those files that Nicholas Reed did not want anyone else seeing?

Try as she might, Vivian could not stop thinking about Lee Reed, his father's murder, and the files he searched for. She knew the dangers of being too curious. Her curiosity led to her parents' deaths. If she hadn't asked so many questions about the cars making regular trips on the ferry between Friday Harbor and Seattle, she'd still have a home. If she hadn't shared her theories with her father, who'd taken them to the county sheriff, they would still be alive today. Her brother would be attending the same high school she'd graduated from. She'd likely already have her degree from UW.

Vivian suddenly looked at her watch. If she hurried, she might catch Father John before her tutoring session with Evan. She quickly packed her things and locked up the department.

CHAPTER TEN

Vivian slipped through the front doors of the church and turned to descend the stairs to the basement. Out of the corner of her eye, she saw Father John speaking with someone near the confessional booth. The man was a few inches taller than the priest, much younger, and, even in the dim light, she could see his curly red-gold hair. Frozen in the shadowed corner near the door, Vivian watched as Father John placed a hand on Nicholas Reed's shoulder. Nicholas bowed his head. Then the priest made the sign of the cross and hugged the younger man. As a cradle-Catholic, Vivian could almost hear his murmured "Go in Peace".

While she walked down the stairs, Vivian wondered about that hug. A handshake was far more common among American Catholics, especially men. It almost looked like Father John had absolved Nicholas, but he wouldn't have come out of the Confessional for that. She also wondered why, given the amount of time she spent in the church, she'd never encountered Nicholas Reed there before. If he'd been a regular parishioner, she'd certainly have seen him at Mass.

Before she could ask Father John about the mysterious encounter with her employer, he distracted her with a sandwich and questions about her weekend. She found herself disclosing her troubled thoughts.

"A friend has asked for your help, but you are not sure if the help you can provide is morally, or legally, proper? But you also feel like you haven't done all that you can, as a friend, to assist this person?"

"Yes, Father. I've made it clear that I won't cross any legal boundaries, but this is more of a... gray area. I know what could come of asking too many questions."

Tears welled in her blue eyes. "Don't I have a duty to help him avoid the pain I went through?"

"I don't believe duty is the right word here, Vivian. The information your friend seeks, is it likely to cause him pain?"

"I think he might feel worse if he never knows." She looked down at her feet. "I certainly do."

The priest leaned his forearms on his desk and smiled softly at her. "Vivian, I can't tell you what to do here. You know, in your heart, what is best." He shook his head when she attempted to interrupt. "Yes, you do. Fear is holding you back."

She left the church without a resolution. She wanted to find those missing files. Mysteries needed to be solved. But, she also didn't need any more danger in her life. The nagging thought that pinged around in her head was: *What if, by not helping, I'm actually putting Lee in more danger?* Sitting alone in her dingy apartment, Vivian finally made her decision. She called Lee.

"I really don't own an evening gown, though. How am I supposed to get one by Saturday?"

"I have no idea. I could ask Jess if you can borrow one of hers...though she's taller than you."

"I'm not showing up to your family Christmas gala wearing a gown I borrowed from your sister. The whole idea is to be inconspicuous. I'll think of something. Do you need to add me to a list or something?"

"I'll come pick you up."

"I thought you had a driver for such things."

He chuckled. "For dates, I drive myself."

"This is not a date, Lee. I'm helping you out, remember?"

"Sure, sure. Where should I pick you up?"

They talked for a few more minutes, planning the details of their not-a-date. When she hung up, for the first time in a week, she felt unburdened. Which, when she thought about it, made no sense. She had a dress to buy, a very ritzy party to attend, and a somewhat-questionable access of the Reeds' personal security system to engineer.

Across Lake Washington, in Medina, Lee sauntered down the hallway from his bedroom, flipped the bird to a security camera in the corner, and bounced down the stairs. Nicholas and his constant shadow, Dom, encountered him in the kitchen.

"What's got you in such a good mood?"

"Life, big bro." Lee patted his brother's cheek—mostly because he knew how much Nicholas hated it. "Perk up, Nicky. It's Christmas."

"Not yet."

"Speaking of, turns out I *will* be attending the thing on Saturday."

Tension suffused Nicholas's features. "Oh? I thought Mom banned you after the latest fiasco."

Lee leaned back to look around the refrigerator door he was holding open. "Only until I found more 'suitable company'." He grinned and shrugged. "I found a nice, quiet girl that won't make a scene."

"You? *You* found a girl that is neither a stripper nor a drunken sorority girl? Where? How? She's not tied up in your trunk, is she?"

Dom interjected, "Should I go check his car, Mr. Reed?"

"Oh har har, you two are hilarious. You'll meet her on Saturday. Oo, steak!"

The two older men watched as Lee piled a plate high with sliced flank steak. He flashed them one more taunting grin before leaving the kitchen.

Nicholas walked over to the fridge and peered inside, much as his brother had. "Did you know he had a girlfriend?"

"Nope. She must be fairly new. Maybe you should ask your sister."

"Eh? Oh no, she'd tell me to mind my business."

"Ah, yeah." Dom chuckled again. "If we're in for the night I can take a little time, see what I can dig up."

"No, I want to..." Nicholas paused to look around the well-lit kitchen. "...make more progress on that project. I just need food first. Sandwich?"

"Sure, thanks. The party Saturday, will it interfere with your other plans?"

Nicholas paused in the act of layering peppered salami and provolone cheese. He frowned. "It might. Damn it... I can't get out of it, though. Mom will be insufferable, and half the board of our publicly traded companies will be in attendance." He sighed and continued to make the sandwiches. "I hate going to these things. My face hurts from pretending to be nice."

Dom rolled his eyes. "You're the one who wanted to return to all of this. It's not like you didn't know what that meant."

"Are you ever going to get tired of saying 'I told you so'?" Nicholas pushed a plate across the counter.

"Thanks. And, probably not."

CHAPTER ELEVEN

The Reed residence sparkled. The afternoon's rain had finally let up, but the puddles, and the damp needles of the towering evergreens, threw back a million reflections of the white lights decorating the gate, front entrance, and the dock. The mast of Nicholas's sailboat, which he hadn't taken out since his accident, blinked a merry red and green. Cars wound around the long drive, pausing long enough to drop off guests attired in tuxedos and sequined gowns. The entire effect dazzled—as intended. No one present could doubt the wealth, or taste, of the Reed family.

The matriarch, fifty-three-year-old Ingrid Reed, stood in the doorway separating the foyer from the ballroom. She wore a floor-length Vera Wang gown of blue silk. Sapphires glinted from her earlobes and around her neck. Her eldest child, Nicholas, stood stiffly beside her, shaking hands.

Lee Reed pulled up outside Vivian's apartment building in a red Ferrari F8 Spider. She met him on the corner so he didn't have to navigate the underground garage of her building. Looking at the expensive sports car, Vivian shook her head.

The passenger side window slowly lowered. Lee leaned over to look out. "Wow, you look fabulous! And cold! Get in!"

Vivian laughed at him as she opened the door and dropped, seemingly to the ground, into the seat. "You look pretty fabulous yourself. You own a car this hot, but let someone drive you around all day?"

Lee gunned the engine. The car shot forward, though he was careful to keep to just two miles over the speed limit. "You think I look fabulous, but my car is hot?

What kind of scale is that?" They stopped at a light. He turned his head to flash his smile. "If you owned a car this 'hot', would you risk it in Seattle traffic?"

"Good point." Vivian ran her hand over the soft leather of the seats. "So, the plan's the same? We go in, make a point to be seen, and then sneak away?"

"For our make-out session."

"For our *imaginary* tryst while I try to access the internal security network. Which action could get me fired," she replied in a repressive tone.

"Only if you get caught."

She snorted.

"You worry too much."

"Someone has to."

When they arrived at the house, Lee pulled up to the back gate. He tapped in a code on the keypad, then leaned farther out of his window and raised his middle finger at the security camera.

"Uh, remember the part about being inconspicuous?"

"Trust me, if I didn't insult them and their stupid paranoid rules, they'd know something was up."

The gate swung open. Lee carefully steered the car into an empty stall in the cavernous detached garage. He walked around the car, opened the passenger door, and reached for Vivian's hand. "Come on. We can go in through the pool deck and avoid the stuffy introductions."

She hesitated just a moment before taking his hand. Clasping her clutch and her pashmina-style wrap with one hand, she concentrated on watching where she walked. Her strappy heels were less than ideal for strolling through rain-soaked grounds. Thankfully, the paving stones leading from the garage to the pool area were broad and perfectly even.

Lee pointed toward the dark lake. "Look. I decorated my boat."

"You sail?"

"When I can. You?"

"I grew up on San Juan Island. My dad..." Her voice caught. Lee slowed his steps. He looked down at her and squeezed her hand. "My dad had a charter fishing boat. I loved going out with him."

"My dad taught Nick, then me and Jess. After he came back from rehab, Nick didn't want to go out on the water anymore. He gave me his boat. Title and everything."

Vivian's head had been turned to look toward the boat dock. When they rounded the corner and the house came fully into view, she gasped.

"I know. Kind of bright, yet somehow boring, right? Mom insists upon all-white Christmas lights. That's why I chose red and green flashing lights for the boat."

Vivian laughed. "Of course you did."

Lee swung open a metal gate. They walked across the paved path with a wall of shrubbery on one side and the pool on the other. Steam rose lazily from the surface of the water. A long veranda extended the length of the pool area. Through the floor-to-ceiling windows, they could see a crowd of elegantly dressed partiers milling around.

"The buffet is on the far side of the ballroom. My family will expect me to head there first."

"You have a ballroom?" She'd stopped walking to stare into the mass of people.

"No, my mother has a ballroom. It's pretentious and snobbish, and I hate it. When we were kids, though, we'd race across it in fuzzy socks and crash into the walls." He gave her hand a light squeeze. "Just a little while in the crowd, then we can disappear."

The idea of being able to slip away unnoticed had seemed like wishful thinking when Lee suggested it. Now, seeing the crowd, Vivian wasn't entirely sure they'd be noticed at all.

The flow of people through the front doors had slowed to a trickle. Nicholas took his cane from Dom, ignoring his bodyguard's sardonic expression. Nicholas carried the cane at social functions because no one bothered to ask him to dance when he leaned on it. Dom took up position just inside the doors, watching the room. He occasionally glanced at his watch as texts from the rest of the security team flowed across it. He also had an earpiece for emergencies.

"Lee pulled in a few minutes ago. He's coming through from the pool deck."

Nicholas looked out over the crowd. "Can you see him yet?"

"Not yet. What do you think? Buffet or bar?"

"Depends on if he wants to get thrown out." Nicholas pushed away from the wall with his shoulders. After a few steps, he remembered to use his cane. Dom followed. They were almost to the bar when they both stopped.

"Oh wow," Dom muttered under his breath.

Standing beside Lee, looking nervous, stood Vivian Richards. This was not the cardigan-wearing, ponytail-sporting IT tech they had encountered at Reed Investments, though. Her blonde hair was piled high on her head to cascade down onto her shoulders. Her gown, a pale peach dress covered with intricate beaded patterns, had a flowing hem that reached to mid-calf, while the round neckline and cap sleeves left her collarbones bare. She wore heels, but still barely came up to Lee's shoulder. She played with the fringe of her wrap. Her head came up and she made eye contact with Nicholas. He was sure her pupils dilated. He was equally certain he was staring.

"Well, that answers our question of what he was doing in the office." Dom looked at his employer's stunned expression, then back at Vivian. "Hey, you might want to..." He trailed off as Nicholas marched toward the couple.

Vivian felt panicked. She had known from the beginning that encountering Nicholas Reed was a near certainty. For some idiotic reason, she'd thought they'd exchange professional handshakes and that would be that. From the moment she felt him staring at her, any idea of a quick encounter had faded.

"Lee," she hissed. "Incoming."

"Eh? What? Oh, hey, Nicky. Smashing party. Thanks for the invite. This is Vivian Richards."

Nicholas's green eyes cut sideways at his brother before resting back on Vivian. "We've met, you idiot. Miss Richards." He held out a hand. His voice dropped slightly and softened as he said her name. He still hadn't broken eye contact.

"Hello, Mr. Reed."

"Welcome to my home."

They lapsed into silence. He towered above her in his black tuxedo. The white of his shirt collar made his freckles stand out a bit more.

Lee looked from Vivian to his brother and back again. "OK, well you've met her. You know she's not a wild-eyed party girl. Let me get the Mom thing over with."

Nicholas finally focused back on his brother. "Maybe offer your date a glass of wine before subjecting her to our mother?"

"Good idea. Vivian? Red or white?"

She swallowed twice. Her logical brain told her it was impossible that Nicholas knew her presence was a ruse, yet her instincts screamed that Nicholas could see inside her very soul. "White, please."

"Be right back. Nicky, stop hovering. Vivian can take care of herself."

"Oh, I know that," Nicholas said, so softly that Vivian barely heard him. He watched his brother weave through the crowd before looking back at Vivian. She was looking at the floor. He bent his head to the side and down, trying to see her face. "Hey. Are you OK?"

"Me?" She winced at her squeaky voice. She took a gulping breath of air. "I... this is not my scene."

Nicholas smiled and winked at her. "Here's a secret: this is no one's preferred scene. It's hot, you can't talk or dance, the wine is only mid-grade, and you don't dare actually eat food. People come to these things to say they've come—and to be seen. Then they escape as soon as they think it's allowed." He looked over her head. "When Lee gets back with your wine, have him take you on a tour of the house. That way you can avoid my mother and get out of this crowd."

Vivian didn't know what to make of his sudden consideration. She couldn't help herself; she smiled. "Are you sure Lee won't get in trouble?"

"Lee is likely to get in more trouble if he stays."

"And you? Can't you escape?"

For a moment, Nicholas thought he saw concern on her features. No trace of pity, though, which he was all too used to, and recognized easily. Ruefully, he shook his head. "For my sins, I am consigned to be here all evening." Pausing, he seemed suddenly unsure. Something about his expression changed enough that Vivian saw the similarities between the brothers. "You look lovely." He nodded his head sharply, then pivoted and walked away.

"Did he scare you?"

Vivian turned to take a glass of wine from Lee. "Scare? No. Confuse? Oh yeah. He also said you should take me on a tour of the house."

Lee's eyes lit up. "Basically giving us permission to disappear."

"Exactly. So—" She winked at the young man. "—take me to your room, Mr. Reed."

He made a face. "Ugh. It's *such* a buzz kill when you call me that." With a gentle pressure on her elbow, he led her across the crowded room.

When they reached the French doors leading to the foyer, Vivian gasped again. There were at least two dozen people in the spacious, three-floor-high foyer, either depositing or picking up coats, talking in small groups, or staring upward in awe. Two curved staircases led up to the second-floor gallery, where real evergreen boughs with massive red ribbons and bows garlanded the railing. Tall windows, with electric candles in each windowsill, were set above the wide oak front door. A massive chandelier decorated with thousands of tiny crystals illuminated the entire space.

Lee leaned over to whisper in her ear. "When I was 16, I hung mistletoe from the tip of that." He motioned with his head at the chandelier. "Mom nearly had a coronary. Dad thought it was hilarious. This way." He led her up the left staircase and down the hallway connecting to the gallery. At the second door on the left, he put his back to the door. "Don't turn your head to look when I tell you this. There is a security camera at the end of the hall. Come really close. I'm going to let you pass me, then make a face at them."

67

"Because they'd expect you to?"

"Exactly."

She brushed past him into the room. Lee's bedroom dwarfed her apartment by comparison. A desk sat near the large windows, which looked out to the front of the house. On the other side of the room was a king-sized bed, neatly made. A small sofa sat in front of an entertainment system. Vivian walked over to the desk and flipped open Lee's laptop. She drained the rest of the wine in her glass.

"Right, let's get started."

CHAPTER TWELVE

Vivian opened her tiny evening clutch and pulled out wire strippers, a coil of CAT6 cable, and a small penlight. Lee looked on, bemused. She sat in his gloriously comfortable desk chair then muttered, more to herself than to him, "Let's try Wi-Fi first." She poked around through various network connections. Occasionally she would stop to tug her wrap higher on her shoulders.

"Hey, stand up a second," Lee said. He pulled off his tuxedo jacket and held it out for her. "That dress is really too flimsy for December."

Her mind too busy figuring out how to access the security servers without being detected, Vivian didn't immediately reply. She cast a rueful eye down at her dress. "I know. I just thought it was really pretty."

"Oh, it is. If this were a real date, I'd be telling you just how good you look in it. This is me respecting the terms of our agreement and not telling you how sexy you are. Please take note of my amazing self-restraint."

She cocked her head to one side. "You make those self-deprecating comparisons to put people at ease. Why?"

Lee shook his head. "No, please, one riddle per night. Focus on the work."

Sighing, she shrugged. "It's no good trying to access the security server through the house Wi-Fi. They have it running on a separate router system. I bet it's air-gapped, meaning they don't even have the server we want on the network. I wouldn't. Mr. Fehr seems very good at his work. I doubt he'd over-look a potential back door."

"So, all of this was for nothing?" Lee threw up his hands in frustration.

Vivian rolled her eyes. "Calm down. I've only just started." She looked around the room. "Did you ever have a landline phone in here?"

"Yeah. The jack is over near the entertainment system."

"Even better. With a house this nice, I bet you have built-in wire channels for things like cable, phone lines, and ethernet."

"OK, you lost me again."

Vivian walked over to his TV and sound system. She dropped down on her knees—making Lee swallow rather self-consciously—to peer behind the TV. "Yup, this is exactly what I need. Does this section of the hutch fold out to... yeah, I see it does."

Lee sat on the loveseat to watch her work, hands clasped together between his knees. "How'd you learn to do this stuff?"

"Well, I always helped my dad with projects around our B&B. Then, at UW, we have computer engineering classes on network infrastructure. A house this big isn't really all that different from an office building. Hand me that multi-tool out of my clutch, please."

He retrieved and handed her the requested tool. "What else do you have in here?"

"Uh, lipstick, my keys, and breath mints. I don't think anything else would fit." She lapsed into silence as she removed the wall plate leading with cable, phone, and ethernet jacks. Nimble fingers pulled on each wire, carefully setting aside the HDMI cable line, un-used phone line, and the ethernet line. Two more lines ran in the conduit. One appeared to be a fiberoptic cable— likely, she thought, for the security cameras. The other line might be what she sought.

Carefully stripping back the protective sheathing of the wires, Vivian grabbed her coil of cable and prepared it in the same way. Then she stopped to explain her process to Lee. "If this works, we will splice into the ethernet cable and be directly connected to the security network. From there, I'm going to see if the computer we're searching for is on that network. Again, it might not be."

He looked at her, sitting there on his bedroom carpet, her fingertips barely protruding from his tuxedo jacket. The hem of her dress twisted around her knees. Her bright blue eyes conveyed her honesty and concern.

"Will anyone know we're snooping?"

She chewed on her lip for a minute. "Maybe. If I am fast enough, I can clone the MAC address of one of their computers and make yours appear to be allowed on the network. They might have a program running that will detect new devices connecting to the network. Hm." She stared down at the cable in her hands. "I'll mask the laptop's identifiers before I connect. It will still show as a new device, but not one that leads directly back to you."

After a few more minutes work, Vivian had the laptop connected to the network. Taking a deep breath, she opened the networking tab, made a quick note of the MAC address of another laptop, and quickly disconnected. She altered Lee's laptop to display the new identifier before reconnecting. Once back in the system, she started hunting for all devices that had been connected to the network within the last week.

Vivian quickly realized they were in very big trouble. She snatched the cord from the jack, closed the laptop and looked at the door in horror, half expecting large men with guns to break it down.

Lee jumped to his feet. "What? What is it?"

"Why," she hissed, "would your brother's bodyguard have top-of-the-line encryption and detection on your home security system? We don't have anything like this on the company servers. They *know*, Lee. They knew I was there probably from the minute I first connected. Every single computer on that network is protected by multiple levels of passwords." Tears welled in her eyes. "I'm so fired."

"Hey. No, hey, Vivian, please don't cry." He reached out to tentatively pull her into a hug. She stiffened at his touch. "You tried. You believed me when no one else would even listen. You're amazing." Lee ran his hands up and down her arms as she stepped back. "I told you my brother is a paranoid freak! Look, see, no one is coming to arrest you or fire you, or even yell at you. You're so good they didn't even know it was my laptop."

Rubbing away her tears with the back of her hand, Vivian shakily nodded. She gathered up her things. When she started to slide out of his jacket, Lee stopped her. "Keep it for the walk to the car at least." He opened the door for her, then stopped. "Turn left, there's a back stairwell. We'll go out that way. I forgot my phone. Be right there."

"OK." Vivian turned from the doorway with her head bent, recalling the security camera at the end of the hall. She didn't need her disappointment recorded for posterity. Unfortunately, the first things she saw as she started down the hall were a cane and a pair of shiny dress shoes. Her head came up in surprise.

"Miss Richards, I..." He reached a hand toward her tear-streaked face but stopped when she drew back. "What's wrong?"

Vivian shook her head so forcefully that some of the pins holding her hair came loose. "I can't." She brushed past her employer and fled down the hall, certain that if she stayed, she'd confess everything. She wanted only to escape.

Lee came out of his bedroom, saw Vivian turn the corner with her head down and shoulders bunched. He glared at his brother—who glared right back.

"What did you do?" Nicholas's tones were clipped.

Lee's carefree, playboy persona slipped. "Fuck you, Nicky. This is your fault." He punctuated his words with a hard shove to his brother's shoulder. Caught off guard, Nicholas stumbled backward. Before he could respond, verbally or physically, Lee had turned the corner and was gone.

CHAPTER THIRTEEN

Vivian spent the entire car ride home fighting back tears. Convinced she would be fired immediately, she stumbled through the next few days in a daze. She let Lee's calls go to voicemail. Even the beauty of the Third Sunday of Advent mass could not penetrate the fog that enveloped her. Instead of staying to help in the soup kitchen, she made an excuse and went directly home.

Seated at her workstation on the Monday after the party, Vivian reminded herself of what was important: finding the truth.

Were her parents killed because of her? Why did the San Juan County Sheriff's department rule the house fire accidental? Why had no one investigated their deaths as murders? And why had the sheriff, a purported friend of her father's, then accused her dad of being part of a criminal network?

Her thoughts skipped away from her list of questions to memories of Simon after the fire. She'd heard his screams for help as she ran toward the only place either of them had ever lived—the farmhouse her parents had lovingly restored into San Juan Island's best bed & breakfast. Her ten-year-old brother, his face and blond hair darkened by soot, sat on the porch stairs back-lit by the flames. Vivian took two steps into the house, screaming for her parents. Her mother lay by the back door, unmoving, as the fire roared around her. Choking on smoke, and her own sobs, Vivian had scooped Simon up and carried him far out into the yard. By the time the firefighters arrived, the roof and second floor of the house had collapsed. Even now, years later,

Vivian could still smell the smoke in Simon's hair and see his tear-stained cheeks. She would also never forget the blood on his feet—their mother's blood.

As a twenty-year-old college student, Vivian knew she wasn't equipped to raise her traumatized ten-year-old brother. That her maternal aunt and uncle had stepped up and taken Simon was a God-send, but, despite knowing that she'd done the right thing, she missed the scamp. She missed his laugh, his trouble-making ways, and his freely given love. She had to get justice—for her parents and for Simon. To succeed, though, she needed investigative resources that she couldn't currently afford. She also couldn't be derailed by drama—particularly drama that could lose her the best job she'd ever had.

"Focus, you moron."

"Excuse me?"

Vivian jumped at the other voice suddenly intruding on her thoughts. *No, wait, I said that last bit out loud. Stupid, stupid, tongue, always moving before the brain kicks in.* She looked up into Nicholas Reed's startled face.

"Oh! I'm sorry. I wasn't talking to you. Obviously. Or anyone else. No morons here, well except me."

His brows drew together. "Do I make you nervous?"

"Nervous?" She laughed, then winced. "Why would you make me nervous?"

Nicholas attempted a smile. "I've been told I can be intimidating." He looked around. "Can I sit?"

"Oh! Yes, sorry, let me get you a chair."

The look Nicholas gave Vivian stopped just short of contemptuous. Without saying a word, he grabbed the nearest chair, rolled it closer to Vivian's workstation, and slid into it.

"I wanted to come check on you. You left the party so suddenly."

She caught her bottom lip with her teeth and looked down at her keyboard. "I'm fine."

"You were crying."

"Too much champagne."

"Miss Richards...Vivian... if Lee hurt you in some way..."

Her head came up. She finally met his eyes. "Oh, no. Lee was a perfect gentleman. Please believe me, your brother did not do anything to upset me."

His green eyes searched her face. He seemed to be deciding whether or not he believed her. Then, he leaned back in the chair. "I don't think you had a chance to meet my sister, Jessie. She's Lee's twin. She owns a nightclub, among other things. It's called Willow. Heard of it?"

"Sorry, no, but I don't get out much."

"Pity. Well, as a Christmas present, I'd like to improve the club's Wi-Fi service and secure their network. Ms. Ghiadello and Mr. Fehr have been raving about your work for us. That's no faint praise. Mr. Fehr used to work for the Feds—and the military. Most of his guys did too."

She blushed.

"So, if you have time, I'd really appreciate your help. I'll pay you, of course. You aren't *required* to help me. I wish you would, though."

Great, thought Vivian. *Now I'm the personal IT girl for the entire Reed clan. So much for avoiding their drama and focusing on my own.*

When Nicholas cleared his throat, she realized she hadn't agreed to help.

"Of course."

Nicholas rose fluidly from his seat. "Great." He pulled an embossed card from his pocket. "Are you free tonight, after work?"

Vivian shook her head ruefully. "I'm sorry, I'm not. I tutor a high-school student on Mondays and Wednesdays. Is tomorrow OK?"

"That works. There's a valet service. Text or call Jessie—number's on the card—when you get to the club." He smiled. Vivian momentarily forgot every qualm she had. His eyes fairly twinkled at her. She had to swallow twice before she could make her mouth work.

"Thank you for the opportunity, Mr. Reed."

"No, thank you. Have a good night."

As he walked away, Vivian blinked, then narrowed her eyes. Nicholas Reed's cane was nowhere in sight.

Detective Suisse used a burner phone to call his CI within the Triad's heroin smuggling ring.

"Are you missing five or six guys and several kilos of H?"

"You know the answer to both questions. Why are you wasting my time?" The voice on the other end of the phone possessed only the slightest Chinese accent.

"We've got the H but haven't found any bodies."

"You won't. These people that are targeting our operations. They don't leave witnesses—or evidence."

"You know who they are?"

"The bosses do. They do not tell us. Only that we have to improve security. Anything else? I am a busy man."

"Yeah. Did you send two idiots to break into the Reed Investments server room?"

Nothing but silence came across the line for almost a minute. "When did this happen?"

"Before Thanksgiving. The third week in November. So it was your organization?"

"If we hacked Reed computers, you wouldn't know about it. We certainly wouldn't send two men so unprofessional as to be caught." With that, the line went dead.

Typical Seattle rain—somewhere between a mist and a steady soaking—made the street and car lights throw off reflections from every sidewalk, tree, and building. Vivian's phone's GPS led her directly to Willow's valet service. She felt exceedingly out of place leaving her keys with the well-dressed valet. She pulled her phone out and called Jessie Reed.

"Yeah?"

Vivian held the phone further from her ear to compensate for Jessie's yelling. "Hi, this is Vivian Richards. I was told to call you when I got here?"

"Oh, yeah! Great! Ignore the line and walk right to the front. A really big man named George is coming to the front door. See you in a sec!"

Vivian tried to make herself smaller as she passed the line of club-goers waiting under the extended awning. She'd felt like a country bumpkin with the valet. The feeling grew as she walked to the front of the line. Three twenty-something women in short skirts, blouses too thin for a December night in Seattle, and clutching the latest phone models, glared at Vivian as she passed. They raked her with their eyes and sneered.

"Vivian Richards?" Jessie Reed hadn't lied. George was indeed a very large man. His impressive musculature dwarfed everyone around.

"That's me."

George smiled down at her with teeth so perfect they had to be capped. "Come with me please." He cut his eyes, just for the briefest of moments, to the women now openly staring at Vivian. "Ms. Reed's waiting for you in the VIP lounge."

She didn't have to duck to walk under his arm as he held the rope out of her way. Inside, the club was crowded, but not as crushed as she'd imagined it might be. Stairs led down to a dance floor intermittently lit with colored lights. From the entry landing, more stairs led to a large loft overlooking the dance floor. Tall tables with stools for seating sat spaced around the loft, allowing patrons to enjoy the music coming up from the bar and dance floor and still hear themselves speak. The bouncer led Vivian through the maze of tables, most of which were occupied. At the end of the L-shaped second floor was a door marked *VIP*. George nodded to the man standing watch by the door, then led Vivian up another flight of stairs.

"How many floors does this club have?"

"Technically, the whole building. She bought it from her brother two years ago. Jessie's office is on the fourth floor, but she wanted me to bring you to the lounge first." He led her through the door at the top of the stairs.

As clean and well-decorated as the lower levels of the club were, the VIP level exuded taste and money. One whole wall of the lounge—which seemed to also be L-shaped, but a mirror of the second floor—consisted of one-way tinted glass. Wall speakers piped in music from the dance floor, but at a muted level. Leather sofas and glass coffee tables replaced the barstools and tables from the loft. Patterned emerald green and gray carpeting complemented the dark wood paneling covering the walls.

"Vivian!" Jessie waved from a horseshoe of couches in the far corner.

"There she is. Have an enjoyable evening, Miss Vivian." George flashed his teeth at her and was gone before she could respond.

The club owner thrust out a long-fingered hand. She wore a silver band around her thumb and another on her pinky finger. "Jessie Reed. My brother, Nicholas, said you're here as part of my Christmas present."

Jessie Reed looked nothing like either of her brothers, except for her green eyes. Dressed in black leather pants and a burgundy silk blouse, she had her long dark hair pulled back in several braids. Her right ear sported an intricately patterned silver ear cuff, while the left had three piercings. Her face was less angular than her brothers' faces—more of an oval shape. The smile she gave Vivian seemed an act of social courtesy rather than truly happy.

As Vivian and Jessie shook hands, a strawberry-blond head of artfully tousled curls suddenly appeared over the back of an adjoining couch.

"Ho there!" Lee Reed, stretched out across the entirety of one leather chaise, pushed himself to a more upright position. "Hey Jess, did you say she's part of your Christmas present?" Despite his quip, Lee's body language projected abject sorrow at seeing Vivian.

"Not in that way, Lee," Jessie snapped. "Ignore my *younger* brother, please. Thank you so much for coming. Would you like a drink?"

"Hi. No, nothing to drink, thank you. Aren't you twins?"

"We are, but I'm older by five whole minutes."

"Oh." Vivian gave Lee a quick nod. "Hello, Lee." She sat on the couch and looked around. "You have a very nice place here."

"Thank you."

"So, ah, your brother, Mr. Reed that is, he wanted me to beef up your Wi-Fi and improve your network security."

"Boring," drawled Lee. He flopped dramatically backward.

Vivian pulled out her phone, noted the password displayed on a card on the table, and connected to the network. She flipped through several social media sites, conscious of two pairs of green eyes focused on her. Every social media site and webpage she opened took significantly longer to load than normal. She looked around the VIP area. There were a few occupied seating groups, but more open tables. "I assume that Tuesday nights are generally slow?"

"This is a slightly larger crowd than typical for a Tuesday, actually. I suppose all the techies want to catch up after the long weekend. Thursday, Friday, and Saturday are our busiest nights."

"I need to see your router and main access point."

Jessie cocked an eyebrow again.

"Where the main phone or cable line comes in."

"Ah. That'd be upstairs." Jessie stood, then frowned at her brother. "You might as well come with us."

"I'm quite comfortable right here, thanks."

Jessie reached over, wrapped her long fingers around one of her twin's ankles, and tugged. He slid halfway into the floor.

"Not cool!"

"Get up or I'll ban you from the entire club."

Through narrowed eyes, Lee scowled at his sister. "You get more like Nicky every day."

"I dare you to say that to his face."

"I might!"

The two of them sniped at each other all the way to the end of the lounge. Jessie pushed open a fire door that led to another stairwell. One floor up, the stairs ended at a door with a keypad. Jessie punched in the code, opened the door, and strode down a wide hallway.

"My office is there." She hooked her thumb over her shoulder. "That—" She pointed to the door across the hall from her office. "—is where all the security systems and cables run to. I'll leave you to it, then?"

Vivian hitched her laptop bag strap a bit higher on her shoulder. "This might take more than one night."

"Fine by me." Jessie hooked her fingers in her brother's collar and tugged. "You leave her alone. I want a word."

Lee cast one pained look at Vivian before the door to Jessie's office shut behind him.

CHAPTER FOURTEEN

The line for entry to Willow consisted of just a few people when Vivian returned that Friday evening. She flashed a smile at the valet, then let herself in the back entrance to the club. She'd changed outfits before leaving work. All her previous "night out" clothing she'd sold to consignment stores during the three months she'd lived out of her car. The dark red jeans and gray V-neck blouse, both purchased during her lunch hour the previous day, definitely did not qualify as appropriate work attire. They would, however, allow her to blend better with the Willow clientele.

Vivian climbed the back stairs to the network room. Hooking her laptop to the system, she started running a few programs to test the network connectivity. She texted Jessie to let her know she was back on-site and working.

Come hang in the VIP lounge for a bit. Drinks on me, the response from Jessie read.

Vivian activated software to ping her phone with any problems and made her way to the exclusive area of Seattle's hottest nightclub.

Jessie Reed's chocolate-brown hair hugged her skull in multiple tight braids. Dark eyeliner and deep red lipstick complimented her naturally flawless complexion. She held court in a corner of the lounge. At least fifteen young men and women clustered around her. Every one of them was gorgeous and expensively dressed. Two of the men, one black-haired, the other dark-skinned and bald with a goatee, eyed Vivian. They didn't leer, but the predatory nature of the looks instantly put her on guard.

Seeing Vivian approach, Jessie flashed a smile and walked forward to take her hands. "Hey. Thanks for coming. Love that blouse."

"Thanks. Uh, not sure I exactly fit in up here."

"Really?" Jessie glanced over her shoulder, saw the men staring at Vivian and rolled her eyes. "They're only dangerous if you want them to be. But if you're uncomfortable, go on down to the loft area. George will grab a table for you. Have a drink or two. Honestly, though, don't expect to go unnoticed down there either." Jessie looked her over again. "You're too hot for that."

"Right." Despite herself, Vivian laughed.

George met her at the bottom of the stairs and motioned to a table. "We have bar runners that will bring you anything you want. I'll be right over there." He pointed toward a corner overlooking the dance floor. "You need something, *anything*, you let me know."

"Thank you, George. Have you worked here long?"

"Since she bought the place. I played ball for the Huskies but blew out my right knee my Senior year. Friend of mine works for her older brother; he told me they were hiring."

"Sorry about your injury. Has there been any trouble? Threats or such?"

People tended to assume that large, muscular, men lacked intelligence. In George's case, that was a mistake. His eyes narrowed. He pulled out one of the chairs across from Vivian and straddled it. "What is it, exactly, you're doing for Jessie?"

"Her brother asked me to improve the network security for the club."

He nodded. "That'd be Nicholas Reed. And now that you're here and working on it, you're asking the head bouncer if there's been any *trouble*. Which leads me to wonder precisely what kind of criminal activity you're worried about. Since you're purposely being vague, I gather that it's possible credit card skimming or something related? You're trying to find out why Mr. Reed sent you here?"

She blushed. "Not very subtly, obviously."

George pushed himself to a standing position and returned the chair to its original place. "Just find out what is happening. Leave the digging to me, or the police. The people that target clubs like this—and those that target people like the Reeds—they don't play games. They're dangerous and they'll swat you like a fly." Grim warning delivered, George nodded and walked away.

Vivian ordered a Coke from the bar and watched the crowd ebb and flow. Two guys she'd met in a previous quarter's class stopped by her table to chat. They exchanged updates on their current courses, complained about a professor they all hated, and shared job leads. The men, somewhat awkwardly, expressed their shock at seeing Vivian in a club. She explained that she was doing a favor for the owner. Just as she considered sharing more details of her task, her phone pinged.

"Sorry, gotta go. Have a good night." She grabbed her purse and worked her way back to the VIP stairs. George stood beside the door. Vivian raised her phone. "More work to do."

"OK. Remember what I said." He pushed open the door for her.

"I will."

"So you sent Vivian Richards to fix Jessie's Wi-Fi issues?" Dom sipped his coffee at the counter in the expansive Reed kitchen.

"Yes."

"No ulterior motives?"

"Something happened at the party. Whether it was Vivian fighting with Lee or Lee being an ass, the quickest way to find out what's going on is to put Jessie on the case. But, I couldn't very well have Jessie just flop down in the IT department and start interrogating the poor girl."

"So, you've decided she's not a threat?"

Nicholas rolled his neck. "For God's sake, Dom, my father's men killed her parents. She's a victim, not a threat."

"Unless she's out for revenge."

"Do you really get that vibe from her?"

Dom pondered. "No. I'm not sure she's really capable of subterfuge. She's smart—scary smart, really—but her emotions and motivations seem to be fairly easy to read." He took another sip of coffee before adding, "Of course, I've been wrong before."

"She could be useful."

At that, the chief of security firmly shook his head. "No. The last thing she needs is to be drawn into our work. You're right: she's a victim. Make restitution and let her get on with her life."

As Vivian left the Christmas morning service, sunlight broke through the clouds. She lifted her face to feel the weak December light.

"It's good to see you smiling, Vivian."

She opened her eyes and turned her smile to the priest. "Merry Christmas, Father."

"Merry Christmas indeed. I've been worried about you. Will you be joining us for Christmas dinner later?"

"Yes, I think I will."

"Good." He patted her hand before turning to the next parishioner.

Evan joined her in the basement. All around them, volunteers and parish staff bustled about, preparing for the Christmas dinner.

"Hey Viv, have you ever thought about getting a cat? I think a cat would be cool. Do they let you have pets in the dorms? One of my foster brothers had a fish but it died. We're not allowed any pets at the home, but maybe when I move out I could get a place that lets me have one, ya know?"

She grinned at the chattering young man. "Here, help me carry these coffee urns. No, I haven't considered getting a cat. Animals are a responsibility. You have to feed them and provide medical care—as well as beds and collars—and a whole lot of expenses I just can't afford."

He pouted. "You're so...*responsible*! Haven't you ever done anything just because it felt good?"

Sister Martha, directing the arrangement of tables, stopped to harrumph at the young man. He tossed her a saucy look in response. Vivian, suddenly recalling her entirely irresponsible and illogical reasons for attempting to help Lee, blushed.

"What do I need a cat for? I have a pet—you!" She ducked as Evan threw a dishtowel at her head.

"Children..." Sister Martha scolded.

Vivian looked at Evan. He looked at her. They both dissolved into giggles.

"Race you to the Christmas cookies?"

"Ha! She hid them." Evan peered at Vivian's face. "Wait... You *know*, don't you?"

Doing her best Yoda imitation, Vivian nodded. "Wise, I am. Know, I do."

"Show me," hissed Evan.

Tossing her head so that her ponytail swung like a cat's tail, Vivian led him to the secret stash. Not only did she know where Sister Martha hid the Christmas cookies, she knew that the sister had made an extra batch just for Evan and the other boys. Her not-so-stealthy hiding of those cookies was probably intentional. The sister wholly subscribed to the notion of "good trouble" and the re-direction of the boys' adventurous instincts.

After helping to feed the hundreds of men and women who streamed through the church basement that evening, Vivian watched Evan open his present from her. She'd ordered a robotics kit for him. He beamed with joy but then looked worried. Vivian, knowing why his mood changed, quickly rushed to explain.

"Father John says you may store it in his office and work on it here." She nodded with her head toward the priest. "I believe he also has a present for you." Laughter bubbled up in her chest as the sixteen-year-old hugged her. As she watched Evan talking with Father John, a sudden longing to hug her brother Simon overcame her.

It was with that sad, wistful, expression on her face that Lee Reed found her.

"Vivian?"

She jumped in her seat. "Lee? What are you doing here?"

"Can I sit?" He waited for her nod, then sat down opposite her. "I wanted to apologize."

"Lee, please. It's Christmas and—"

"I know. That's why I came. And I promise that after this, if you never want to speak to me again, that's OK.

I will not bother you again. I just couldn't leave things like they are."

Too afraid of what she might say, Vivian waited.

"I should never have bothered you with this. I put you in danger of losing your job, and in actual danger—"

"What?" She interrupted him. "What do you mean *actual danger?*"

He looked over his shoulder. Confirming that they were alone, he continued. "I..." He stopped to look down at his hands, which he clenched and un-clenched on the tabletop. "I, uh, I'm behind the break-in at the office last month."

"What?" Vivian screeched the question so loudly that everyone in the basement turned to stare. Father John's green eyes locked on her and Lee. He frowned and started toward them, Evan right behind him. "Come on." Vivian grabbed Lee's arm and dragged him from the room. She turned twice down a narrow hallway before pulling him into a storage room. Pushing him farther into the room, she put her back to the door. "What do you mean? *You* hired those goons? The ones who brought a gun and pointed it at my head?"

He took a step toward her. Vivian thrust out her hand, palm facing him. He stopped.

"I didn't know they would bring a gun. I didn't think anyone would be there! I just wanted those files."

"So, you hired two complete morons to literally brute-force their way in?" Vivian's chest heaved underneath her green Christmas sweater. She worked extremely hard not to scream her frustration at Lee. "And when that failed, you thought... what, exactly? Might as well go to the source? Maybe I can charm this girl into doing what I want? I mean, who cares if she gets fired from her job—a job she desperately needs! But you don't care, do you? You've never been evicted.

You've never had to get your meals from a church soup kitchen. You've never had to send your brother to live with relatives because you can't afford to feed the both of you. You selfish asshole!"

She stood there, panting with anger, unsure whether she should leave the room or throttle him. Lee, too ashamed to meet her eyes, began to pace.

"You're right. I am selfish. I am an asshole. That's why I came to apologize. I promise I won't do anything else to put you, or your job, in danger. My brother will never find out what you did to help me."

"You can't promise that."

He sighed. "Fine, he'll never find out from me."

They stood in silence. The room smelt of mildew, wet cardboard, and cleaning products. The fluorescent lights flickered. Lee scuffed one boot across the concrete floor.

"Why?" Vivian had to take three deep breaths before asking the question. She managed to whisper, rather than yell.

"Does it matter?"

"If you want me to accept your apology, it does."

"I decided to forget the whole thing."

Vivian snorted. "Bullshit."

Lee cocked his head to one side. Just for an instant, the care-free play-boy, grin slipped through. "Are you supposed to swear in a church?"

She narrowed her eyes.

"Sorry. But, really, I don't need to find those files. I have other leads. But, nothing that will involve you."

They lapsed back into silence. His expression was pleading, hers dubious. Finally, he whispered "Can I go?"

"Yes." She opened the door and stepped aside. As he passed her, she laid her hand on his arm. "Lee? I forgive you. Merry Christmas."

"Merry Christmas," he whispered sadly.

CHAPTER FIFTEEN

The week between Christmas and New Year's Eve passed uneventfully. Vivian went to work for three nights during which she mostly read a book or surfed through social media.

On the night after Christmas, she spent almost an hour on the phone with her brother. Simon was learning to ski and wanted to attend a horse-back trail ride in the summer. He sounded as happy as any fourteen-year-old boy ever did. Several times during their talk, Vivian started to tell him that she was saving her money so that he could come live with her. But, she always stopped herself from bringing it up. Simon was happy with their aunt and uncle. It wouldn't be fair to drag him back to Seattle just because she was lonely.

Vivian spent her Christmas bonus on two new work outfits. One was an entirely practical pantsuit in dark blue with cream pinstripes. Crawling around on the floor in tight, short, skirts while checking computer wiring just wasn't a good idea. The dress she bought, though, did have a tight skirt. It was something she never could have afforded before starting at Reed Investments. Nor would she have had anywhere to wear it. When she brought the dress home and hung it up in the closet, she stopped to run her fingers over the silky white material. The large blue polka dots perfectly matched her eyes. She'd also splurged on new blue pumps that matched both outfits.

On Wednesday night, the third of January, Vivian wore the new pantsuit to work. She had new software to install on all the building's computers. Mr. Fehr had promised to drop off Mr. Reed's laptop before he left for the evening. By 8 p.m., Vivian realized that the security chief had forgotten. She grabbed her building pass and made her way to the executive offices. As she'd expected, Fehr's office was dark with the door locked. She'd just turned toward Mr. Reed's office door when she heard the first crash.

Vivian threw open the door and immediately got crushed between it and the frame as a large body bounced off her. The man grunted; she yelped. Bright lights flashed in her peripheral vision as her head slammed against the wall. By the time she blinked away her confusion, the man had lunged back across the room. In the dim light, Vivian could see Nicholas Reed flat on his back atop his desk as another man attempted to choke him. Inset shelving above her position on the floor held several trophies. Vivian pulled herself to her feet, grabbed a trophy, and swung it at head of the man strangling her employer.

"Vivian, no," Nicholas croaked out as the pressure on his throat let up. The attacker who'd been strangling him lurched sideways from the force of Vivian's blow. Only then did she see the third man, in the corner. He raised a gun. She gaped. Then Nicholas did the most extraordinary thing: he arched his back and sprang to his feet. Bouncing once on the floor directly between Vivian and the gunman, he spun through the air like a top and kicked the gun from the man's hand. There was a bright flash just before he made contact. Nicholas's body jerked fractionally to one side even as he brought a two-handed hammer blow down on the gunman's collarbones. As the man fell, Nicholas put both feet against his office wall and sprang back in the opposite direction.

Vivian, still holding the trophy, saw the man who'd originally collided with her move to grab her. She swung the trophy blindly in his direction. Then a muscled arm

93

encircled her waist and spun her out of the way. She awkwardly fell, again. Nicholas punched one man so hard, Vivian heard the bones of his face break. The one she'd originally bludgeoned tried to stand, took two wobbly steps toward his partner's abandoned gun, then pitched head-first onto the floor. Crouched like a tiger waiting to spring, Nicholas eyed his three opponents. Everyone remained frozen in place for several long seconds. The man with the presumably broken collarbones started to wheeze.

Nicholas stood straight in one sinuous move and crossed to his desk. He pulled open a drawer and withdrew several zip-ties. Vivian started to question her sanity. She'd once watched a mixed-martial-arts match on a campus television. What Nicholas Reed had just done far eclipsed the athleticism she'd seen on the TV. He moved efficiently, at one point dragging two of his attackers across the room at the same time. He didn't once limp, much less use his cane. She watched warily when he walked to her and extended a hand.

As he pulled her to her feet, his features briefly tensed. "Are you hurt?"

"I don't think so." She pulled her hand from his. "Where's Mr. Fehr?"

"I gave him the night off."

"Well, that seems pretty short-sighted."

He huffed in annoyance. "Why were you up here?"

"I needed your laptop to install new software updates. Mr. Fehr was supposed to bring it to me. I came to get it and heard the commotion." She looked at the three men, two of whom seemed unconscious, tied in the corner. "How did they get in here? What do we do now?"

"You seem awfully calm."

"*You* seem awfully spry for a guy with shattered vertebrae and a hip replacement."

His green eyes seemed to pin her in place. "Any chance you hit your head and just imagined all of that?"

She rubbed her right temple. "Not likely."

"I was afraid of that." He stared down at her. His expression looked almost sad. "What am I going to do with you, Vivian Richards?"

Totally unsure of how to answer that ominous question, she kept her mouth shut.

Obvious pain suffused Nicholas's features. He suddenly looked very pale, even in the dim office light. He pressed a hand against his side, then looked down at it.

"Oh!" Vivian stepped forward. "You're shot!"

"Just a graze. No serious damage."

"You're bleeding!"

His eyes cut sideways at her even as he leaned against the wall. "That does tend to follow being shot."

"Among other things."

His lips quirked at her comment.

"Miss Richards, I think I'm going to have to impose on you."

"Impose?"

"I need a ride. I shouldn't drive."

"Should I call an ambulance?"

"No!" He'd shouted the response. Seeing her flinch, he immediately apologized. "I'm sorry. No, I don't need an ambulance. This is just a graze, and I don't have time to answer a thousand questions from ER doctors or the police. I'll call Dom and have him send someone over to collect these goons. If you could take me home, Dom can stitch me up."

She peered at him skeptically. "You want me to take you to your house so that your bodyguard can stitch you up—after you've been shot and half-strangled. And you're wondering if *I* have a head wound?"

He responded with another side-eye glance.

"Well, I can't let you bleed to death. Come along, Mr. Reed. I need to go back to my desk and grab my keys." She spared one last look at the pile of men in the corner. "You're sure we should leave them?"

Nicholas leaned against the wall, now obviously in pain. "They're breathing. They'll be fine until Dom's guys get here."

As the elevator doors closed, Nicholas watched Vivian closely. She wasn't shaking yet, but he would bet half his fortune she wouldn't make it to the house before she started. He would also bet the same amount of money she would have a lot more questions for him. The circle of people who knew his secret was, it seemed, about to expand.

CHAPTER SIXTEEN

Alerted by a brief phone conversation with Nicholas, Dominick Fehr remotely opened the gate as soon as Vivian's car appeared on the camera. Rather than pulling up the main drive to the house, Nicholas directed her to park outside the guest house on the back portion of the property. He leaned on her shoulder more than he had at the office, as she helped him out of the car. The bodyguard and head of corporate security met them at the door. He slid Nicholas's right arm over his shoulder and took most of his weight, freeing Vivian. She trailed behind as they made their way through a reinforced steel door.

What would have been a large private office contained a reclining examination table, an IV stand, and several medical devices. Bright, directional lights hung from the ceiling. Dom led Nicholas to the table. He said something in a voice so low Vivian couldn't hear. Nicholas glanced at her, then shook his head.

"Miss Richards, is that your blood or Mr. Reed's?"

"Huh?" She looked down at her new suit jacket. "Oh no," she cried in a dismayed tone. "This was brand new."

"I'll buy you a new one," Nicholas said, dryly. "She took a nasty knock to the head, Dom. Check her over please."

"*You're* bleeding. My headache can wait!" Her snappish tone accompanied a blue-eyed glare.

Trying to be the peacemaker, Dom motioned to a nearby chair. "If you'll have a seat over here, I'll be right with you. Let me triage Mr. Reed."

Nicholas snorted. "I think we're way past the "mister" and "miss" stage. I just bled all over her new suit and car."

"Be that as it may, if you'll have a seat?"

She sat, suddenly tired. Nicholas noted her shaking hands and realized he'd lost his bet. She'd lasted way longer than he'd expected. As Dom stepped closer, he met Nicholas's eyes.

"So, she knows?" He kept his voice pitched low.

"She saw enough. I don't think we can easily explain it away."

Dom sighed. "OK. First stitches. Then we deal with fall-out."

"Who'd you send to the office?"

"This will burn." Dom dabbed antiseptic onto the gash the bullet had carved just above Nicholas's left hip. "I sent Ramirez and Kekoa. They're taking your un-invited guests to the holding area. Did you recognize any of them? Stretch out on your right side so I can stitch this."

"One of them was vaguely familiar, but I can't place him. Maybe if I looked through our database, I could pick him out. He was trying to strangle me."

"They were all alive when our guys got there." Dom worked in silence for a few minutes. "Done. IV time." He shook his head at Nicholas's petulant expression. "No arguments. You lost blood and expended a lot of energy. I don't want the doc calling me at 2 a.m. irate because your vitals are all screwy. Sit here and recharge while I deal with Miss Richards."

"Vivian," Nicholas corrected.

"As you say, Mr. Reed."

From across the room, Vivian watched Nicholas glare at Mr. Fehr's back. Her head hurt, and exhaustion seemed to flood her whole body. If two large—and certainly dangerous—men hadn't shared the room with her, she would have curled into a ball on the tile floor. She wanted nothing more than her bed and time to think.

Dominick Fehr blinked in surprise when the petite blonde rose out of her chair as he approached.

"I need to go."

"Whoa there. I'd like to check your vitals and make sure you don't have a concussion."

"Are you a doctor?"

"No ma'am. I received field medic training in the service and then again once I joined... the company I worked for prior to my employment with Mr. Reed."

Vivian narrowed her eyes. "That's rather evasive."

"Yes, it is. Follow my finger with your eyes please. Now stare straight ahead. Touch your chin to your chest. Now look at the ceiling. Any pain or bright flashes in your vision?"

"No."

"May I exam your head and jaw for signs of fracture?"

"Do I have a choice?"

His brown eyes looked right at her. "Yes, Vivian, you have a choice. You can, and probably should, walk out of here, quit your job at Reed Investments tomorrow morning, and move far away from Seattle. But—" He smiled softly. "—I don't think you're going to do any of that, are you?"

"Hells no. Also, yes, you may examine my head. Which is only the fifth weirdest thing I've said tonight."

"No talking now." Dom prodded and massaged her skull and jaw. "You have a nasty bruise above your right eyebrow. Any pain while taking deep breaths or moving your arms?"

"A little sore, but more like being stiff. Why do you have a full medical suite in the guest house? Is there a bathroom? That's some really expensive hardware." She motioned with her chin at the medical equipment.

Dom chuckled. "There's a bathroom through there." He pointed to a door. "When you're back, I'll see which of your questions Mr. Reed feels like answering."

Vivian walked back to Nicholas's side a few minutes later. She'd re-done her ponytail and splashed some water on her face. Her employer was just sliding his arms into a casual button-down shirt. His bodyguard-turned-nurse re-attached the IV as soon as he was settled. Vivian got a quick glimpse of Nicholas's bare chest. While well-muscled, it was mottled with burn and incision scars. With the open collar, she could just see a hint of a scar at the base of his Adam's apple.

"Feeling better?"

He motioned to a chair Dom had pulled to the side of the exam table. "Yes. Thank you for asking. How are you? Would you like some water?" Dom handed her a bottle of water before she could reply. "You have some questions, I imagine?"

She sighed. "So many. First, you should know that I'm not going to forget what I saw."

Nicholas looked at Dom, then back at her. "I didn't think you would."

"You have really scary security for a trust-fund guy."

Nicholas coughed. He shifted uncomfortably. Vivian looked from him to Dom and back again. "So... why? Why have all this set-up in your quest house? Why have a bodyguard who is also a medic? *Why* do you have such high-level security?"

"Because this isn't the first time someone has tried to kill me."

"So you *didn't* go on a week-long bender in Vegas, four years ago, and wreck your car?"

"No. There was a bomb in my car. I should be dead."

"You were dead," Dom interjected. He walked over to remove Nicholas's IV.

"What is that you gave him?"

Dom waited until Nicholas nodded before he answered. "A proprietary mixture of electrolytes, creatine, and plasma, created by my employers."

"The Reed family dabbles in bio-chemistry?"

Dom sighed. "Sorry, my *former* employers. I was previously employed by Cheyenne Consortium Services." He raised his hand. "Before you ask, the less you know about them the better. Suffice it to say, their technology and research helped save Mr. Reed's—" Nicholas grunted at the return to formality, so Dom amended his words. "—Nicholas's life."

"And in return, I am their not-entirely-willing lab rat."

"Is that why you can move like you did in the office?"

Both men's expressions became, somehow, even more somber. Nicholas briefly rubbed his right hand, now free from the IV, over his short, curly, hair. "One of the unexpected benefits of the treatments I endured is greater strength in my arms and legs and greater flexibility in my joints. Most of my joints."

"So the cane is not totally an act?"

"No. My right femur and the right side of my pelvis are titanium. The ligaments, tendons, and cartilage in the joint are all artificial. Occasionally, my body tries to reject some part of that list. It hurts."

"Does it hurt now?"

He tilted his head, studying her. "You genuinely care, don't you?"

"Of course I care. What kind of monster do you think I am?"

"The normal human variety."

"You need a better class of friends," she snapped.

"So I'm learning."

Suddenly filled with nervous energy, Vivian rose from her chair and started to pace. Nicholas watched her ponytail swinging back and forth and briefly ignored her questions. He snapped back to alertness when she said, "I think you should know, Lee is in serious trouble. Those men were likely looking to hurt you because of him."

Nicholas didn't raise his voice. He spoke in clipped, staccato tones. "I'll ask you to keep your uninformed suspicions to yourself. Whatever Lee did to hurt your feelings, he's blameless in this matter."

"Hurt my feelings? Don't be ridiculous! He is perfectly capable of hiring men with guns. He admitted as much to me on Christmas—at which point I told him I wanted nothing more to do with him! It's you who shouldn't be making assumptions, *Mister* Reed."

"Let's everyone take a breath here." Dominick gently pushed Nicholas back onto the exam table. "You need to rest." He turned to Vivian. She stood there— in her crumpled blouse, pinstriped slacks, and blue pumps—looking small, scared, and utterly miserable. She crossed her arms over her stomach. "Vivian. Look at me. Take a deep breath. Now another. That's good. It's late. Why don't I take you home and we can pick this up tomorrow?"

"Take the offer, Vivian."

She immediately bristled at Nicholas's tone. Before she could tell him what she thought of his order, Dom laid a hand on her arm.

"Please," he said. "If he comes off that table again, I might not get him back on it. Anything you need to say to him can wait until tomorrow."

"Fine, but I *will* get some answers." Vivian addressed the statement more to Nicholas than to his bodyguard.

"So will I," Nicholas responded.

CHAPTER SEVENTEEN

Nicholas fidgeted with the papers on his desk. He glanced at his watch. Within the office, there was no sign of the previous night's struggle. He sighed, then winced as the medical tape over his wound tugged at his skin. That reminded him, yet again, of the woman sitting five floors below him, in the IT department.

Vivian's knowledge of his abilities—and what he chose to do with those abilities—presented a danger to them both. She was an innocent caught up in a perilous web. She was also far too curious and intelligent. If he tried to hide secrets from her, she'd find them. When she did, those blue eyes would burn holes through him. He needed to find out exactly what her involvement, personal or otherwise, with his brother entailed. What had she meant when she'd said Lee was in trouble?

"You still have another hour to figure out how much you'll tell her."

Nicholas glared at Dom. "I know how much—how little, really—I *want* to tell her."

"So, what's the problem?"

"She won't stop asking questions. If she doesn't get answers from me, what lengths do you think she'll go to in order to find the truth?" Seeing Dom's considering expression, Nicholas nodded. "Exactly. Therefore, we answer the minimum we reasonably can, find out exactly what she and Lee have been up to, and then..."

"We find a nice farm for her to go and live on?"

Nicholas's glance spoke volumes—of profanity. "You wish."

"What did the good Father have to say about our Miss Richards?"

"Would you please stop calling her that?"

"Nope," Dom replied. He popped the "p" for added annoyance-factor.

"Asshole," Nicholas muttered. "Father John said she was an orphan. She's been putting herself through school. He passed on her resume to Ghiadello. Otherwise, he repeated the basic details of what you found out."

"So she doesn't know the truth."

"Not yet."

Nicholas trod softly across the tiled floor of the IT department. Vivian sat at her table, her blonde head turned away from him. He stopped a few feet away. Attempting to appear as non-threatening as possible, he shoved his hands in his pockets. She looked up. He stood there in expensive slacks and dress shoes, shirt sleeves rolled to his elbows and his tie loose about his neck.

"Hey."

"Hey," she replied.

"Ready for that talk?"

When she nodded, Nicholas turned sideways and gestured toward the door. She walked down the white concrete block hallway to the elevator. He kept walking. When she made a questioning sound, he smiled and motioned with his head, indicating the end of the hallway. He stopped beside the fire extinguisher, then looked down at her upturned face. He just managed to avoid wincing at the sight of the bruise near her temple.

"I'd ask you to forget this, but you won't." Nicholas ran his fingers along both sides of the box holding the fire extinguisher. There was a click, and the entire box swung away from the wall. Behind it was a palm scanner. Never breaking eye contact with Vivian, Nicholas placed his left hand on the scanner.

A three-foot-wide section of the wall, from floor to ceiling, recessed half a foot before moving sideways. Behind the missing section of wall was another reinforced metal door. This one had a keypad beside it.

"Getting a *super* strong villain's lair vibe, here."

He grinned. "No, for that we'd have built it in Mount Rainier."

Vivian couldn't help herself. She grinned back. "Oh, obviously. Silly me."

Nicholas keyed in the code. The door clicked before swinging open. He stepped closer to her, until only inches separated them. Her perfume, a light citrus scent, wafted into his nose. She could see the pale puckered line of a scar near his right eyebrow.

"Last chance to turn around. You can go back to your quiet life."

Vivian tilted her head back until she could stare him down. "I'd rather risk my life knowing than spend the rest of my life wondering."

He peered down at her as if trying to memorize every inch of her face. "Very well. Follow me."

He led her down metal stairs to a sub-basement. The air was noticeably cooler but did not smell of dampness. The floor, when they stepped off the bottom stair, gave slightly under Vivian's heels. She looked down.

"It's the same tiling they use on submarines. It dampens static electricity, is non-slip, and helps reduce noise." Dominick Fehr crossed his trunk-like arms over his chest. He was wearing a shoulder holster, and, like Nicholas, had dispensed with his suit coat. "Good evening, Miss Richards."

"Mr. Fehr. You're doing that just to irritate him, aren't you?"

"Don't encourage him," Nicholas growled. "Come sit down over here. I think you'll be most comfortable in this section of our workshop." He gestured toward a bank of computer towers, wide-screen monitors, and several keyboards. When she made a soft squeak of joy at seeing the computers, Nicholas smiled behind her back.

"Workshop? Seriously? That's way too mundane for whatever this... Is that the new Lenovo tower? I thought only the military had access to those. But, of course, billionaires and super-secret shadow organizations with scary names can get whatever they want. Can I touch it?"

"Focus please."

Nicholas sat in the other high-backed, and sinfully comfortable, office chair facing Vivian. Dominick leaned his hip against the table holding the keyboards. Both men stared at her. The younger one spoke first.

"You have questions."

"Uh..." She opened her mouth to say more, then looked around the sub-basement room in wonder.

"OK, I'll start. Are you dating my brother?"

"What? Oh, no. I am—I *was*—helping him on a project. That's all. These are really comfortable chairs. I'd like one of these. Not," she hurried to say, "that I'm making demands. I uh, what was your question?"

"Lee?"

"Your brother."

"Nervous?"

"Yes!" Vivian clutched the arms of the chair. "Wouldn't you be? Well, of course you wouldn't.

Nothing makes you two nervous. You can just smash anything that threatens you."

"I don't know—you're making me pretty nervous right now," Dom stated.

Nicholas threw him a quick over-the-shoulder glare. "He will not be smashing anything right now, including you. If you're not dating Lee, why were you attending my family party as his date? And why did you two sneak off to his bedroom?"

Vivian sighed. Confession was supposed to be good for the soul, but at that moment she felt trapped and despondent. "Lee came to me asking for help. He wanted to find security videos from the Reed building the night your father was killed. He was convinced those videos were on the servers at the office."

"And you helped him look?"

She nodded. "I... I thought he was obsessed with an Internet conspiracy and that seeing a bit of old footage would help him move on. I know what it's like to believe something to be true but not be able to prove it."

Dominick looked at the floor for a minute. Nicholas winced. If Vivian picked up on either man's expression, she gave no indication.

"I couldn't show him any footage, as it turns out. And you know why."

Nicholas winced again.

"You and—" She looked at Dom. "—you, moved the files right after you came back from rehab. I thought you moved them to your house. Now, I'm thinking they're on these computers right here. Which makes me wonder why you went through the trouble of moving them via portable hard-drive when you just needed a quick cable run from upstairs."

"Because we didn't have this place setup yet. So, you attended the party to...?"

"I still thought I could help him. I thought I could connect him to your back-up server at the house and it would all be over."

"But it wasn't. You left there crying. Scared?"

"Yes." She looked down at her feet. They barely touched the floor, since the chair she sat in was obviously adjusted for the height of the two tall men in the room.

"Ah," Dom said. "That was you." He met her eyes and nodded in acknowledgment. "Well played. I didn't even notice the intrusion until the next day."

"Well, after that, I told Lee I was done. He came to the church, on Christmas, to apologize. He said he didn't need my help anymore. I don't think he's stopped trying to find out who killed your father. I think either he's hired people to beat the information out of you, or he's asked the wrong questions of the wrong people."

"Lee did not hire those men to attack me."

"How can you be so sure?"

Nicholas just stared at her in response.

"He told those intruders how to get in here. The night we met, remember?"

"I'm not likely to forget," Nicholas said softly.

"Oh." Vivian peered at him. "Did you know Lee was up to something?

Both men nodded. "We suspected. You've filled in some missing pieces. Thank you for that. Now, about the answers you sought?"

"I'm still unclear on why you have scary spy-type encryption on your computers and hidden 'workshops'." She made air quotes. "Does the President even have this level of paranoia surrounding him?"

"I couldn't say, having never met him. After the bomb in my car, I was—as Dom loves to remind me—dead. Prior to that, though, I was already on the Justice

Department's radar. One of their agents knows a guy at Cheyenne. The team from Cheyenne Consortium arrived at the ER in time to get my heart started again. The rest is rather gruesome and second-hand information. I was unconscious for all of it, of course."

"Well, yeah."

He blinked as he inhaled—looking slightly exasperated yet amused. "Once they saved my life, I spent eighteen months learning how to walk again and then learning about the, uh, side-effects of my treatments."

"Super strength and Gumby-like flexibility?"

Nicholas rolled his eyes, but Dom chuckled.

"Why where you on Justice's radar?"

Before he replied, Nicholas leaned forward and clasped his hands between his knees. Knowing what he knew about her past, he didn't want to scare her. "Because my father was the head of the largest criminal syndicate in the Pacific North-West. I found out what he'd been doing—where our money had come from for at least two generations—and I foolishly confronted him. The FBI had a wiretap in his office. They heard our argument and arranged to meet me. I was in Vegas that week not on some frat-boy bender but to work out an agreement for my testimony."

"You don't think..."

"That my father arranged to have me killed? No. Unfortunately, there was a mole in the US Attorney's office who reported to one of my father's... associates. A Chinese triad member planted the bomb in my car."

"We learned all this later," Dom clarified. "At the time, the world thought Nicholas was still in a coma. My employers made alternate arrangements with the Justice Department, since there was little he could do from a hospital bed."

"Then, worried that my father would seek retribution for the hit on me, the Triad shot him."

"So he *was* murdered. Lee was right."

"Yes. The footage he's looking for doesn't exist anymore, though. I erased it last year."

"And the criminal organization? The deal to testify?"

"That—" Nicholas leaned back in his chair and waved his hand to indicate the room. "—is what all of this is for. Since I've been home, Cheyenne Consortium's own little bionic boy has been steadily dismantling the mess my father created."

"So, you run around fighting crime and stuff?" Vivian looked skeptical. "Do you have outfits and capes?"

They both sneered.

"Hey, think about how it sounds." She ticked off a list on her fingers. "You have superpowers. You have a hidden lair. You're a billionaire. You fight crime."

"OK, one, it's not a 'lair'."

"I prefer to think of it as a well-designed man-cave," Dom interjected.

"Not helping, Dom," Nicholas growled through clenched teeth. "Two, I don't really have superpowers."

Vivian grabbed a tablet stylus from the table and flung it at his face.

Nicholas snatched it out of the air, closed his fist, and snapped the stylus in half.

"You were saying?"

Suppressing a grin, Dom continued the explanation. "We track down criminal elements and deport them if they are non-citizens. We provide extra security for business owners willing to cut ties with the Triad. The Reed family fortune is being used to drive up profits for legitimate enterprises while squeezing out bad actors. And, yes, we occasionally participate in physical apprehensions."

"But no capes," Nicholas snapped.

Vivian turned in her chair to look at the monitors. Every screen was black. "Surveillance?"

"Yes."

"Video, audio, data mining?"

"All of it."

"Have you ever killed anyone?" She didn't look at them as she asked.

They paused. Dom answered first. "Yes. As a soldier and in my time with Cheyenne. Killing those men saved lives. I didn't like it. Still don't. Expect to have to answer to God for it at some point. Until then..." He trailed off before shrugging.

Nicholas wouldn't meet her eyes. "Yes. Right before I came home, Dom and I were... Well, where it was doesn't matter. We encountered a piece of garbage who'd been raping and trafficking little girls. I started punching him. Dom pulled me off, but it was too late." Nicholas looked at his hands. "I wasn't used to being a weapon."

CHAPTER EIGHTEEN

Vivian started to respond to Nicholas's bleak statement but was stopped by her cell phone ringing. She looked at the thick ceiling and walls before asking, "Signal booster?"

"Of course," Dom replied, sounding slightly offended.

Vivian looked at the screen and immediately accepted the call. "Lee? What? Why? No. No!"

As her voice rose, Dom stepped forward. Nicholas came out of his chair.

"Come to the office. Don't argue with me! Lee? Lee! OK. Go to..." She looked at Nicholas, who mouthed one word to her. "Go to the church. Yes, I'll be there soon. Lee?" She pulled the phone from her ear and looked at it. "He hung up. He said someone's chasing him."

Dominick walked to the other side of the room, opened a rectangular safe and pulled out two pistols and several extra magazines. Nicholas collected those, and a shoulder holster, while the bodyguard pulled out several zip-tie cuffs and a baton. Nicholas motioned toward the stairs.

"Go back to your office. We'll call you when it's over."

Vivian snorted. "The hell I will. I'm going with you."

Nicholas crossed the room in two long strides. He loomed over her to the extent that she stepped back. "No, you are not."

"Listen here, *Mister* Reed. He asked *me* to come. It's *my* church." She jabbed a finger in the hard chest filling her vision. "He's *my* friend."

"He's my brother!"

Dominick ended the argument by grasping Vivian's elbow and steering her toward the stairs. "She'll just follow us in her own car. We're wasting time." He marched up the stairs with Vivian. Nicholas trailed behind. The security professional pushed Vivian, gently, into the back seat. The two men stopped to slide into Kevlar vests before climbing into the front seat of the SUV.

Nicholas turned around to glare at the woman in the back seat. "You'll do exactly what I say, when I say it, without argument." He continued quickly, in order to stifle her protest. "Otherwise, I will tie you to that armrest."

She gaped at him. "You're serious."

"I am. Now, tell me what Lee said. *Exactly* what he said."

She relayed their brief conversation. "He sounded scared."

"He should be."

Dominick caught her eye in the rear-view mirror. "This is going to be fast and loud. I don't have a vest or helmet for you. You must listen to us, OK? If you can't promise me that, you need to stay in the car."

Suddenly realizing how far in over her head she was, Vivian nodded mutely.

"How many people will be at the church?"

Vivian checked her watch. "At this hour on a Thursday, not many. The kitchen staff will have finished cleaning. Father John will be in the rectory. That's—"

"We know the layout." Nicholas shifted in his seat. He pressed one hand to the wound in his side.

Never taking his eyes off the road, Dominick asked, "That going to be a problem?"

"No," was the clipped response. Nicholas opened the bag he'd grabbed on their way out of the workshop.

Opening a black zipper case, he withdrew a pen-like injector. After turning the dial twice, he jabbed the needle through his pants into the meat of his thigh.

"How many times has the doc told you not to do that through clothing?"

Nicholas leaned his head back against the headrest and closed his eyes. "Don't know. I've been tuning both of you out for years."

Dom grunted in response and made an illegal U-turn. The SUV rocked before stabilizing and speeding down the alley beside the church. The priest's old Volvo sat parked in its usual spot. Beside it was a sedan with tinted windows. Nicholas turned around in his seat.

"Fold that seat beside you forward and reach into the case behind it. There are two helmets. Pass them up to me please."

Vivian followed his directions. She watched as both men fastened the motorcycle-style helmets over their heads and checked their weapons.

"We're going to check out that car over there. Get down on the floor and stay there until I come get you." Nicholas made direct eye contact. "You getting shot will not help Lee. We'll be right back."

Vivian slid into the floor. She heard the SUV doors click shut and the locks engage. The usual city sounds were muted by the thick windows. The church parking lot wasn't particularly well lit. She sat in the darkness for what felt like ten minutes. Then the door locks clicked open.

"Parking lot is clear. Nicholas is going through the rectory. You're with me." Dom held out his right hand while he kept his gun in his left. "Phone still on?"

He whispered the question as they jogged across the small parking area.

"Yes." She tapped on the broad back in front of her. "Look. That's Lee's car."

Dom nodded in acknowledgment before asking, "Will these side doors be locked?"

"For the church, but the door to the basement will be unlocked. It's winter. We leave it open for the homeless."

"Roger that. Stay behind me now." Looking every bit the soldier he once was, Dom placed her hand on his hip. "Keep this right here."

They only made it a few steps into the basement before Vivian's phone buzzed in her pocket. Dom stopped his forward progress as she pulled the phone out. She read the text message then, hand shaking, passed the device forward to Dom.

The text read: *If you want him back alive, toss your gun into the room.*

Vivian, trying to control her shaking, pointed at the double doors that divided the hallway from the large common room. Dom pointed to the door beside them.

"The kitchen," she whispered.

"Go in there, stay down."

She nodded. Right before she stepped through the door, she squeezed Dom's hand as he handed back her phone. She crouched down, moving between the prep tables and rolling carts, trying her best to stay quiet. Just as she rose beside the door leading to the common room, a large calloused hand covered her mouth. Warm breath tickled against her ear.

"Shh. It's me. Dom went in there?"

Vivian nodded.

"You stay here. No matter what you hear, you *stay*."

Her blue eyes flashed up at him. He removed his hand and stepped around her.

Lee's captors had only flipped a few of the light switches, so only every third row of fluorescent lights illuminated the room. It gave the whole place an odd, flickering, shadowed effect. As Dom entered the room, he placed his gun on the floor and kicked it across the floor.

"Good. Now where is Reed? We know he's come."

"I'm right here." Nicholas stepped through the door from the kitchen. He held both hands aloft.

The tall, rotund man who had Lee in a choke-hold stepped farther into the light. Lee's face was already bruised and bleeding. His right knee bent at an odd angle, obviously not able to support his weight. Beside them stood a shorter man with a runner's physique. He was the one speaking. He held a 9mm automatic by his side.

"Very good. Your brother needs to learn a lesson. We leave here now. Once he's taught, we return him. If he is a good pupil, he might even get to keep all his fingers and teeth."

"You're not taking him anywhere, and you can stop lying about returning him. He doesn't have any information to share with you. I'm the one taking your men. I've been raiding your stash houses and destroying your dope."

The gunman chuckled, but it was a mirthless sound. "As if we do not know this. You dishonored your father and got him killed. Now this boy asks too many questions." The gun came up, pointed directly at Nicholas. "Perhaps if you stop interfering, you can keep your sister and mother safe. If you fight us tonight, your whole family will die."

Nicholas pulled his helmet off, dropped it on the floor, and spread his arms wide. "You've already failed to kill me once. Do you enjoy failure?"

At the first echoing gunshot, Vivian jumped. She pushed open the kitchen door in time to see Dominick Fehr slide like a baseball player across the floor, snatch up his gun, and shoot a very fat man right between the eyes. Lee—whom the man had been holding—collapsed to the ground, gasping for air.

The wiry gunman fired at Nicholas's chest. The round hit him in the center of his vest. Using the kinetic force of the bullet and his hyper-mobility, Nicholas somersaulted backward in the air. He bounced once on the balls of his feet even as he drew his gun and fired across the room. His opponent pulled the trigger an instant after Nicholas's bullet hit him in the shoulder. The shot went wide, pinging off the door frame to the kitchen.

Vivian had been crawling toward Lee when the errant bullet whizzed by her head. She cried out and retreated to the kitchen.

Blood gushing from his shoulder, his escape routes cut off, and his kidnapping plot obviously foiled, the Asian man glared at Nicholas. He couldn't raise his arm enough to take aim at the elder Reed brother, but the younger one lay at his feet. Right before both Nicholas and Dom shot him, the Triad gunman fired two shots into Lee's chest.

Vivian heard the last gunshots followed by a heavy thump. She pushed open the door again. The first thing she saw was Lee on the floor, bleeding. A strangled scream escaped her as she stumbled forward. Though she pushed down hard on the wounds, blood seeped through her fingers. Lee tried to say something. Only bloody bubbles escaped his mouth.

Everything after that was a mad kaleidoscope of sound and light. Someone, either Dom or Nicholas, picked her up by the waist and moved her away from Lee. All the lights in the room came on. Dom started doing CPR. Father John was there. At some point, a blanket fell over Vivian's shoulders. Paramedics arrived, but only after Dom had inserted a plastic tube into a hole in Lee's right side. Nicholas followed the ambulance to Harborview Medical Center. Police flooded the room with a lot of questions for Dom. Vivian was relocated to the priest's office.

Sister Martha had just finished helping Vivian wash the blood from under her fingernails when Johann— one of the Reeds' drivers—showed up. He whispered a few things to Father John, then walked Vivian out to a waiting town car. He drove her back to her apartment and walked her to her the door. Zombie-like, Vivian locked the door, pulled off her ruined clothing, and fell into bed. She cried herself to sleep.

CHAPTER NINETEEN

After a few hours of fitful sleep, Vivian called Johann. She needed a ride since her car was still at the Reed building. The driver took her to Harborview. Father John met her in the private waiting room. He pulled her into a long hug.

"You poor child. Did you sleep at all? Have you eaten?"

"I slept. I'm not hungry. Where's Nicholas? How's Lee?"

"Nicholas is meeting with the doctors right now. He'll be back to relay their news. Come, sit down. I believe you know my niece, Jessie."

In a week crammed full of surprises, finding out that Father John was an uncle to Nicholas, Lee, and Jessie barely made Vivian blink. She simply nodded and followed him. Jessie Reed looked haggard. Her long, curly brown hair hung in a sloppy ponytail with strands escaping above her ears. Her mascara had run at some point during the night, highlighting her parlor.

Jessie swiped at her eyes, further smearing her mascara. "I freaking hate hospitals. Why didn't Lee just come to us for help?"

Realizing that Nicholas hadn't told his sister the whole story, Vivian shook her head. "I don't know. I wish I did."

The door that led to the trauma center swung open. Nicholas came through leading an older woman. He wasn't wearing a tie, but his white dress shirt was clean and crisp. His usual one-day beard looked a touch longer, but otherwise, he could have just come from a board meeting. Right hand gripping the top of his cane, he supported the woman on his free arm. She had platinum-blonde hair, one-carat diamond studs in her ears, and wore expensive heels. The woman's skin looked tight under her exquisitely applied makeup.

Vivian stood up as the pair approached.

Nicholas made introductions. "Mother, this is Vivian Richards. She's a friend of Lee's and one of my employees. Vivian, my mother, Ingrid Reed."

Mrs. Reed's vacant expression did not change.

"Ingrid, come sit down so Nicholas can tell us what the doctors said." Father John didn't wait for her response. He simply removed her arm from Nicholas's and led her to a chair.

In the moment that passed as Father John seated Ingrid, Nicholas stepped closer to Vivian. His green eyes swept over her drooping eyelids, makeup-free face, cable-knit sweater, and jeans. "Thank you for coming."

"Thank you for not asking if I'm OK."

The barest hint of a smile touched the corners of his mouth. "I try not to ask questions with obvious answers." He motioned to the empty chairs, then waited for Vivian to sit before speaking. "Lee is out of surgery. He was shot twice in the chest—"

Jessie made a soft mewling sound.

"His right lung collapsed and one of his arteries was damaged. The surgeons repaired all of that. They had to remove a small segment of his lung tissue, but they otherwise expect him to make a full recovery. He's going to be in a coma and on a respirator for a few days." Nicholas took a deep breath. "Once he is released, he'll need some rehab. I'm going to contact the facility that helped me and reserve him a spot."

Vivian's head snapped sideways. Her pupils dilated. Nicholas wanted to let Cheyenne *rehabilitate* Lee? He met her eyes and gave an almost imperceptible shake of his head.

"When can we see him, Nick?" Jessie, Vivian noted, used a different diminutive of her elder brother's name than Lee did.

"They're most worried about infection right now, so no visitors for another forty-eight hours. Again, he won't be awake for at least two more days. Vivian will return to the office with me. Jessie, Johann will drive you and mother back to the house."

Jessie and her mother departed. Nicholas extended his hand to his uncle. Father John clasped it in both of his. Though neither spoke, something passed between them. Nicholas nodded. The priest turned to Vivian. Eyes bright with sudden tears, she took a shuddering breath and tried to smile.

"I don't think I'll make Evan's session tonight."

"Understood. I will find some suitable occupation for him. Please get some rest." He looked over her head to his nephew. "Both of you." He walked out, leaving Vivian alone with Nicholas.

"Dom's waiting downstairs. We promised the detectives from SPD that we'd bring you by for an interview. If you're up for it?"

She shrugged. They walked in silence to the parking garage. Once in the backseat of the same SUV they'd ridden in the previous night, Vivian closed her eyes and leaned against the seat. Nicholas sat beside her while Dom drove.

"So, Father John is your uncle?" She didn't bother opening her eyes to ask the question.

"My mother's older brother."

"Is that how I got hired by your company?"

"John's friendly with Mrs. Ghiadello. But no, he didn't ask me to hire you. I had no idea we'd hired a blonde spitfire for the IT department until the night I met you."

She snorted in response to his description. Then, taking a deep breath, she opened her eyes and faced her boss. "What am I supposed to tell the police?"

"The truth."

Her face contorted in an expression of contemptuous disbelief. "Right. I'll just tell them my employer is a super soldier on a one-man—" She paused and made eye contact with Dom via the rear-view mirror. "—sorry, *two*-man, crusade to eliminate an international crime syndicate. Oh, and that his younger brother is convinced—rightly, it turns out—that there's a conspiracy covering up his father's murder."

"Well, you can certainly include that background if you like," Nicholas said dryly. "But, I was referring to the specific events of last night. Your friend Lee called you sounding distressed. You arranged to meet him at the church. Mr. Fehr, the chief of security for Reed Investments and Mr. Reed were still at the office when you received the call. You asked them to accompany you. Once in the building, you heard sounds of a struggle. Mr. Fehr left you in a place of safety. You did not see any of the shootings, only the aftermath."

"But I did."

"What?"

Vivian squeezed her eyes shut. She clenched her hands until her nails stung against her palms. "I saw the big man. I saw him die. I just didn't see who shot him."

She was in such obvious pain. Nicholas wanted to soothe her but had no idea how. Saying he was sorry seemed wholly inadequate. She looked so fragile; he feared she would shatter like spun glass if he touched her. A muscle in his jaw twitched. He stared out the window.

"My lawyer will meet us at the station. Consider him your lawyer for the purposes of this interview."

"Do I need a lawyer? Am I in trouble?"

"You're not in trouble. Mr. Garvey is there to make sure that the detectives do not attempt to mislead you or otherwise entrap you. You have done nothing wrong. You're there to make a statement."

"What *did* happen?"

It was Dom's turn to answer. "We'll save that for after. There's no sense clouding your memory with anything you didn't witness." He put the SUV in park, then came around to open her door. "That's Mr. Garvey. We'll be right here when you're finished." Once Vivian and the attorney entered the precinct, Dom climbed back into the driver's seat. "Man, we have got to find a way to extricate her from all this."

"How do you propose I do that? You think I want to put her through this? *I* wanted to leave her behind last night."

"She would have gone on her own. You know that."

"Exactly," hissed Nicholas. "She chose to help Lee. She chose to continue helping him. Even in my office— God, was it really just two nights ago—she could have run screaming. Instead, she ran toward the danger."

"And if she comes apart in a fit of conscience and tells everything she knows? What then, Nicholas? You know Cheyenne won't let her tell their secrets."

"So we keep her close—for our protection and hers." He saw Dom's expression. "You disagree?"

"No. I think it's our only option. That doesn't make me like it, though."

Nicholas wanted to make a witty retort, but the truth of his friend's words prevented it. He went back to staring out the window. Cold rain fell from slate-gray clouds. With the decorative lights of the

Christmas season packed away, the dominant color of a Seattle January was gray. Clouds, buildings, streets, even the flat, reflective, waters of the Puget Sound and Lake Washington were varying shades of that most depressing of colors. It all just made him feel weary.

Vivian exited the police station an hour later. She stopped to thank Mr. Garvey. Dom stood waiting beside the SUV. He opened the door for her. As she slid onto the seat beside him, Nicholas closed the laptop he'd been typing on.

"Any problems?"

"No. They wanted to ask more questions, but Mr. Garvey wouldn't let them."

"Good. That's what he's paid for. Now, Dom's going to drive us to the office. You can pick up your car and go home. I'm giving you the night off." He shook his head at her. "No arguments, please. I'm not freezing you out. Come see me on Monday evening. If anything changes with Lee, one of us will call you."

Too tired to argue, Vivian merely nodded. "I need to know how much Father John knows. If I say the wrong thing in front of him..."

"My uncle knows about my father's criminal activities. Actually, I think he knew long before I did. He knows that the Triad tried to kill me. He believes I'm still working with government agencies to make amends. As for who exactly I work with, what my abilities are, or why, I do not think he knows."

"OK." Realizing they were back in the Reed building's parking garage, Vivian opened her door. "I will see you on Monday, then. Thanks for the ride."

As Dom pulled around to the executive side of the garage, Nicholas asked, "Did she seem subdued to you?"

"You'd rather she argued with you? Don't we have enough to deal with? If you're really spoiling for a fight, don't forget you have to explain increased security to your sister."

Nicholas groaned. "Isn't that why I have you?"

Stone-faced, Dom replied "You'd have to triple my hazard pay before I'd even consider it. Your sister terrifies me."

"Try growing up with her."

CHAPTER TWENTY

It was Monday morning, rather than evening, when Vivian next saw Nicholas and Dominick. At 6 a.m., her phone buzzed with a text message.

Lee is awake and off the vent. Asking for you. —*N*

She dressed as quickly as possible and raced to Harborview. Dom met her in the lobby, vouched for her, and escorted her upstairs. As they rode in the elevator, Vivian smiled up at him.

"I'm sorry that I didn't ask on Friday. Are you...You know, Nicholas is right. Asking someone if they are OK after something like...that...seems almost insulting."

Dom didn't return her smile, but he did nod. "I don't regret killing those men. I do regret the actions that led to me having to make that choice."

"Oh." Guilt suffused her. "I'm so sorry. I tried—"

"Vivian, please. You did everything you could to keep Lee out of trouble. Had he listened to you, last night wouldn't have happened. *You* did not kidnap him, beat him, or threaten his life. If anyone should apologize, it's Lee to you."

Just before the elevator doors opened, Vivian flashed a quick grin at Dom. "So, no more *Miss Richards*?"

"Only in front of *Mister* Reed. I have to get *some* enjoyment out of my day."

The head of Lee's bed was slightly elevated. Dozens of wires and tubes snaked around his chest and head. His right leg was immobilized in a brace. When the pretty IT tech entered the room, he attempted a smile.

"Vivian," he croaked.

"Use the board, you idiot." Nicholas rose from his seat in the corner. He touched Vivian's elbow lightly and bent his head closer. "Good morning. Sorry to call you so early, but he insisted upon seeing you. Keep it brief, though. He's weak and needs to rest."

Lee watched his brother lead Vivian to a chair, his hand at the small of her back. He narrowed his eyes at Nicholas and scrawled a curse on the small whiteboard he'd been given to aid communication. Nicholas did not bother to respond. Instead, he walked to the door where he conferred with Dom in low whispers.

Vivian reached out and touched Lee's hand. "Hey you."

Hey, he wrote. *I tried to keep you out of this.*

"And look where that got you. Oh Lee, I'd rather you broke your promise to me than gotten into all of this. Why didn't you just ask your brother for help?"

He scowled at her before writing: *He would just lie to me again. He's been lying for years! To all of us! Did you see what he did? What he can do?*

"Lee." Nicholas's voice from right over her shoulder made Vivian jump. "I didn't bring Vivian here to make you more upset. Your blood pressure is way too high."

Vivian glanced at the monitor. She squeezed Lee's hand. "We don't need to discuss this right now. There will be plenty of time later. I'll visit you tomorrow and bring a tablet loaded with apps. All you have to do is lie here and heal. You *can* do lazy, right?"

Lee tried to laugh but started coughing. *Sorry*, he wrote, then underlined it.

Vivian rolled her eyes. "What is this defect in Reed men that they're constantly apologizing for things that aren't their fault?" She leaned over and lightly kissed Lee's forehead. "Rest. Get better."

When she straightened and turned to the door, she found herself the subject of intense scrutiny. Tawny brows furrowed over Nicholas's green eyes. She couldn't determine what his expression meant, but the attention definitely made her nervous. She left without saying anything.

Just after 6 p.m., Dominick appeared at the door of the IT department.

"Almost finished?"

"Almost. You know, I still need to install that software update on Mister... Nicholas's laptop."

"Yeah, that's not happening. How much longer do you need and are you hungry?"

"Fifteen minutes? Thirty, tops. And, starving."

"Burgers or Chinese?"

"Five Guys?" Seeing his nod in the affirmative, she continued. "Definitely burgers. Little cheeseburger, lettuce, mayo, ketchup. Let me get you some money." She leaned over to grab her purse.

Dom rolled his eyes. "Also not happening. We work for a billionaire. Finish up. I'll be back in thirty."

It took him forty-five minutes. Vivian waited at the parking garage entrance to the basement. She took the bag of food from the security chief so that he could work the mechanism to enter the workshop. Looking up at the security camera attached to the ceiling, she asked, "Won't the other guard staff see? Or do they all know?"

Dom opened the second door and waved her forward.Dom opened the second door and waved her forward. "They don't all know, and no, they won't notice. That feed comes down here, not to the main building. Watch your step, please. These stairs were not designed for heels."

Vivian focused on her steps as she asked, "Don't they wonder why they have one fewer feed than cameras?"

Slightly exasperated, Dom answered, "No. It's never come up."

"What's never come up?" Nicholas stepped forward and took the food from Vivian. He indicated a table deeper in the workshop with three chairs pulled up to it.

"Miss Richards has kindly pointed out that we have one more security camera than video feeds, in the basement."

French fry halfway to his mouth, Nicholas paused. "Yeah?"

"I mean, if an entry level IT gal can point it out, you'd think some super scary security guys would." Vivian looked at them for confirmation.

"Maybe the IT gal is far more scary than the security guys?"

Dom brought three bottles of water to the table before sitting down. They ate in relative silence. The men finished well before Vivian, who kept looking around her in wonder. Her previous visit to the workshop had been cut short by Lee's call for help. Now, between French fries, she took it all in.

Five feet from the base of the stairs, a dividing wall funneled anyone entering the room toward the bank of computers and monitors. Underneath the stairs were several tall gun cabinets. The entire workshop was a long rectangle. On the other side of the wall at the base of the stairs, Vivian could see a miniature version of the medical suite she'd encountered at the Reeds' guest house. That area was bracketed by another wall that came two-thirds of the way out into the room. The walls and ceiling were made of white concrete blocks. The furnishings, with the exception of the two computer chairs with excellent lumbar support—Vivian really lusted after those chairs—were stainless steel. A table identical to the one they were eating on sat against the wall. File folders, a whetstone, a microscope, a gun-cleaning kit, and an unopened pair of boot laces cluttered the top. Rows of directional LED lights illuminated the half of the room where they sat.

Vivian turned around in her chair, peering into the shadowed area on the other side of the dividing wall. "What's back there?"

"Workout equipment." Rising smoothly from his chair, Nicholas led the way. As he passed the edge of the wall, the lights in the rest of the workshop came on. A quick bag and a long punching bag hung from the ceiling. There was a weight bench as well as several pieces of equipment Vivian could not identify. Thick mats in the center of the room formed a sparring area. Wooden boards with human outlines—and a lot of holes—hung on the wall that separated the area from the medical set up.

"And that?" She pointed to closed door. "Super-secret costume storage?"

He chuckled even as he tried to sneer. "The bathroom."

"Oh. Well, in that case, I'll be right back."

When she returned to the table, Vivian stopped halfway and removed her heels. At Nicholas's raised brows, she explained, "These tiles may be impact and noise absorbing, but I'm going to break my ankle." He noted that, when she sat, she tucked one leg underneath her. "Now." She leaned forward, pinning them both with her blue eyes. "What are we going to do about Lee?"

Nicholas glanced at Dom with a quirked eyebrow. "We?"

"Yes, we. There must be something I can do to help him. I may not be a super-soldier, or even a really bad soldier, but there's got to be something."

Before Nicholas could say anything, Dom asked "Aren't you about to start your last quarter at UW? Won't you be too busy?"

The look of disgust she gave him would have curdled milk. "I have a capstone course. Singular. That's it."

"And the boy you tutor—Evan, I believe?" Nicholas asked.

She looked from one to the other. Dom had darkly tanned skin with golden undertones, a dark beard and mustache, and chocolate-colored eyes. Nicholas's pale skin was dotted with freckles, his jaw covered with red-gold stubble. Despite those differences, their expressions were identical.

"So your concern is that there's too *much* for me to do?"

"Uh, that's not—"

"Great." She stood up, leaving her shoes behind, and pulled her chair back to its position in front of the computers. With a tap of one key, a log-in screen appeared on the monitor directly in front of her. She looked up at Dom.

He folded his arms over his chest. "Show me what ya got."

Nicholas, still seated at the table, swallowed hard when Vivian slid out of the chair and bent over to look at the back of the computer towers. Realizing he was ogling her, he leaned back to stare at the ceiling.

"Ah, two factor authentication. Smart." She sat down again, then slowly pivoted to face Nicholas. She reached into her purse, pulled out her phone, and tapped out a quick text message. Across the room, Nicholas's phone chirped. He looked up at her, but she had her head bent over her phone. He shrugged and typed a reply. Vivian's phone buzzed a second later. Ever so slowly, she raised her head and smiled at Dom. He looked from her to Nicholas and back again.

"No way."

She shrugged.

Ignoring their discussion, Nicholas retrieved his laptop and flipped it open. Eyes widening, Dom started forward. Vivian made a soft tutting noise. Dom stopped. Nicholas tapped a key, waited, then looked at his phone. The blonde woman looked down at her phone. She rolled forward, pressed a button on the computer keyboard, and waited.

Nicholas's phone chirped again. He looked at it, then at the pair in front of the computers. "What the hell are you two doing?"

"Well, I'm standing here getting schooled, and Miss Richards just broke into our system."

"Really?" Comprehension dawned on Nicholas's face. "Nice. But I thought you weren't a hacker?"

"That doesn't mean I don't know *how* to hack. I have to know how hackers operate in order to stop them."

"But I didn't click on a link or open a website. How'd you get the malware on my phone?"

"I sent you my contact information card. It just had an extra line of code in it. We worked it up in a class I took last year."

He walked over and dropped his phone on the table beside her. "Well, now you can take it off."

She wrinkled her nose at him. "That depends. Does this mean I can help?"

He cocked his head to one side as if considering. "Will you promise to listen to instructions?"

"If they're reasonable."

Nicholas cast his eyes at the ceiling while shaking his head. "You're exasperating."

"So wouldn't you rather I be on your side?"

He held out his hand. "Welcome aboard, Vivian."

After shaking, then retrieving her hand from his grasp, Vivian said, "Great. Now, about Lee."

"What about him? He will need to be protected until he heals. Maybe longer."

"But you killed the men who tried to hurt him." She shifted in her chair as she said the word "killed".

Dom, apparently deciding he wasn't needed, removed his gun from his shoulder holster and began cleaning it. Nicholas leaned against the table beside where Vivian sat.

"Those guys were just hired help. We don't know who the bosses are. It's not like the Triads have a website where we can look up their org chart."

"Thank you. Being exceedingly stupid, I had no idea that was the case," she retorted. "Speaking of Triad bosses, they know you're the one interfering in their business. Is that not a problem?"

"They think I have an army of mercenaries working for me."

"Cheyenne Consortium?"

He nodded.

"But they don't know what you can do. Your special skills, I mean."

"I don't believe they've made that connection yet, no. But they definitely know I'm behind the dismantling of their organization here in Seattle. It's why I have so much security for the family as well as me personally."

"I get the need for security, but the way you talk about Cheyenne... You said you were their guinea pig. But you still want to send Lee to them?"

"Lab rat," he muttered while rubbing his hand over his hair. "Lee's not in as bad shape as I was. They won't need to rebuild him."

"That knee might need it," Dom interjected.

"OK, his knee might need some work. But it won't be rehab in the sense that I went through rehab. They have private hospitals. Private, *remote*, hospitals. Places where he can heal and be safe." Seeing that she still looked worried, and skeptical, Nicholas straightened. "It's the best of a very short list of options. Help me find and dismantle this particular Triad branch. It will mean less time in hiding for Lee as well as less risk for the rest of my family... and you."

"Right." She pulled the keyboard fractionally closer. "I'd better get started."

CHAPTER TWENTY-ONE

By the end of the following week, Vivian had settled into a new routine. Her new class—her final class, she had to keep reminding herself—was on Tuesday and Thursday mornings. She left class and drove immediately to work. As soon as the rest of the department staff went home, usually by 6:30, Vivian decamped to the workshop. The only exceptions were on Monday and Wednesday evenings, when she left work at 7 p.m. in order to tutor Evan at the church.

Dominick and Nicholas, having explained the outline of their surveillance and data-mining operation, generally left her to her own work. During the first week, they only let her in while they were present. By the second week, her palm print was added to the scanner. She came and went as she pleased. If the men were already in the sub-basement when she arrived, they'd exchange greetings before returning to their tasks. That those tasks often involved excessive grunting, sweating, and the removal of shirts, still made Vivian blush.

It wasn't as if she'd never seen a half-naked man, Vivian reminded herself. So, why was the sight of Nicholas's scarred, muscled, sweaty chest so distracting? She was certain that her musings fell under the category of "impure thoughts", but there was no way in hell she was going to bring them up in the Confessional. Especially, she thought wryly, when her priest also happened to be Nicholas's uncle.

"Vivian!"

She jumped. "Sorry!"

Both of his brows inched upward. "What's wrong?"

"Just thinking."

He misinterpreted her blush. "Lee will be all right. I promise you."

"Lee? Oh. That's tonight."

"That's what I was trying to tell you. We're going to go home now and get cleaned up. Why don't you come with us? The fewer cars pulling into the airfield at midnight, the better."

"Let me grab my stuff."

She slid into the back seat. Dom drove while Nicholas rode in the front passenger seat. As they crossed the 520 bridge, Dom asked if she'd had dinner.

"Do you also cook?"

"Me? No. He does." Dom cocked his head to the side to indicate Nicholas.

"Really?"

"Hey!"

"Yes, really. He's actually very good. Must have been all those hours of cooking shows while he was in traction."

Vivian giggled, which made Dom and Nicholas smile.

While Dom retreated to the guest house to shower, Nicholas led Vivian through a side door of the main house. She followed him down two hallways before they arrived at the kitchen. He indicated the two commercial-sized fridges. "Grab yourself a drink. I need to shower."

"Yes, you do. I mean, um, because you're sweating, not because you smell—obviously."

He laughed. "You're in a mood tonight. I'll be right back." He stopped and turned around. "Maybe don't wander. I'd hate for my mother to corner you."

"She doesn't come in here?"

This time, the sound he made contained no joy or amusement. "My mother, here? In the kitchen? I'm not entirely sure she knows this room exists. Be right back."

Vivian looked around at the gleaming countertops, prep tables, and expensive gadgets. Killing time, she paced from one side of the room to the other. She had just worked up the nerve to open one of the refrigerators when a female voice directly behind her said, "Oh, hi Vivian."

Once recovered from jumping nearly out of her skin, Vivian nodded. "Hi Jessie."

This time, Jessie's curly hair was held up with two jade sticks jabbed into a messy bun. She wore artfully ripped jeans with a pale green lightweight sweater. "You're going with us to see Lee off?"

Vivian nodded.

"Nick just left you here in the kitchen? Didn't even offer you a drink? That man..." Jessie rolled her eyes before jerking open one door of the nearest fridge. "Water, soda, juice, beer, or white wine? Sorry, no red up here and I'm not braving the wine cellar—even for you."

"Uh..."

"If it matters, I'm having a beer."

"I'll just have water."

"You sure? Suit yourself."

"He's coming back."

Jessie popped the cap off her beer using the countertop. "Eh?"

"Nicholas. He just went to shower."

"Oh, is he cooking?"

"He is," intoned Nicholas as he walked up behind his sister, reached over her head and snagged her beer. He took a long swallow before offering it back to her.

"Gross. It's yours now."

"Excellent." He peered at the label. "This one of yours?" To Vivian, he asked, "Did my sister mention that she also owns a micro-brewery?"

"Lee did mention that his twin got all the brains."

Jessie smirked. "Right before he said he got all the looks, right?" She pursed her lips and nodded at Nicholas. He nodded right back. "That idiot. Anyway, no, that's a competitor's IPA. I really like it, though." She retrieved another bottle from the fridge.

Nicholas pushed the sleeves of his woven cotton shirt up to his elbows in order to wash his hands. "Staying for food?"

Jessie rose up on her toes to kiss her elder brother's cheek. "No, thank you. I've already eaten. I'm going to go watch TV until it's time to go to the airport." She whispered something to her brother, then smiled at Vivian. "See you in a bit."

Dom, his dark hair still looking damp, came in just as Jessie left. "Vivian, come sit down." He pulled a stool up to one of the prep tables. "Was that Jessie I heard?"

Nicholas, busy butterflying chicken breasts, nodded. "It was. She's already eaten. She said my mother is on her second bottle."

"Well, good for tonight, then."

"But bad for the rest of the month when she wakes up tomorrow and realizes she missed putting her baby on a plane."

"True" Dom stretched. "Speaking of, I need coffee. Vivian, why are you drinking water?"

"I like it?"

They stared at her.

"What? I do."

"Well, if you change your mind, there's a beautifully crisp Chardonnay in there. Can you chop onions?"

Nicholas asked the question as he laid out a new cutting board and moved the chicken closer to the stovetop.

"I volunteer at a soup kitchen several nights a week."

Nicholas pointed a knife at her, then flipped it neatly around to offer the handle.

"How fine do you want them?"

"Mmm." He looked down at the oil heating in his sauté pan, then at the large onion on the cutting board. "Half diced fine and half in thin slices. Wish I had time to caramelize them."

"Told you the boy can cook," Dom said from his position in front of the coffee maker.

Vivian completed her task. Nicholas nodded his thanks as he turned the chicken to brown the opposite side. She stood close by, watching him work. When he smiled down at her, she blinked. It took her a minute to realize that she was seeing a part of Nicholas Reed the rest of the world never did. His right arm snaked around her shoulders even as his hip brushed against hers. He grabbed his beer bottle from the counter to her right and dipped his head close to her ear.

"Excuse me."

Vivian looked up at him. He raised his arm to take a long swig from the bottle. She slipped away to the safety of her seat by Dom.

The sauteed chicken breasts and onions, served with a sun-dried tomato cream sauce and a spinach salad, felt like fine dining to Vivian. After setting the plates on the prep table where they'd arranged their barstool seats, Nicholas pulled another beer from the fridge for himself. He also poured a glass of Chardonnay for Vivian.

"In case you change your mind."

She sighed but accepted the drink.

"Johann will drive you over to the airfield. Dom will drive Jessie and me. That way, Johann can take you straight home."

While Dom and Nicholas discussed the evening's logistics, Vivian concentrated on eating. After the first bite, she gave a small moan of pleasure. She looked up to see Dom grinning and Nicholas's green eyes staring, fascinated, over his raised bottle.

"Sorry," she mumbled as heat flooded across her cheeks. "This—" She gestured at her plate. "—this is your real super-power."

"You're welcome. Just remember this the next time I piss you off."

"Mm. I think I'm in love." She coughed. Somehow, her cheeks felt even hotter. "With the food!"

"Eat," replied Nicholas in a jovial tone.

A light, misty, rain fell on the city. The private terminal at Boeing Field, despite being well lit, felt shrouded in fog. The ambulance carrying Lee from Harborview pulled up right after the Reeds' SUV and town car. They waited in the vehicles as the medical team carried Lee up the stairs and got him settled. Once the medics left—except for the flight nurse that Cheyenne Consortium had contracted to fly with him—Dom opened the SUV doors. Nicholas walked his sister to the plane, holding an umbrella over their heads. Vivian waited in the car.

"You warm enough, Miss Richards?"

"I've told you to call me Vivian, Johann. Yes, thank you, I'm fine."

"Mr. Reed said you were to wait here until Miss Reed is back in the SUV."

"Yes, he told me as much. Sorry we're keeping you out so late."

"Hey, no skin off my back. I get paid. Here he comes."

Nicholas gave Jessie a hand up so that she could step up into the high-profile vehicle. He frowned with concern when she curled against the seat with her hands and jaw clenched.

"I'll be right back."

Her emotional turmoil crept into her voice. "Nick, just go."

Nicholas shut the door. He raised his head, eyes searching the darkness on the edge of the terminal building and runways. Satisfied that no immediate threats lurked, he opened Vivian's door and reached one hand inside.

Vivian saw the tension in his features. She kept her thoughts to herself and tried to be as unobtrusive as possible. Nimbly climbing the stairs into the executive jet, she ducked through the doorway and turned down the center aisle. Lee reclined in a medical bed where two rows of seats usually sat. He managed a grin. Vivian reached out to squeeze his hand.

"You're sure you're OK with this?"

"Do I have a choice?" If he attempted to make the comment light-hearted, he failed.

"Yes, you have a choice, but the alternatives don't seem much better." She squeezed his hand again. "You'll be safe. We'll find the guys who did this. Then, you can come home and return to working your way through the U-dub sororities."

Lee leaned his head back and closed his eyes. His chest shook with the briefest of chuckles at her barb. "Is this your way of breaking up with me?"

"Silly boy," she murmured. "You've always been out of my league."

"Yeah," he said as he re-opened his eyes. "Because you're in the majors and I'm playing double-A ball."

"Precisely." She leaned forward and brushed a kiss on his forehead. "May the Lord bless and keep you, Lee Reed. I'll see you again."

Energy obviously waning, he gave the briefest of nods and released her hand. "Count on it."

Nicholas escorted her back down the stairs. They stood in the rain, under an umbrella, and watched the plane taxi down the runway. He thought he heard her sniff. She turned her head to brush away a tear. Given how raw his own emotions were, Nicholas refrained from any comment. When the jet's lights rose into the night sky, he finally spoke.

"Thank you for being a friend to my brother. It means more than I can say."

"I have a brother, too. He lives in Colorado with my aunt and uncle. I had to send him away because I couldn't protect him. Simon and Lee are sweet boys who don't deserve this level of pain in their lives."

Her comment startled him. He looked down to find the lights of the terminal reflected in her eyes so that they seemed to leap with blue fire.

"Promise me that we are going to find these bastards, lock them in a deep dark hole where they cannot hurt another soul, and purge all trace of them from the city."

"You have my word on it."

CHAPTER TWENTY-TWO

Detective Kwon waited. He watched his partner closely after Lee Reed was shot by Triad members. Despite the official story—that Dominick Fehr had killed both of the kidnappers—Kwon did not for an instant believe Nicholas Reed hadn't played an active role in the incident. What he couldn't determine was whether the incident represented a break between Reed and the Triad or if it had all been part of some internal power struggle. The detective also wanted to know why Vivian Richards had been present in the church that night—and why his young partner was so obsessed about the woman's role in the Reed crime syndicate.

So, Kwon kept his thoughts to himself. He followed his partner when they were off duty. He noted Suisse's body language as they were called to crime scene after crime scene with drugs and weapons left behind—but no bodies. Detective Kwon also noted when Suisse became very interested in busting Reed. That his partner suddenly bought in to Kwon's own theory—of Nicholas Reed becoming Seattle's richest criminal—should have been a relief. Instead, it just raised the senior detective's suspicions.

Vivian parked in the rear church lot. For once, she was early for her session with Evan. As she walked to the exterior stairs leading to the basement entrance, she noted movement from the corner of her eye. A dark sedan rolled slowly past the alley mouth. The windows were tinted. Six months previously, she'd have brushed off her unease as paranoia. Now, though, some instinct made her hurry into the church.

She mentioned the odd encounter to Dom the following day.

"Have you noticed anything similar, or felt like you were being watched? Any strange phone calls? Is your phone battery draining too quickly? Has anyone at the soup kitchen been staring at you, or purposely not making eye contact? Acting abnormally?"

Slightly flummoxed by his rapid-fire questions, Vivian made a dramatic "time-out" gesture with her hands. "It's a soup kitchen catering to homeless people. You're really going to have to define *abnormal*. I haven't noticed anyone following me, but I also wasn't really looking for it. How would I even know, the way traffic is right now?" She pursed her lips before continuing. "The only time I'm feeling watched is when I'm here, and I'm not even going to dignify that phone question with a response."

"I'll need a copy of your schedule. Dave or Johann can shadow you for a few days, see if they can pick up this tail."

"No!" She planted her hands on her hips and tilted her head as far back as she could in an effort to stare down the much taller man. "They have important jobs, not the least of which is keeping Jessie and Nicholas safe and finding the guys behind the hit on Lee. The last thing they need to do is follow me on a grocery run."

Amused by her stance, but also entirely serious about his commitment to her safety, Dom crossed his arms over his broad chest. He leaned over so she could hear his whispered threat. "Or, I could just tell Nicholas."

"Fine!" Vivian threw her hands in the air before stalking off.

Nicholas came down the workshop stairs a few minutes later to find her smashing keys on the keyboard and muttering under her breath. Giving the blonde a wide berth, he hopped onto the medical-area exam table and bared his forearm.

"Dare I ask which one of us she's pissed at?"

Dom attached an IV bag to the stand and deftly slid the needle into his boss's arm. "Oh, definitely me."

"Anything I should be aware of?"

"Not right now. Shirt please. Doc wants a cardiac tape."

"Screw the doc."

"I'd really rather not."

"We could just send her *your* cardiac tape, see how long it takes her to figure it out."

"Thank you, Mr. Reed, but I prefer to limit the number of terrifying women I annoy to one per week." He slapped the EKG leads into Nicholas's palm. "Put these on, then I'm checking your blood sugar."

Nicholas grudgingly held out one finger. "Seriously," he whispered, "I think she may break that keyboard. Maybe I should talk to her."

Dom shook his head while widening his eyes. "I'd rather you walked into a Triad stash house un-armored and alone than go over there right now. Let her cool off."

His comment had the desired effect of distracting Nicholas. "Speaking of which, I think we're going to have to explore other avenues. The heroin busts haven't yielded anything useful. If we follow the chain up on the gambling side of things, might have more luck."

"Possible. I'll send a few of the newer guys out, try to find some threads to pull."

As busy as Nicholas and Dom's quest kept her, Vivian refused to give up her work with Evan. A few nights later, she leaned over the cafeteria table to point at a trigonometry equation. "You need to use the inverse function there. Remember, inverse is for when you need the angle and already know the sine, cosine, or tangent."

Evan stared, open mouthed, at something over her shoulder. Vivian reached up and tapped his forehead with her index finger. "Hey. Am I boring you?"

"Is that... oh wow, it totally is. And he's coming over here."

A warm flush spread over Vivian. She knew before she turned who was crossing the floor toward them. She could feel his gaze.

"Do you *know* Nicholas Reed?" Evan's starstruck expression flitted from the man in question to her.

Vivian rolled her eyes. "He's my boss, you dork. Now pay attention. This problem calls for—"

"Yeah, yeah, inverse function. I wonder if he drives a cool car. He has to, right?"

Realizing that she'd get no more work out of the teenager, Vivian flopped her head backward as far as her neck would allow. Lips quirking, she asked in a teasing tone, "Well, Mr. Reed, *do* you drive a *cool* car?"

Nicholas smiled down at her. Words pitched as a rumbling purr, he replied, "Actually, I rode my bike over. Good evening, Vivian." Fluidly switching both stance and tone, he held out his right hand to her student. "Nicholas Reed. You must be Evan. Vivian speaks highly of you."

"She does?" Evan's voice broke, making his question more of a squeak.

Nicholas didn't even blink. "Of course she does. Trig huh?"

"Yeah," the teenager moaned. "It *sucks*!"

"Really?" Nichols canted his head to one side, smiling with good-natured ease. "I always liked basic algebra, geometry, and trig. They made sense. Differential equations, though..." He shuddered dramatically. "Evan, can I borrow your tutor for a moment? There's a work matter we need to discuss. I promise to return her."

Evan's smile faded. He straightened his shoulders. "Viv, why don't you two talk here? I'll take a walk."

Vivian looked at him like he'd spoken in Ancient Greek. "Uh... what?" She looked from Nicholas to Evan and back. The boy and the man appeared to be staring each other down. Her eyes widened as she realized what Evan meant. "Nicholas, I'll meet you by the kitchen doors in just a moment."

Nicholas nodded curtly. "Pleasure meeting you, Evan."

As soon as he was a decent distance away, Vivian leaned toward her pupil. "Evan, what's bothering you?"

"Viv, you do not have to go anywhere with him if you don't want to. If he's your boss, he shouldn't be making you work after hours."

She blinked.

"You've shown up bruised and looking like you've cried yourself to sleep more than once since you started working for him. I remember what that looks like, Viv." A bit of the starving nine-year-old watching his mother being abused by pimps crept into his voice.

Tears welled in her eyes. "Honey, Nicholas did not give me those bruises. He's actually helping me."

"Truth?"

"I'll swear it by whichever saint you pick. Now, I'm going to go over there and see what he wants. Meanwhile, I want you to re-do these five problems. I'll expect them when I get back. And show your work,"

Vivian called over her shoulder as she walked toward Nicholas.

"That boy has a serious crush on you."

Vivian rolled her eyes. "No, but he is very protective—something the two of you have in common."

Nicholas raised his brows and cupped her elbow with one hand. "Is there any place with a modicum of privacy?"

While he hadn't actually whispered the question *in* her ear, Vivian still fought a shiver. "This way. There's a closet where we keep the cleaning supplies."

Vivian shut the door behind her and leaned against the door handle. Nicholas paced in the small space.

"Once again, I find myself in the janitor's closet with a Reed."

Nicholas stopped his idle perusal of the paper towel shelf to slowly turn and cock one sandy-auburn brow at her. "Oh?" His lips twitched at her blush.

Vivian opened her mouth to explain but hissed instead. "You're bleeding!" She crossed the room and pulled his left hand to her.

Nicholas tried, though not very hard, to pull his hand away. "Guy had a knife. Sliced through my new gloves."

She peered at the thin slice on the back of his hand. "Why do you sound more peeved about the gloves than the knife wound?"

"Because I liked those gloves. Also, this barely qualifies as a cut, much less a wound. Stop fussing." This time he did pull away. "I came to ask a favor."

Perfectly mimicking the incredulous head-tilt he so often used on her, Vivian stayed mute.

"OK, and to check up on you."

Her chest expanded with her deep inhale. "I specifically told Dom not to involve you—"

"It wasn't Dom. I passed Johann lurking in a parking lot two blocks over. He's more scared of me than he is of you."

"I can fix that," she snapped.

Nicholas laughed. "Have pity on the man. I do pay his salary, after all." Dropping the teasing tone, he asked, "Why didn't you want me to know you were being followed?"

"I only thought I *might* be being followed. You have enough to do, as evidenced by your hand tonight. Now, what's this favor?"

If his narrowed eyes didn't make clear he knew she was changing the subject, his words did. "We *will* continue the discussion of increased security for you. But, for tonight, I wanted to see if you could scrub through these cell phones. Tomorrow, obviously."

Vivian took the two phones from him. She shrugged. "I might as well go back to the workshop tonight. I'll see what I can find."

"Really, there's no rush. You should finish up here and get some rest. The phones will wait."

"Now who's fussing? I suppose I could take them back to my apartment and work on them there. Anything I should know?"

"The guys I took them from won't be talking to anyone for a while." At her wide-eyed stare, he sighed. "They have broken jaws."

"I don't suppose the Triad have a great dental, or medical, plan?"

"They ought to." His mood suddenly soured at the mention of the violence he'd done, Nicholas motioned toward the door. "I'll check in with you tomorrow night?"

Brain already turning over which programs she'd use on the phones, Vivian nodded absently.

Nicholas shoved his hands in his bike jacket and slipped out of the church. Staying in the shadows, he made his way to the rear of the rectory building. The light from the closest streetlight didn't reach the corner where he crouched. He waited for ten minutes, controlling his breathing, allowing his heightened senses to experience every smell, sound, and image of the wintry Seattle night. Finally sure he was alone, Nicholas jumped up, grabbed the corner gutter bracket and swung his body onto the roof. A normal man's joints would have snapped at the strain. He merely grunted.

Sure-footed, he stayed just below the roof peak as he moved toward the front of the church building. There, crouched like a gargoyle, he watched Vivian and Evan walk to her car. The boy chattered the whole way. She pulled out of the lot, drove to the end of the block and turned left. The black SUV driven by Johann followed fifty feet behind. Only two other cars were visible. Both went the opposite direction. Nicholas waited another twenty minutes before leaving his perch.

CHAPTER TWENTY-THREE

Dave Kaskoy buzzed his boss into the small security room of Reed Investments. While Dave, and several of the other team members, knew of the workshop under the building, they did not operate from there. Some secrets Nicholas Reed kept very close to his scarred chest.

"Good evening, sir."

"Evening. I've asked Kekoa to come in and cover the rest of your shift."

Rather than ask unnecessary questions, Dave nodded and rose from his chair. "I'll grab my rifle."

"Earbuds for tonight." Nicholas laid a small object on the desk. "Vivian tweaked the signal a bit on them."

"Talented gal," Dave said with obvious warmth. He didn't miss his boss's sharp look. "Do we also have her to thank for the new GPS-tracking software?"

"She, correctly, pointed out that using Cheyenne's software left us vulnerable to being tracked by Cheyenne."

Dave keyed in the code for the gun case mounted to one wall. He withdrew a custom rifle with a high powered scope. "Non-lethal ROE?" He needed to know the rules of engagement for the night's mission.

"Yes. I sincerely hope it will just be over-watch."

Before closing and re-locking the case, Dave withdrew a box of specialized non-lethal rounds. They were designed to deliver an electrical pulse via a non-penetrating projectile. Anything fired at high speed could be lethal, though, if it hit the wrong part of the body. "God-willing, sir."

Nicholas sent the coordinates of their destination to Dave's phone before they left the office building. They parked the black SUV three blocks from their target. The former Army sniper turned off down a side street while Nicholas continued walking toward a ten-story office building.

Dave sauntered through the lobby of a mixed-use office and apartment complex. No security guard sat behind the reception desk. He pulled a ball cap down to hide his face as he entered an elevator. The keypad for the upper floors was locked with an RFID scanner. Dave waved a fob in front of it. On the second pass, green lights came on. He selected the top floor with one gloved finger.

Exiting the elevator on the fifteenth floor, Dave walked to the end of the hallway with his head down. He turned and walked another twenty feet before pushing open the fire door leading to the stairwell. From there, he went up to the roof access, picked the lock, and stepped out into the windy night. He took only a moment to orient himself before laying his case down and assembling his rifle. After two brief adjustments to the scope, he keyed his mic.

"Over-watch established. I have you."

"Roger. Beginning ascent."

Through his rifle's scope, Dave watched Nicholas scale the outside of a building. Though he'd seen his boss in action before, the physical strength demonstrated as Nicholas swung from crevice to crevice still awed the young veteran. Nicholas made sure to avoid the street-facing sides of the building—to prevent detection by anyone driving or walking past.

When he reached the ninth floor, Nicholas wedged his titanium hip into the narrow crevice beside a window. Quickly, before he lost his balance and tumbled to the street below, he broke the window and dropped into the office on the other side. He made sure he was alone before beginning to methodically search the location.

Dave's shoulder muscles tensed as every light in the building suddenly came on. He saw Nicholas whip around, then crouch defensively. There was no visible threat that Dave could see, though. He moved his rifle, trying to see into the other offices and the floors below and above. Just as he trained his rifle back to the right, he caught movement in the office closest to Nicholas.

"You're blown. Bug out. Repeat, you're blown. Recommend egress via adjacent building. Rooftop is no-go."

Nicholas was already moving. He'd heard people whispering nearby. He leapt straight out the window he'd entered through. Turning his shoulder at the last minute to hit a window on the next building over, he slid toward the ground. Before he fell more than two floors, though, he arrested his fall and swung hand over hand around the corner of the building.

"No eyes," Dave said into his mic, letting Nicholas know that he was out of sight. He put his rifle to the side and pulled out a combination camera and directional microphone. He began rapidly snapping pictures of Seattle police officers swarming over the roof, entrance, and ninth floor of the building Nicholas had just vacated.

A few tense minutes later, he heard through his earbud, "Evac complete. RTB."

"Moving."

Once they were both back in the SUV and driving away, Dave asked, "Bad intel, or a trap?"

Nicholas stripped off his gloves and grunted. "Trap, apparently. The location came off the phones of those

Triad guys we busted a few nights ago. Vivian even electronically scouted the building beforehand. We have good reason to suspect the import-export company run out of that office is a shell corp." He flexed his hands and rolled his shoulders.

"Not like the Triads to use the police that way," Dave observed.

"No, it really isn't. But, I also highly doubt the phones and the cutting warehouse we raided were some elaborate false flag by the SPD. Which means the Triad worked fast getting the police set up on that location."

"Inside man?"

"Likely." He rubbed his shoulder again. "Damn it. Dom is going to be all over my case if I've messed up this arm again."

"Did you mean to slide down that side-window?"

Nicholas shot him a rueful grimace. "I was hoping it would break when I hit it. Damn thing was reinforced. It was like bouncing off marble. Thank God for decorative window ledges." He leaned his head back and closed his eyes. "All the same, maybe leave that part out of your report."

"As you say, sir."

"Well?"

"Well, what?" Adam Suisse snapped at his partner. "He was here and then he was gone. We've searched vents, security cameras, and every inch of this building."

Detective Kwon walked around the tiny shards of tempered glass—all that remained of the office window. He looked out onto the street below. The flashing lights of three police cruisers cast strange patterns against the buildings and alleyway.

"You're telling me he just Peter Pan-ed out this window and... what? Flew away?"

"Hey, smart guy, I didn't say that. Maybe he had a rope to the other building already. He had to get in here through that window."

"This CI who gave you the tip about the guy attacking heroin dealers—do you trust her?"

"Yeah, I do. She works in a laundry and heard a couple of their lieutenants talking about how this guy, or guys, might hit this office next."

"Mm. Well, it's a crime scene now. Inventory everything. Maybe we'll get a drug bust out of this fiasco."

Kwon stared out into the moonless night, wondering how their mysterious vigilante had escaped.

CHAPTER TWENTY-FOUR

Working their way up the chain of Triad connections to find the man, or men, who'd ordered the hit on Lee didn't keep Vivian so busy she didn't have time to work on her own little quest. She took full advantage of the networks, systems, and hardware available in the workshop. It only took her two nights of searching to find that no digital records of her parents' murder case existed. She could find neither autopsy reports nor fire marshal's investigation files.

Her first actionable lead came from reviewing old research files from Nicholas and Dom's earliest actions against the city's criminal forces. Her mouth made an "o" of surprise when she realized they'd dismantled the ferry smuggling ring she'd unwittingly discovered as a teen. From there, she followed several back-door links to the San Juan County Sheriff's database. There, she still didn't find any of the information she sought, but she did learn that the files *had* existed. Some of them had been moved, or deleted, six months after her parents' deaths. The other files, though, had only been removed the previous November. Right after the break-in at Reed Investments that led to her meeting Nicholas and Dom...

Vivian glared at the monitor screen. It'd taken several days of meticulously tracing file moves and copies through the workshop's servers, but she'd found the files she sought. Well, she *hoped* she had. She couldn't tell for sure, though, because the file folders were protected by password access.

Except for the overnight security staff, the rest of the Reed Investments employees had left the office an hour earlier. The CEO and his security chief were still on the fourth floor. Vivian, Dom thought, was probably already in the workshop trawling through social media and traffic cameras for leads. Nicholas finally hung up his phone call with a Cheyenne executive. Dom had just opened his mouth to ask what was said on the call when the door to the executive office flew open.

"How dare you lock me out!"

"Excuse me?" Nicholas's tone dripped with all the arrogance a lifetime of privilege could instill. His eyes, though, wouldn't meet either the irate blonde's or Dom's.

"You heard me." Vivian's hair danced behind her head like the tail of an agitated cat.

"Well I can't very well answer you if you won't tell me exactly what you're ranting about!"

"Ranting?" She nearly spat the word at him. "My entirely justified anger—which is not yet a rant but will be very soon—is over the section of password protected files on the server down there. What's in there you don't want me to see?"

Dread clawed its way up Nicholas's spine. He shot a glance at Dom, but no help would come from his bodyguard. Dom had specifically warned him against trying to hide information from Vivian. Trying for a conciliatory tone, he explained, "The information in those files doesn't pertain to our investigation. I sealed them for your protection."

Vivian stepped back like she'd been slapped. "You arrogant ass! I made the decision to help you. I can see that was a mistake, but that does not mean that you can just tell me I'm finished!"

Nicholas invaded Vivian's personal space, towering over her. "I will not put you in any more danger. If you can't follow the rules of our agreement, your assistance is no longer required."

She flung her head back, glared at him over her pert little nose, and pushed on his chest with her hands. "I was in danger long before I met you! Contrary to your conceited worldview, not everything happens because of your involvement! So, knock it off and unlock the files!"

"Will you, for once, just listen to me?"

"No! I want to know what you think I can't handle."

"I told you those files don't have anything to do with Lee," snapped Nicholas. Tension made the tendons in his neck and shoulders stand out.

"And Lee is not our only focus! How could knowing the truth possibly put me in danger? I'm not your responsibility, *Mister* Reed. You think you're the only one hurting? Are you honestly so self-absorbed that you think you're the only one who's lost someone to these bastards?"

"They were my father's men," Nicholas blurted.

Silence fell so suddenly it had physical weight.

"What?" Vivian whispered her question.

Nicholas couldn't meet her eyes. His shoulders slumped. "The information in those files is about a drug smuggling ring. My father's employees were running drug cars on a ferry. The ferry you worked on four years ago. When you reported it to the sheriff, one of his deputies called my father. He in turn told the Triad and they..."

Vivian's face had been flushed when she stormed into the office. Now it drained of color. She shook her head, trying to ward off tears. A buzzing sound filled her ears. "You knew? You knew who murdered my parents? All this time?"

"No! I didn't put it all together until right before Lee... Vivian, please." Nicholas's hand flashed out to grab her wrist as she tried to walk past him. Dom, already moving to separate the two of them, didn't get there fast enough. Vivian whipped around and punched Nicholas as hard as she could.

"Ow!" She cried out and cradled her right hand while backing toward the door.

"Vivian, let me see your hand." Dom kept one eye on Nicholas just in case, but he was more worried about the woman.

"No." Tears welled in her eyes. She swallowed several times, still backing up. Tears fell down her cheeks.

"Vivian, please let me—"

Dom's plea was cut off by another sobbing "No." The door slammed closed behind her, leaving an eerie quiet.

Dom turned around, arms crossed over his chest. "So much for protecting her feelings."

"What did you want me to do? Let her read it all by herself in a cold sub-basement?"

"Don't be an idiot. You could've explained it to her. You could have laid the evidence out, showing her she's been right all these years. She lost *everything*, man."

"I know that!"

"Yeah you know it, but do you understand? How can you? You've never lost your parents and your home in one night. She was *alone*. She had to drop out of school, and she got evicted. Everything that woman has done for the past four and a half years has been through sheer will-power. Vivian's the bravest person I know."

Dom let his statement hang in the air. Nicholas knew what a high honor the former soldier had just bestowed on their IT tech. On, Nicholas realized, their friend.

When Nicholas pushed past him, headed for the elevator, Dom asked, "Where are you going?"

"I need to think."

"You're going to go apologize to her now, right?"

Nicholas's shoulders bunched. He'd been alternately moping and beating the crap out of a punching bag for the past few hours. He knew he was wrong. He felt like the asshole Vivian accused him of being. The look of pain on her face after she'd punched him tore at something deep inside him—something he'd thought long dead. How was it possible that a ponytail twitching in anger and soft blue eyes clouding with tears could hurt so much?

"I thought I'd give her some time to cool off."

"Man, you know nothing about women."

That comment made Nicholas's eyebrows slant upward. "Glass houses, Dom?"

"Remember that we just met her in November and sprang all of this on her barely a month ago." Dom motioned to the workshop as he spoke. "She's been fighting the city's villains and your demons and never asked for anything in return except our respect. So, ask yourself Nicholas, would any of this be worth it without Vivian?" Dom laid the car keys on a nearby table. "Besides, your billion-dollar face probably broke her hand. You at least owe her the cost of an ice pack and a few x-rays."

Nicholas watched his friend walk away, knowing the older man was disappointed with him. "Join the club," he murmured. Realizing he'd been left to sulk alone, Nicholas made a decision. He left the basement quickly, before he changed his mind.

Vivian sat on her couch holding a bag of frozen pizza rolls on her throbbing hand. She'd cried until her eyes hurt and her nose ran. Now, she was just miserable. Well, miserable with a good dollop of still-angry.

"I can't even claim workman's comp! How awesome would that be: walking into the ER and saying, 'Yeah I broke my hand on my boss's pretty face.' What would he do? Probably yell at me some more or treat me like I'm a delinquent child. Come to think of it, both of those concurrently would be the best bet." She paused in her rant to hiccup. "What was I thinking, getting involved with Nicholas-freaking-Reed in the first place? Billionaires with hero complexes are the definition of bad news. Bad boys are bad enough but good guys pretending to be bad boys—except he hasn't been pretending, has he? I've just been fooling myself into believing he isn't damaged goods on a vengeance streak." Choking back a sob, she shook her head. "I am so, so, so monumentally, incredibly, totally, stupid."

She hopped off the couch at the knock on her door. She kept talking, though, even before the door was fully open. "Oh yea, pizza. Pizza and wine, just what the doctor ordered, or would have if I'd gone to the doctor which I can't because... Nicholas?"

Nicholas had to force his expression into a friendly smile. Vivian's babbling usually lightened his mood, but he was too distracted by her swollen eyes, disheeveled appearance, and the bruised hand she held against her chest. If anyone else had done this to her, made her feel this way, he'd have beaten them senseless. "Hi."

"You are not the pizza guy."

He shook his head. "No. Does the pizza guy also owe you an abject apology?"

"He might if he doesn't get here soon and interrupt what promises to be a very awkward scene. You can't just show up here, Nicholas."

"I had to." He glanced to his right. "Do I have to do this in the hallway?"

"Do what?" She chewed on her lip.

"Apologize. Check on you. Apologize some more and at great length. Give you dinner. Take you to get that hand x-rayed." His lips quirked upward. "Did I mention apologizing?"

"You brought food?"

"And wine."

She stepped aside, letting him in. "This doesn't mean I can be appeased with carry-out and alcohol, mister. I'm not a cheap date. Not that this is a date. Or that you'd... never mind."

"Who were you talking to?"

"Huh?"

"When I walked up, I could hear you talking."

"Oh. I was, um, having a debate. Out loud. Verbally. With myself."

"Who won?"

She looked up from the corner of the couch where she'd re-buried herself. "Stop being charming. I'm still really mad at you."

"I'm trying to not be an asshole. Charming is all I have left in my repertoire."

Vivian shook her head and swallowed the lump in her throat. "I don't need charming, especially not from you. Right after... after they were murdered, everyone was so polite. Very *charming* men explained to me that it was just a fire. They explained away everything I saw and everything Simon heard. They smiled and patted my hand and *lied* to me. They told me it would all be OK. But it wasn't OK when Simon went away. It wasn't OK when insurance refused to pay for the house, or when the *charming* judge seized all our remaining property. It definitely wasn't OK when I spent months living out of my car." She blinked back tears as she met his gaze. "I don't want lies. Not from you, Nicholas. I don't need to be protected from the truth."

"I never meant to hurt you—" He stopped talking when Vivian waved her hand in a silencing gesture. She'd forgotten and used her bruised one. Nicholas made a hissing sound and reached out to close his fingers, gently this time, around her wrist. "God, Vivian. I'm so sorry."

"I guess I should have paid better attention when Dom was teaching me how to throw a punch. Also, I really hate your stupid, beautiful, square, hard, stupid, jaw."

"It's doubly stupid?"

"Yes." She tried to pull her hand away but couldn't.

"And beautiful? Really? Can't I get handsome instead? Or rugged?"

"No. Rugged would have the decency to have at least a teeny tiny mark."

"Would it help if I said it hurt?"

"No, because you'd be lying." She tried to ignore the tingling warmth on her skin from the grasp of his fingers.

Nicholas sat on the opposite end of the couch, his body turned toward her. "No, Vivian, I wouldn't be lying."

She blinked at him rather owlishly.

"It hurt to see you in pain. It hurt to realize how badly I've treated you. I need to apologize for that. I also need to thank you." He waited for her to say something. "Are you all right? You're too quiet."

"I think I'm in shock."

"It's been a shocking day."

She winced. "About that. I'm sorry. I should never have... you have to know that I'd never have said or done that... just finding out like that..." She looked away. "I've really got to control my temper."

He ruefully shook his head. "If you do that, who will keep me honest?" Nicholas stood and held out a hand to her. "Come on. Let's get that hand looked at."

CHAPTER TWENTY-FIVE

"Nicholas, you can't go in there with me!" Vivian tried to step in front of him and stop his forward momentum before they reached the doors of the ER.

"Vivian, move." He placed his hands very gently on her shoulders and turned her around like she was a small child.

"Seriously, I cannot go into the emergency room with Nicholas Reed! The paparazzi will be here within five minutes. How are you going to explain bringing one of your company employees to the hospital at... What time is it anyway? I forgot to put on my watch because you were distracting me by apologizing, and I'm possibly suffering from low blood sugar. That food you brought smelled really good. Let's go eat it. I'm sure my hand's fine. What?" Vivian blinked at the intake nurse. "Oh, um, hi. Yes. I, um, punched—"

"A punching bag while I was showing her a few self-defense moves. She hits harder than you might expect." Nicholas turned on the charm, with predictable effect. Two minutes later, they were seated in the triage waiting area. He spent less than a minute watching the blonde beside him try to fill out the forms with her left hand before he gently slid the clipboard from her grasp. "You misspelled your own name, Vivian. Now, let's see. Social security number?"

"Like I'm giving you that information. Who knows what you would do with it? Not that you are a cyber-criminal, or any kind of criminal..." She glanced around frantically before rattling off the numbers. "Really, I can do this. I'm pretty ambidextrous. You'd be amazed what I can do with my left hand."

He looked up from the form and smiled softly.

"Unlike my mouth, which is apparently just stuck on overdrive because I really hate hospitals. And you're making me nervous. And there's questions on there I am NOT answering in front of you and please, please, please, just leave me here to die of shame all by my lonesome, OK?"

"Hush." He filled in most of the information about her address, phone number, employment, and insurance status without needing her input. "Height: 5'4."

"Hey! I'm 5'5."

He turned his head and just stared at her.

She ducked her head and mumbled, "Fine, five-three and three-quarters."

"We'll round up, then. Next, weight: 121 pounds."

"How do you know that?" She fairly squeaked the question.

Nicholas leaned over so he could whisper in her ear. "Because I picked you up and threw you across my office, remember?" He took a moment to savor her adorable blush before returning his attention to the form. "Last menstru—"

Vivian suddenly found the clipboard back in her lap. She stared in shock at her boss. "You're blushing."

"I do not blush."

"Yeah, you do. It's an involuntary vascular response. It doesn't make you less of a man."

A muscle in his jaw twitched.

"I'm going to enjoy this right now. Mostly because the alternative involves sliding under the chair in embarrassment. I can't wait to tell Dom about—"

He growled.

"Or not. I'll just keep this one all to myself. Store it away in my Nicholas vault and only take it out when

I'm alone. All for me and my personal enjoyment. Not that I have a mental Nicholas stash, because that would be way too... They really need to just sew my mouth shut while we're here."

"Now who's blushing?"

She smiled at him, and suddenly Nicholas felt like he was standing in bright sunlight. His chest tightened but not with the all-too-familiar sense of loneliness. He felt...happy. *Just because she smiled at me?* He would think about that later.

He kept her chattering in nervous tangents while first the triage nurse talked to her and then when the doctor finally came in to look at her hand. She clearly hated hospitals, the way she kept fidgeting. When the doctor started manipulating her fingers and pressing on the bruises of her right hand, Nicholas stood beside her and folded her left hand into his.

"Vivian, look at me. Breathe." He stroked his thumb back and forth over hers. "No, don't look at him. Breathe. That's right. You're fine."

When they took her back to the x-ray suite, Nicholas pulled out his phone and typed out a quick message to Dom. Then he flipped through a year-old copy of *People*. He was still miserably behind on popular culture—probably always would be. He was seconds away from storming to radiology to make sure Vivian hadn't been kidnapped by nefarious doctors when she walked back into the curtained cubicle.

"Hey."

"Sit. You look tired."

Her nose wrinkled. "What happened to *charming* Nicholas?"

"You told me to stop it."

"Oh, sure, now you listen to me."

"I always listen to you, Vivian." He noticed how the stark truth made her uncomfortable and changed the subject. "What did the x-ray show?"

"Oh, you know, I have bones. They never tell you anything until the doctor gets a look at it anyway. You don't have to stay. I can get a cab home. No need for you to wait in ER-limbo for the rest of the night. Surely you have better things to do with your time. Important, hero-type things."

He leaned back in his chair, crossed his arms over his chest, and said, "This is where I need to be right now."

As a shocking admission of her exhaustion, Vivian lapsed into silence. Nicholas was used to quiet contemplation, though he'd never managed it with the bouncy blonde nearby. They waited another twenty minutes before she suddenly turned her head toward him.

"When we were walking back there, the nurse asked me something. She asked if I felt safe at home—if I had a safe place to go back to." She noticed the way he clenched his jaw but didn't look away. "Of course, I told her yes. I didn't even hesitate. I've got you and Dom and even Johann. It's just, it made me remember. How horrible it was in the shelter. To live in a constant state of fight or flight."

If Nicholas's teeth clamped down any harder, they would break off. Of course, he had no idea what it was like to be homeless—or a woman. Knowing that his father's crime syndicate had caused Vivian to know exactly how that felt caused his guts to clench. That people—women in particular—in his city had to endure such misery made him furious.

Before Nicholas could respond, the doctor walked in. "Ms. Richards, you appear to have a transverse

169

fracture of your fourth metacarpal. We call this a boxer's fracture. It usually occurs when a punch is improperly delivered. So, next time your boyfriend decides to teach you self-defense—"

"Oh, he's not my boyfriend. He's kind of my boss. Not directly, just... he owns the company."

The doctor looked at Nicholas. Nicholas gave him the blandest smile he could muster.

"Well, next time, have a trained martial artist show you self-defense moves. For now, I'm going to immobilize the injured hand in a splint. It's not as restrictive as a cast, but you will have to keep your finger immobilized for several weeks and return for follow-up x-rays to make sure the bone has fused properly."

Vivian nodded with due sincerity while trying not to laugh at the flicker of annoyance on Nicholas's face at the "trained martial artist" comment.

Her good mood lasted until they were walking out of the hospital. Nicholas leaned fractionally closer and muttered, "You'll train with me from now on. No more improper punches." When she squeaked in protest, he replied, "Or you learn to control your temper and not throw punches at people out of your weight class."

She murmured something about pots and kettles, but he closed her car door and walked around to the driver's side just so he didn't have to hear her—or think about why he suddenly wanted to spend more time with her.

He couldn't let her see it; there'd be no living with her. He needed to find a way to delete the entire website and erase every social media post referencing it. She could probably handle the latter task in her sleep and one handed, but that would require telling her in the first place. And, really, Vivian would not hesitate to pull out the "I told you so" face. It was not his favorite of her varied expressions.

Nicholas looked up at Dom with something akin to pleading. "Is there any chance this is an advance copy sent as a blackmail attempt? Because I will pay whatever they want just so this doesn't go live."

The bodyguard snorted. "Hannah saw it online this morning before the coffee was even made."

The man most feared by the city's underworld turned in a panic toward the bank of computers. He took two steps in that direction, clearly intent on trying his own luck at digital skullduggery, before his friend's voice pulled him up short.

"If you think you're in trouble now, it is nothing compared to what will happen if she finds you touching her system."

"It's my system," he said, petulantly.

"Sure it is. And she's one quarter of your size, injured, and your employee."

Nicholas's eyebrow quirked.

"So why are you terrified, man?"

He picked up a stray tennis ball from the table and lobbed it at Dom's head. "Like you aren't terrified of her."

Dominick Fehr's face lost all traces of laughter. "I'm terrified *for* her. There's a notable difference. It's good that you're acting this way, though."

"Huh?" Nicholas was still thinking about trying his luck with hacking. Maybe he'd use his laptop.

"If you didn't care for her, you wouldn't be so worried about her reaction. It's just one photo and five sentences on a trashy website. She, and you, have weathered far worse. Relax."

Nicholas took a deep breath. He closed his eyes and willed himself to be still. Dom was right. This was nothing, a trifle. He could smooth this over with a grin. At worst, it'd cost him another pricey bottle of wine. As the sounds of the workshop swirled around him and helped to center his focus, Nicholas opened one eye.

"Dom?"

"Mm?"

"You were at Hannah's *before* the coffee was made this morning?"

There was a loud bang followed by a clattering on the metal steps. Before the on-coming storm blasted them both, Dom turned, mouth twitching. "Yes, I was. Where did *you* spend the night, Mr. Reed?"

Vivian stalked across the basement, blue eyes fixed on her target. She wore white Capri pants, a pink button-down shirt, and pink ballet flats with white polka dots. Her blonde hair was pulled back in a tight ponytail that swayed with every step. She would've been adorable, if adorable could be combined with a quantifiable level of focused anger.

Because Nicholas was still—despite hardship, loss, and enough family drama to fill a reality TV show—a guy, his first thought was not about self-preservation. All he could think for several seconds was: *How did she do up all of those tiny buttons with just one hand*?

Dom glanced at Nicholas, noted the slightly vacant expression, and decided to save the poor boy. Stepping forward, he said, "Hey, Vivian. How's the hand feeling this morning?"

"Good morning, Dom. You cannot save him by distracting me."

He shrugged and chuckled simultaneously. "Had to try. I'll go grab some coffee. Just leave the blood and mess; I don't want you to further hurt your hand trying to hide evidence of a murder." As he walked by the seething woman, Dom tried one more time to diffuse her mood. "Go easy on him. He's genuinely sorry."

Vivian turned her head and blinked. She suddenly threw her arms around the taller man and pulled herself to the tips of her toes in order to kiss his cheek. "You're a good man, Dominick Fehr." Smiling at his shocked expression, she pushed him toward the door. "Hazelnut soy latte for me, please?"

"Only for you." He winked as he left.

When Vivian turned around from watching the security chief leave, Nicholas was standing right in front of her. "I'm a good guy."

She snorted—a noise as disconcerting as it was rude—and rolled her eyes. "Angling for a kiss too? I think the gossip columns have enough fodder."

He tried charm, his default setting for dealing with the women in his life. "There's no one down here to take a picture. They didn't get a picture of that kiss last night either."

Her pupils dilated. She poked him, hard, in the chest with an extended finger from her uninjured left hand. "I—Told—You—So." Each staccato word was punctuated with a prod from her finger.

"You don't babble when you're angry. Really angry, that is."

"What?"

"You ramble-on when you're nervous, or excited, or happy—but when you're really mad at me, you sound like a drill instructor."

"How would you know what a drill instructor sounds like, Nicholas Reed?"

He tilted his head. "TV." A new thought occurred to him. "Have you been rehearsing this tirade on the drive over here? Wait. You're not supposed to be driving while on those painkillers!"

"I might have gone over a few lines of attack while driving over here. It was a perfectly safe drive because I didn't take any painkillers since I woke up and also because no one is driving around the city at this hour on a Saturday morning. That did not count as a kiss last night!"

Nervous Vivian had made a roaring return. Nicholas felt like he could handle her better when she was like this. The coldly rational Vivian snapping at him was far too... scary. But then, he'd always associated her babbling with happiness and secret smiles and twinkling blue eyes and... *Snap out of it, dude. Now you're sounding like her in your own head!* He focused on keeping the beautiful woman distracted. Leaning slightly forward, he dropped his voice to a throaty whisper. "Would you like to show me the difference between a real kiss and what happened last night?"

She backed up several steps. "Oh no, you're not going to distract me by being all sexy, Nicholas Reed. Not that I find you sexy..."

A red-brown brow shot upward.

"...any more than any other heterosexual woman—or homosexual man for that matter—does. You know you're hot. Don't think I don't know that you know when I'm watching you parade around with your shirt off, and... Oh God, you're doing it again."

"I haven't done anything, Vivian."

"Except not listen to me!" She saw him wince. "I told you that the paparazzi would find out about our trip to the ER. Didn't I? Didn't I tell you it was a bad idea and to leave me there alone?"

"It was two photos and five sentences, Vivian."

"In which we are both clearly visible leaving the hospital and climbing into your car! And don't get me started on the text you so blithely—"

"Good word. I think it was on the crossword I worked last week."

"Nicholas!"

"Vivian, please—"

She rushed on, reciting: "Nicholas Reed was seen leaving the ER early this morning with a young woman named Vivian Richards. Hospital sources confide that there was a "sparring" accident that led to a broken hand. Mr. Reed managed to slip the woman in and out of the hospital in the middle of the night without answering any of our questions. The woman declined to file any charges related to the injury. She has not been previously seen with Nicholas Reed but was seen around town with Lee Reed." She sucked in a breath. "Nicholas, they all but accused you of domestic violence!"

He stared at her. "You're worried about my reputation." The realization hit him like a physical blow. His incredulity was not helped by her expression.

"Of course I'm worried about your reputation! You're the head of a multi-billion-dollar business enterprise! You can't afford to be branded as an abuser. Also, it's just not fair. Never mind that it's stupidly not true and the exact opposite of what happened! I hit you, remember?"

He rubbed his jaw as if the blow still pained him. "I seem to recall that, yes."

Vivian came forward until she was toe-to-toe with him. Head back, her voice quieter, she said, "And you really are a good person, Nicholas. The best person I know—"

Unable to bear having her finish such a sentence, Nicholas placed the pad of his thumb over her lips. He moved his hand to the back of her head and used his other arm to hug her to his chest. "Hush, Vivian. I'll fix this, I promise." He kissed her forehead.

She made a choked giggling sound, which made him glance down in confusion. "Now what?"

"That's why it's not a real kiss. That's your "I'm going to fix it and protect you. Every thing's all right. Now go to sleep—there are no monsters under the bed," kiss. I bet you do the same thing to Jessie."

He couldn't help it; he laughed. "What did I do to deserve you, Vivian Reed?"

She wriggled out of his grasp and moved toward her computers. "Bled all over my new pantsuit."

CHAPTER TWENTY-SIX

Needing to get out and think of anything besides her increasing entanglement with the Reed family, Vivian pulled on her coat and went for a walk. While the Reed Investments building wasn't in the best Seattle neighborhood, it certainly felt safe enough in broad daylight. As she turned the corner at the end of the block, two men exited a black sedan.

"Hello again, Vivian." Detective Suisse stepped up on her right.

"You remember us, of course." Detective Kwon walked on her left.

She expelled her breath through her nose while looking heavenward. Not seeing any sign that an avenging angel planned to intervene, she simply replied "How could I forget?"

"How's your hand?" Suisse reached out to touch her splinted right hand. She jerked it away and shoved both hands in her coat pockets.

"Perfectly fine, thank you. Did you really drive all the way down here to walk around the block with me?"

Kwon answered. "We did. We thought this might be a better place to chat than surrounded by your boss's security detail and lawyers." The detective looked around. "They let you out without an escort?"

"I am a systems administrator for Reed Investments, not a political prisoner." Vivian stopped and faced the older detective. "Why don't you tell me the truth? What do you really want?"

Detective Suisse stepped up so close behind her she could feel his breath brush across the top of her

right ear. "But Vivian, we've always been truthful with you."

Kwon frowned at his partner. "I—we—are worried for your safety."

"Please forgive my skepticism." She turned and resumed walking.

"How'd you really hurt your hand, Vivian?" Suisse's question was followed by his partner stating a fact she'd hoped everyone had forgotten.

"The day you came in for the interview, after Lee Reed was shot, you had a bruise on your temple."

Vivian stilled. She took a deep breath, trying to maintain her composure. "As I explained during my interview, I fell against a worktable in the kitchen."

His dark brows furrowing, Detective Kwon shook his head. "That bruise was starting to yellow, Miss Richards. It was at least a few days old."

"You're mistaken. Now, it seems you've escorted me all the way around the block and ruined my walk. Good-bye, detectives."

"Nicholas Reed is a dangerous man, Vivian. If he's hurting you—if he's pulled you into his criminal enterprises—let us help you." Detective Suisse once again reached out, this time snagging the sleeve of her coat.

Vivian looked down at his fingers then, stone-faced, looked up at the tall blond policeman. "Let go of me. I do not need your protection from Nicholas Reed or anyone else."

As she walked into the office building, Detective Kwon shouted one last question: "Where is Lee Reed?"

"Nicholas, we might have a problem. Detective Kwon is—Oh!" Vivian found herself plucked off the floor, swung through the air, and plopped down on a table. She wriggled, trying to escape the large hands clamped around her waist and move off of whatever instrument of war was between her butt and the tabletop.

"Stay," growled Nicholas. He flexed his grip on her hips to emphasize his point.

"Vivian how many times have we told you not to just walk in?" Dom ranted from across the room. "I nearly took your head off with that throw!" He pointed to a throwing knife still quivering in the wooden target board nearby.

"Well, why do you have to throw toward the door? That's just silly! I mean, you could impale anyone who happened to walk through! And I don't appreciate being ordered around like your prize spaniel, Nicholas Reed! I'm most definitely not a spaniel. Have you ever met one? They are gorgeous, sure, but as dumb as a box of rocks. I'm definitely more of a border collie, if I was a dog at all—which I'm not—so stop telling me to stay. And stop swinging me through the air like a child. Tucking me into bed one night does not make you my big brother. I bet Jessie doesn't let you manhandle her—"

He leaned in closer. "Enough." It was his dangerous voice and worked to shut her up long enough that they both heard Dom's quiet chuckles. Nicholas threw a glare over his shoulder at the other man, but it had no effect. He returned to staring down his blonde IT whiz. "Apologize to Dom for scaring him."

Her mouth dropped open. "I will not! You can't order me around, Nicholas. This is exactly what I was talking about! You act like you own the two of us, and it's obnoxious and totally unfair—"

"You were wrong, and you know it. Apologize to Dom."

Vivian glared at him, but she was increasingly aware of the large, rough, hot hands holding her hips. He still hadn't let go of her. Her feet didn't quite touch the floor. She felt the toes of her flats brush against Nicholas's shins. His bare chest and angry face filled her vision. She hesitated a second too long; he stepped closer. His muscular thighs pushed apart her knees so that he was between her legs. His breath teased across the bridge of her nose.

"Apologize."

She leaned back and shook her head. Her ponytail swung like a metronome. Later, she wouldn't be able to explain what made the words escape her mouth. Apparently, Nicholas brought out the petulant streak in her. "Say please."

The set of his jaw didn't change. His breathing remained slightly faster than normal, his pupils dilated. But, his thumbs moved from pressing into her hipbones to smoothing across the sides of her waist. His fingers tugged her closer. Her lower body pressed against his upper thighs. His eyelids lowered a fraction. The tenor of his voice changed from an irritated snarl to a sensual growl. "You're going to make me beg?"

"Y...yes."

They stared at each other. She caught her lower lip between her teeth. His eyes flicked to her lips. He bent his head.

Vivian arched her back and turned her head. Panicked, she all but yelped, "Sorry, Dom! I'll wear bells or something!" She pressed her palms, gently, against Nicholas's chest. When he backed up enough for her to move, she jumped down. "I'm hungry. I'm thinking Chinese. That good for you two? Yeah, I'll just order the usual. Apparently, I am a good dog after all, because I'll even fetch dinner and, yeah... later"

Nicholas watched her scurry back to her computers. When he turned and saw Dom's expression, his frown returned. "What?"

"Nothing, man, didn't say a thing."

"I'm going to shower."

"Copy that. She was talking about Detective Kwon when she came in. I'll find out what that was about."

Nicholas cursed under his breath. "She was, wasn't she? I should ask her about it before she bolts."

Dom coughed. "Shower. I'll chat with Vivian."

"I'm not going to hurt her, Dom."

"You sure? Look, take a break. Cool off and let me handle this. What's the use of having a sidekick if he can't tackle the pesky policeman and irritated employee situations?"

Nicholas's eyes flicked uncertainly toward the door. "You're positive?"

"I got this. Oh, but, Nicholas? I don't do bedtime tuck-ins, so save your strength."

The look on the younger man's face would keep Dom chuckling for several days.

Vivian sat in her rolling chair, one leg curled underneath her, eating her Chinese with chopsticks. She answered all of Dom's questions but pointedly ignored Nicholas. For his part, the playboy-turned-detective sat on the floor, his back against a table leg, and tried to ignore his response every time the slim bamboo sticks touched those glossed pink lips. *Forget how she managed to button that shirt; how does she* manage to use chopsticks with her hand in a splint? Is there anything she can't do?

"So," Dom asked, "the detectives showed up and started asking questions about Lee?"

"Yes, and not very politely. Then Kwon left a voicemail on my phone. He wants me to come in for a chat." Her blue eyes rolled upward. "It sounded less like a request and more of a mandatory thing."

"Did he outright ask where Lee is?"

"Yes. He also wants to talk about Nicholas." Her eyes flicked, briefly, to the man in question. "He and his partner seem to be under the delusion that I am in danger because I am wrapped up in Nicholas's criminal enterprise. The nerve, really! Where does he get off believing that Nicholas would be that kind of person, and then to act like anything he read in the press is true?"

"Vivian." Nicholas's quiet tone, laced with just the right amount of guilt, regret, and exasperation, silenced her diatribe.

Dom waited a few minutes before asking, "What are you going to do?"

He'd meant the question for Nicholas, but Vivian answered. "I'll call him back and tell him exactly what comes of making assumptions."

"No." Nicholas stood up. "I'll take care of this. It's my mess, and I'll handle it." He gave the other man a soft smile. "Dom, I need a few minutes with Vivian. After that, can you take her home, please? I don't think she should be driving." He caught her eye, then nodded toward the computers.

Vivian followed him at a distance. She frowned as he rubbed a hand over his right hip.

"Hurting?"

"No more than usual."

They sat. Vivian kicked her feet back and forth. The tips of her ballet flats made soft swishing noises on the tiles.

"I unlocked those files. Please understand, I didn't want you reading all of that alone, without context."

"So, springing it on me was better?"

He shook his head and grimaced. "Definitely not. I messed up. I'm sorry. Vivian..." He wanted to reach out to her, to offer some physical comfort. After the sexually charged incident earlier, though, Nicholas didn't think being close to her was wise. "The details in there are grim. Are you sure you want to read this?"

She looked down at the keyboard, then at the corner. She looked anywhere except at his face. That would have broken her. "I have to know."

"Do you want me to sit with you?"

Vivian took a deep breath. "Thank you, but I think I need to do this on my own. Do you understand?"

He shook his head. "I don't, but I'll respect your request. If you need *anything*, I'll be over there."

She tensed as he walked away. For several minutes, she sat staring at the keyboard. Then she gripped the mouse, moved the cursor to the folder in question, and started opening documents. She read it all—even the autopsy reports. Four years previously, she'd asked to see the reports, but the San Juan County Sheriff had denied her request. He'd told her the details were too upsetting and that she needed to grieve. More upsetting, she'd been told by everyone in authority that her parents' bodies were too badly burned to determine a cause of death. The autopsy report only said that for her mother. Her father's autopsy revealed two shattered kneecaps displaying "damage consistent with gunshot wounds".

After over an hour of wading through all the documents, Vivian closed the file and rose. She wasn't surprised to find Dom waiting for her.

"Your carriage awaits, mi'lady."

"I can drive myself."

"Maybe, but please let me do this for you. He'll just pitch a fit if you argue." He held up a hand, eyes fairly twinkling with good humor. "Now before you take a swing at me, let me say that I know he's been a royal dick lately. He's deserved everything you've thrown at him. Just keep in mind, please, that the Cheyenne docs didn't make his brain bigger when they fixed him up."

"Uh, did they make anything bigger?" She looked up at him with a twinkle in her eyes and a blush on her cheeks.

Walking up the stairs to exit the workshop, Vivian started giggling.

"What's so funny?"

"You called Nicholas a dick—a *royal* dick"

Dom reached up to tug on her ponytail. "No tattle-telling, young lady."

CHAPTER TWENTY-SEVEN

He'd tucked her into bed. Try as she might to concentrate on her work, Vivian's thoughts kept coming back to that detail of her Friday night. Well, it had actually been Saturday morning. *And why shouldn't I think about it,* she thought. *If I have to suffer the embarrassment of paparazzi speculation, I might as well savor what I can.*

The trouble was, savoring those memories meant several days of distraction.

Nicholas had driven her, from the hospital to her apartment, in silence. She'd gratefully accepted it. By then it was close to 3 a.m., and she was physically and emotionally exhausted. Leaning her head against the window, Vivian dozed off before they reached her assigned parking space. Nicholas spent several minutes looking around the dark interior of the garage, his frown deepening.

"I don't like your parking situation."

Vivian lifted her head from the window. "Really? You want to do this now?"

His frown hadn't disappeared, but he apparently decided to postpone any argument. Before she could get her suddenly heavy limbs to move in the correct fashion, Nicholas was around the side of the car and opening her door. He led her to the elevator, and then her door, with a firm hand on the middle of her back.

Once inside her apartment, he'd gently divested her of her purse and dropped it, with her keys, on the couch.

"I usually leave it on the table by the door."

His head tilted. "I doubt that."

She'd frowned as she tried to understand what he meant. Her fuzzy brain gave up quickly. She sighed and leaned in enough to pat his bicep. "Stop worrying so much, Nick'las."

His lips quirked when he heard her verbally trip over his name. "I'll put these pain pills on the counter. Why don't you go get ready for bed?"

"K. G'night." She hadn't moved, though, because he was standing there with that bemused expression on his face—the one he so often wore in her presence. "This is the bit where you leave?"

He put his hands gently on her shoulders and turned her toward the back of the small apartment. Unlike earlier, at the hospital, he didn't let go but carefully guided her along the hallway.

"Really, I'm cool. I can sleep in this."

He made a sound indicating agreement even as he nudged her to sit on the bed. "Feet up." Before she'd had time to think about it, Nicholas had knelt and removed her tennis shoes. Then he gently pulled her cardigan down her arms, leaving her in a tank-top. Her drugged, sleep-deprived, brain registered that she should be embarrassed but then decided that expressing that emotion required too much effort. Nicholas pulled her hair from its usual ponytail. He cupped the back of her neck while slipping an arm under her knees and moving her to a prone position.

After pulling the covers over her shoulders, his rough-padded fingers brushed her hair from her face.

"I'm sorry I hit you," she whispered.

"Shh. Get some sleep now. Tomorrow you'll remember why you aren't really sorry." Her eyes were already sliding shut when she felt his lips brush across her forehead.

"Remember indeed," Vivian whispered.

"Still talking to yourself?"

Vivian jumped, then glared at the woman standing beside her desk. "Jessie! Seriously, are all you Reeds ninjas?"

"Maybe." Mirth made Jessie's eyes twinkle before her expression sobered. She motioned with her chin at Vivian's splinted hand. "You want to tell me what really happened?"

Vivian made a rapid mental calculation. Jessie Reed was no fool. She'd see through any half-hearted lies. "Your brother, as I'm sure you know, has an over-protective streak. It's gotten far worse since Lee was shot."

Jessie's nose wrinkled. "I'm aware. So he decided to show you some of his moves?"

Vivian coughed at the suddenly vivid image of a half-nude Nicholas Reed showing her some moves. "Yeah. It didn't end well." She held up her splinted hand.

"Good. I mean, not good that your hand is broken, but good that it wasn't your fault. I'm sorry, are you choking on something?"

Vivian tried to control another coughing fit. "Yes, sorry. Dry air. Have to keep the computers cool and all."

Lee's twin was back to looking dubious. "You're sure you're all right? You're looking flushed."

"Fine, really."

"Well, I have a favor to ask."

"Oh no." Vivian groaned. "Every time a Reed comes in here asking for a favor, my life gets severely more complicated." She noted Jessie's frown and relented. "Let's hear it."

"There's been a lot of chatter at my club about some women—and girls—going missing. You did such a great job with the club's systems, I was wondering if…"

"I don't think boosting a Wi-Fi signal is going to help find missing women."

Jessie replied, "I know you work *closely* with my brother and Dom. That has to entail more than just fixing Wi-Fi." She held up her left hand to stop Vivian's imminent protest. "I don't want to know exactly what you do for my brother. I think you *can* help me find out what's going on."

Vivian leaned back in her chair. "OK. Tell me what you know."

"The first I heard of it was from a group of sorority sisters. They were semi-regulars at Willow. One night, right after New Year's, two of them went out to a different club—Kuzzo—and never came back. The car they drove that night was found down in Portland two weeks later. No sign of either woman."

"Did either of them have ties to Portland?"

"According to their friends, no. The police have no leads and without any signs of obvious foul play, have just kind of ignored it."

"You said there were others?"

"Are you going to help?"

Vivian narrowed her eyes. "I kind of have to, now. Not knowing will bug the shit out of me."

Jessie's eyes flashed. "Join the club. Hey, do they give you a lunch break in this sweatshop?"

"Well, sort of. Coffee and sandwiches at the cafe around the corner?"

"Works for me!"

"One more thing. Nicholas, Dom, and anyone on the security staff, can *not* know I'm helping you with this."

"Understand completely. Last thing I need is Nick acting even more paranoid."

"What good is hacking into phones going to do?"

"I'll record conversations and be able to track the phone owner's movements. Then I can collate that data to see if anyone in the club interacted with our missing women on the days they disappeared."

"Ah. So, do you have any?"

Despite being asked around a mouthful of croissant, Jessie's question was perfectly intelligible. Yet, Vivian had no idea what she meant. "Huh?"

"Club clothes. You can't wear that." Jessie gave a contemptuous nod at Vivian's work attire.

"Oh. Not beyond that one outfit I wore last December. I really haven't had the chance to..."

"Have fun? Ever?"

Vivian giggled around the straw in her mouth.

"Jessie?"

Both women looked up to see Nicholas and Dom standing at the end of the restaurant booth. Nicholas looked dumbfounded. Dom appeared concerned.

"Hi Nick!"

Vivian felt the tangible weight of Nicholas's stare on her face. *No, he's staring directly at my lips. That's weird. Why would he be staring at me while I'm sucking on a... crapsickles! I'm sucking on this damn straw like it's a... Please, please, please let the world end right now. Stop sucking on the damn straw, Vivian!* She forced herself to release her death grip on the cup and give the men an innocent smile. "Hi. We're having lunch."

His head angled to the side. Green eyes focused on her, searching for signs of deception. His whole body seemed to still and fade into the background of the cafe. Vivian realized she was holding her breath. Abruptly, he turned on the mega-watt smile and nodded at his sister. "So I see. I wasn't aware you two were lunch buddies."

"Oh, more than that! Clubbing buddies too! We're going out tonight," Jessie gleefully replied.

Vivian was frantically shaking her head and trying to signal Jessie with her eyes, but either Nicholas Reed's little sister was oblivious to the world around her or she just didn't care.

"Oh?" The haughty stare was back.

"Yup! We're going shopping too. Vivian needs to fit in with my crew."

"Why?"

Vivian just wanted to die, slide under the table, and fade from history. Her feelings were exacerbated by the half-amused, half-pitying look on Dom's face.

"Mr. Reed, we really need to get our lunch and be going if you're going to make that meeting this afternoon."

Thank you, Dom. Thank you, thank you, thank you. I will name my first son Dom. OK, maybe Dominick. Just get Nicholas out of here before Jessie tells him everything.

Nicholas couldn't leave without a parting shot. "Have fun ladies. Jessie, no ducking the security detail tonight."

"Sure." Insincerity dripped from the single word.

"I'm serious." His eyebrows were arched—never a good sign. Even as Dom took his arm and forcefully pulled him to the counter, Nicholas glared at Jessie and Vivian.

"Did you have to tell him?" Vivian hissed.

Jessie nodded emphatically. "Uh huh. You done? We should head out before he comes back and interrogates us."

Vivian whimpered softly.

CHAPTER TWENTY-EIGHT

Nicholas and Dom ate in Nicholas's office because the older man refused to let anyone eat in the company car. No matter how many times Nicholas protested that they could have it cleaned, the rule remained in place. They ate like military men: quickly, chewing carefully, and swallowing each bite, but doing it with an efficiency that suggested they had more important things to be doing.

"Did you know they were going out? Did you know they were even friends?"

"Man, I cannot keep track of your social calendar, much less Vivian's. And forget about Jessie. That's why I keep telling you we need a separate detail for her."

"I don't have a social life. Neither does Vivian. At least... I didn't think she did."

"Girl's got a life besides work. Maybe Jessie has a guy friend and is arranging a hook-up."

"Has she mentioned someone to you? A boyfriend, I mean?"

Dom wadded up the wrapper from his burger and tossed it into the wastebasket across the room. "What is this, high school? Why are you so worried? Do we have work for Vivian tonight? Something I didn't hear about?"

"No," Nicholas admitted. "I just thought she'd tell me something like this. Don't you think it's a bit soon? It's only been a week since she broke her hand."

Rolling his eyes, Dom walked toward the door. "They're going to a club, not leaving town with the circus. Also, she's with your sister—who is a force of nature. Relax. Now, about tonight. Hannah is making dinner for me. You're supposed to meet with your uncle, right?"

Nicholas nodded, still distracted by the disquieting feeling of having his sister and Vivian hanging out together. "I'll take my bike to the church."

They met in the rectory office. Father John poured himself a drink then looked at his nephew.

"No, thank you. I'm driving."

The priest nodded, then settled behind his desk. "Have you heard from Lee?"

"Yes. The surgery on his knee went well. He'll be starting physical therapy in another week. Docs say he'll make a full recovery."

"How is he, emotionally?"

Nicholas shrugged, unwittingly looking more like his younger brother. "He's pissed at me. That's not necessarily a bad thing." John eyed him over the rim of his glass. "Anger can be a great motivator. Let him be pissed at me if it gets him out of bed every morning and doing the rehab. I'd rather he wants to fight me than try to run off and take on the Triad by himself."

"Again."

"Right. Again."

"And Vivian?"

Nicholas's head came up. "What about her? She's fine." Even to his own ears, it sounded like a dodge.

"So how'd she break her hand?"

"You read gossip sites?"

John's lips briefly twitched to a smile. "When you were teens and your mother cut off all contact between us, I resorted to reading about my niece's and nephews' lives through whatever medium I could find. Now I just have a Google keyword search running. It alerts me any time one of you is mentioned."

Despite his rueful expression and shaking head, there was a touch of laughter in Nicholas voice as he said, "My uncle: priest and Internet stalker."

"Stop stalling, young man. Exactly how did Vivian hurt her hand?"

Father John did not know the extent of Nicholas's enhanced abilities or his efforts to fight criminal activity. He'd made it clear when Nicholas had returned from rehab that he did not wish to know details. He probably didn't know the exact manner of the Richards's deaths, either. Still, Nicholas didn't feel comfortable lying to his uncle.

"She punched me."

John choked. He coughed several times before sputtering, "Vivian punched you? What did you do?"

"Oh nice. You assume I was the one at fault?"

The priest quirked a brow.

"A few weeks back, before Lee was shot, I found out about how—and why—Vivian's parents died. I kept that information from her. She, predictably, found out and was... upset."

"That sounds like the mother of all understatements. It also sounds like an over-reaction on her part. Police and attorneys have been stonewalling her for years. She never punched any of them."

"My father's men were at least involved, if not the actual murders."

Sadness suffused John's features. "Oh no. Oh Nicholas, I am so sorry."

Staring off into space, Nicholas said in a monotone, "I'd have punched a friend if I found out something like that. I can hardly blame her. Worse, she keeps apologizing for hitting me."

"And that makes you feel more guilty."

"Precisely. I can't seem to do anything right where she's concerned. If I hide something from her, I am an over-protective bully. If I tell her what I know, if I let her deeper into... what I do... it puts her at more risk. You know her. You know how much pain she's been through. Shouldn't I try to keep her from going through more?"

"No." Father John's voice was as somber as his expression. "You should let her make that decision for herself. Too many people, too many *men*, in her life have tried to shield her. All that has done is expose her to danger and grief. Vivian has a heart bigger than any other person I've encountered. She also has a spine of steel. You've already let her into your life—even if at first it was unintentional. Vivian doesn't do anything half-way. She's all-in, whether you want her to be or not."

Nicholas rubbed his hand over his hair. "So she gets a choice but I don't? What if I choose not to be the reason she gets hurt?"

"Then you have to cut her out of your life completely." He gave his nephew a shrewd look. "Are you ready to do that?"

When he left a few minutes later, Nicholas's mind swirled with questions. His mood matched the reined-in fury of his bike's engines as he navigated the warren of Seattle's streets. The Ducati Diavel roared in satisfaction as soon as Nicholas turned onto the bridge over Lake Washington. The wind-whipped whitecaps glinted in and out of focus across the dark lake. He'd almost managed to mellow out and forget about his troubles when he pulled around the drive and slid to a stop.

Vivian's car idled in the drive. Nicholas secured his bike in the garage and returned outside in time to meet Vivian as she slipped out of the mansion.

She looked... His brain short circuited trying to find an adjective. Half of the blame for that could be attributed to her tight red skirt and filmy white blouse. The other half rested solidly on her shoe-less feet and terrified expression. Nicholas's emotions rocketed from lust to concern to blinding rage in less than a second.

"What happened?"

She flinched when he stepped near. He immediately noticed that she sported matching bruises on her upper arms—bruises that closely resembled handprints.

"How'd you get here so fast? They just called you. I didn't want to call Dom because he has a date, but I had to because I'm scared, and I don't know what to do now, and I knew you'd be mad..." Her words trailed off. He'd heard this tone of voice from her before: the night Lee was shot. Anger wasn't his dominant emotion now; he was sick with worry.

"Vivian? What's wrong? Where's Jessie?"

"In the house. I was so scared, and they were so much bigger than us, and my hand..." She trailed off again but not before motioning with her splinted right hand.

"Come on!" He was already striding toward the nearest entrance to the house. When he realized Vivian wasn't behind him, Nicholas stopped, annoyed. Then he saw her pained—shoe-less—progress across the same ground she'd just covered. He retraced his steps and stopped right in front of her. Without saying a word, he bent and hooked an arm under her knees. She squeaked when he lifted her. That one sound, just for a moment, made his lips twitch toward a smile. "Hold on tight," he whispered against her hair.

Nicholas pulled Vivian tighter against his chest so he could work the door handle. Turning sideways to get through the doorway, he instantly heard the low drone of voices from a nearby room. He didn't pause to put Vivian down until they were in one of the informal sitting rooms off the kitchen.

"Mr. Reed, I was just calling you..." A stocky Pacific-Islander in business attire, but wearing a shoulder holster, stopped talking. Everyone in the room could hear Nicholas's phone buzzing away inside his jacket pocket.

"Just a moment, Kekoa." Nicholas knelt as he placed his blonde bundle in a large wing chair. He grasped her good hand and placed his free hand on her knee. A muscle in his jaw ticked as he noted her torn stockings. "Vivian, look at me."

She didn't want to look into those piercing eyes. He saw too much. He'd know instantly that she'd let him down.

"Vi-vi-an." When she finally raised her gaze to his face, he spoke again. "I need to check on Jessie. I want— no—I *need* you to stay right here. I'll be right back."

She nodded once.

Nicholas turned and stood in one fluid motion. Jessie lay on the couch, eyes wide open but unseeing. Her breathing was a little too shallow for Nicholas's comfort, but she didn't appear to be in immediate danger. He looked at the waiting security detail.

"From the brief description of events from Miss Richards, we believe that Miss Reed was drugged. Her symptoms are similar to rohypnol, but there are a few key differences that indicate this might be a designer drug. Her vital signs are not ideal, but she doesn't appear to be in respiratory or cardiac danger. I would still recommend taking her to a hospital for monitoring."

Nicholas sat on the couch beside Jessie. She was half-reclining with several pillows supporting her upper body. "Hey, sis. Can you hear me?" He released a breath he hadn't realized he was holding when his sister smiled faintly. Without looking away from her, Nicholas asked "Is Mr. Fehr on his way?"

"He should be here shortly, sir."

"When he gets here, we can decide if she needs a hospital. He knows where the basic medical supplies are." He saw a flicker of movement to his left. Nicholas's arm shot sideways, finger pointed at Vivian. "I told you to stay still."

She was too tired to argue, but her eyes narrowed with a promise that she'd bring this up later. "My car is still running."

"Kekoa, please take care of Miss Richards's car. She won't be needing it for the rest of the evening." When she opened her mouth to reply, he turned and stared her down.

Several tense minutes passed with Nicholas keeping his attention split between Jessie and Vivian. When both women shifted, Nicholas's muscles bunched. He was obviously ready to spring but couldn't decide in which direction. His sister smiled again before her eyes drifted shut. She appeared to be sleeping peacefully. Vivian rested her head against one of the chair-back wings. She did not appear to be doing anything peacefully.

Dominick Fehr didn't precisely storm into the room, but he moved with a deadly efficiency of purpose. His concerned expression upon seeing Jessie went blank when he saw the damage to Vivian's wardrobe.

A novice, or a fool, would have mistaken the bland set of his features for casual indifference. A closer examination of his stance and eyes would have shown how very—terrifyingly—angry Dom was. He stood beside Nicholas, looking down at Jessie.

"What do you need?"

"Triage and privacy."

The former soldier nodded once. He quickly debriefed the other bodyguards, then issued an order for the medical kit to be fetched. Once that was done, he returned to Jessie's side. The extraneous security men were dismissed. He took her blood pressure, measured her pulse, and verified her respiration rate. Finished, he reported to his employer. "She's sleeping peacefully. I don't think they could do anything more for her at a hospital. The drug is obviously already in her system, so pumping her stomach won't help. I can take a blood sample and run it through the machines." He paused, throwing a quick look at Vivian. She was staring into the distance. "Should I call in additional support?"

"We might need one or two more guys tonight."

"Want me to wake Elena?" Elena Diernstad worked as the Reeds' housekeeper.

"Good idea. Once we get Jessie upstairs, can you coordinate that? Elena can help get her changed and stay with her while we talk to Vivian. I'll need you on duty after that."

"You don't want to go after these guys tonight?"

"No. We need more information." He brushed a curl off his sister's pale face. "And I'm not leaving them alone tonight."

CHAPTER TWENTY-NINE

Dom gently carried Jessie from the room. Nicholas crouched in front of Vivian. His worry deepened when her eyes darted around the room, never focusing on him.

"You're not going to argue with me about staying here tonight?"

She shrugged listlessly.

His fears ratcheted up another notch. "Let's go upstairs. We'll get you cleaned up and you can tell us what happened."

"I can walk."

He nodded smartly to acknowledge her defiance. He still, however, hovered just behind her as they navigated the stairs and corridors of the Reed mansion. Nicholas showed her to a guest suite right next to his room.

"Be right back."

While Nicholas ducked down the hall to gather first aid supplies from his room, Vivian looked around. She really ought to be, she thought, impressed by the size and décor of the bedroom. But, exhaustion and the crash from her adrenaline high were definitely taking their toll. She half-sat, half-collapsed, into yet another wing chair. A small, still active, part of her brain wondered if the Reeds got a bulk deal on expensive furniture items.

The air was cooler. She started to rub her arms through her see-through sleeves, only to stop when the bruises painfully reminded her of their presence. The thought of how she'd earned the marks made her shudder with something other than cold. Nicholas walked in, saw her, and quickly stripped out of his leather bike jacket. He'd been so busy, he'd barely paused to unzip it.

"Hey," he said as he carefully draped the coat over her shoulders. "Elena is grabbing some spare clothes of Jessie's. Dom will bring them in a second." He reached out a hand to stroke her hair but hesitated and moved back instead. "Vivian? Do you need to see a doctor? Or... um... the police?"

She realized what he was asking. "No. I..." She shuddered again. "Nothing that bad happened. I'm just over-reacting, you know? I've been through worse, and obviously I should just..."

A return to her rambling cheered him, but the emotion was short lived when she stopped talking and started staring into the distance again.

"Hey girl." Dominick's large but comforting presence suddenly filled the space around her. He cupped her elbow and helped her rise. "These should fit you." He looked down at her, dark eyes taking in every scratch. "You take as long as you need, OK? But before you go in there, you're going to promise me that there's nothing physically wrong beyond what we can see." It was his turn to ask the difficult question without directly asking it. The pointed look he gave her torn blouse was enough.

"Honestly, I wish you two would just ask. I'm flattered that you think I could be raped and still manage to get Jessie home safely. Trust me, I wouldn't be talking—or walking."

Both men grimaced. They prowled the room while she was ensconced in the bathroom.

"I had to ask. Her blouse—"

"I know. I already asked her." They paced some more. "Her left knee is skinned." Nicholas sucked in a deep breath and jerked his head around, searching for a target. He needed to be calm for Vivian's sake. The urge to destroy everything in the bedroom seethed just below the surface.

"She called me while she was driving back here. Every word out of her mouth was about Jessie, or you, or apologizing for interrupting my date. She never said a thing about being hurt." Dom glanced at the closed door. "Who apologizes for interrupting a date after she's been attacked?"

"Apparently, Vivian."

As if summoned by their conversation, the blonde woman slipped back into the room, wearing loose fitting shorts and a t-shirt. She perched on the edge of the chair with her neatly folded—though completely ruined—clothes in her lap. The black leather bike jacket she'd left on the bed. Nicholas snickered as he took the pile and moved it to a nearby table.

"What?" She might have been battered and exhausted, but she could still snap at him.

"You constantly surprise me, is all." He crossed his arms over his chest. "Those cuts need to be cleaned and bandaged. Dom or me?"

She nearly yelped her response. Dom smirked while Nicholas remained standing nearby.

"Start at the beginning."

"Where else would I start?"

He sighed. "Vivian..."

"Jessie wanted to scout out 757. That's the new club at the corner of—"

"I know where and what 757 is."

"Fine." She jerked slightly as Dom used tweezers to remove a sliver of glass from her foot. "Also, she didn't feel right spying on her own patrons."

"Spying on..."

"We were eavesdropping, physically and electronically, on club patrons." She winced. "Hoping we could get a lead on the missing women."

"Missing women?"

"In the past year, twenty-six women have disappeared after a night-out clubbing. The police have no leads."

Nicholas took a deep breath, trying very hard to not roar at her. "So you two thought you'd investigate on your own? Two attractive young women who are already in danger?"

"Well I didn't hear you come up with anything better!"

"Because you didn't bother to ask!" This time he did yell.

Dom raised his head to eye them both. "This argument can wait." The look he gave his employer was scathing.

Vivian huffed. "Well, anyway, we went there. It was loud and crowded. It felt... dirty, I guess. Not like, health-code-violation dirty, although I'm certain that I wouldn't want to eat anything served there. Neither one of us drank anything other than soda. Jessie said she wanted to be sober so she could notice the details of their operation. I was the designated driver."

"And my guys? Jessie's additional security?" Dom asked the question.

"Uh, Jessie said they weren't necessary."

"You know better, Vivian!" Nicholas tried again not to shout, but fear and anger made it hard.

"Look," she huffed. "If you two are going to interrupt with criticisms, I'll just catch a cab and go home."

"No you won't." Arrogant and authoritarian Nicholas had resurfaced. He was so busy trying to control the urge to wrap both women in packing peanuts and never let them leave his sight again, that he didn't think about moderating his tone.

"Hey, Vivian." Dom pressed lightly on the knee he was bandaging. "We're sorry. No more interruptions. Please tell us what happened."

"We were standing at a corner table drinking and chatting with people Jessie knew—I think she knows half of Seattle under the age of 30—lots of men and women. They were all young, well-off, and kind of vacuous. None of them could carry on a coherent conversation. They were seriously boring me to tears. I don't understand how you grew up with people like that. Or, why anyone, knowing who you and Lee typically date, would think you'd be interested in a girl like me."

Nicholas stared at her. He kept his arms crossed. His head tilted to one side. There were several points he wanted to make about that ridiculous statement, but Dom had promised her silence.

"Some older guys came over. Not creepy-weird-mid-life-crisis, just older than everyone else gathered around. They recognized Jessie." Her eyes narrowed. "And they recognized me as 'that girl from the pictures'. It felt like... Well, it felt like they were focused on me, not Jessie. They made me uncomfortable." She shivered again. "I ignored the feeling because it was loud, and I'm not used to all that attention. Also, my feet were hurting."

Dom noticed her shivering and how crossing her arms made her wince. He also noticed how the pulse point at Nicholas's left temple throbbed as he looked at her bruised arms. The nearest covering at hand was Nicholas's jacket. Dom held it out so she could slide her arms into it. When she clutched the engulfing black leather over her chest, she looked younger and more fragile. Finished dressing her cuts, he settled on the floor at her feet. The last thing she needed just then was two men standing over her.

"After a few minutes, Jessie said she was feeling dizzy and nauseated. I helped her to the ladies' room. She splashed some water on her face but she looked really pale. I didn't like it, so we decided to leave. I tried to tell them that when they stopped us in the hallway."

"They?"

"Sorry, those same two guys from the table."

"Wait. I know we promised no interruptions," Dom said. "But I want to record your description of these two. I need as much detail as you can remember." He pulled out his phone and hit the "record" button.

"One of them had pale blond hair. He was very Nordic looking. Blue eyes, really pale skin, and he's tall. Taller than either of you, but not as muscular. Sort of lean, like a runner, maybe? The other guy has really big hands and a stocky build. He's got dark eyes and hair, cut short. The hair I mean." She took a deep breath. "He's got a broken nose now too, so he'll be easier to find."

"You broke his nose?"

For a brief moment, Vivian's eyes lit up. "Oh hells yeah. He might have a limp, too."

Nicholas grinned while Dom choked on a laugh. "Maybe you better tell us the rest of the story."

"When we came out of the bathroom, Jessie was unsteady. The blond guy put his arm around her waist and pulled her away from me. I told him to let her go and that's when the short one grabbed me from behind. He gave me these." She rubbed her bruised upper arms. "Blondie said we were invited to a private party. They started dragging us toward the back of the club. We got to a locked door. While Blondie was unlocking it, Jessie leaned over and puked all over his shoes. The guy behind me was distracted, so I did what you taught me." Her smile was for Dom. "I was wearing heels, so I stomped down on his foot, slammed my head back against his face, and elbowed him."

Nicholas stepped closer. His long fingers gently examined the back of her head. "Good-size lump back here, but no blood."

Distracted by how very good it felt to have Nicholas touching her, Vivian quipped, "Well you have told me I'm hardheaded."

He splayed his fingers over her head. "Go on."

"Um, well, Blondie was jumping around trying not to get sick; Thuggy was spurting blood from his face and hopping on one foot. So, I grabbed Jessie's hand and dragged her out a door. I think that's where I lost my first shoe. Pure dumb luck, the door was an emergency exit that led right to the parking lot. I always carry a spare key in my purse, because I had this habit of leaving my keys in random places and then being too embarrassed to have to call Triple-A to get in my car for the umpteenth time. I got Jessie in the car—she's heavier than she looks, you know—and sped out of there. Huh. I guess I didn't tip the valet. He probably hates me now."

Both men stared at her, dumbfounded.

"What? It's rude not to tip."

Nicholas couldn't contain his laughter any longer. "You're obviously loopy from exhaustion. I think we have all the description we need for now. Dom, will you check on Jessie? I'll join you in a minute."

Dom patted her knee again as he rose. As the door shut behind him, Nicholas removed his hand from Vivian's hair. He stepped back, holding out his hand to help her stand. He pulled her into a tight hug.

"Thank you."

Vivian squirmed until she could look up at him. "I'm sorry. I should have never le—"

Nicholas moved his hands to cup her cheeks. "Shh." He leaned forward and kissed her forehead. "You are brave, smart, and utterly perfect."

CHAPTER THIRTY

Nicholas used his thumbs to tip her chin up. "Why didn't you want to tell Dom how your knee got skinned?"

Vivian blinked and tried to jerk her head from his grasp. Failing to physically evade his question, she tried verbal evasion. "I told you, nothing bad happened."

"I beg to differ." A full minute of silence passed as he waited, and she looked everywhere but at his face. "Are you afraid of what I'll do?"

"Yes!" She half-sobbed the exclamation. "Not afraid for them, because right now I'm so bloodthirsty I want you to beat them to a pulp." Her hands came up to grip his forearms, although her splinted right hand merely rested on his shirtsleeve. "But you *can't* go after these guys. Don't you see? Detective Kwon already asks too many uncomfortable questions. If your employee and sister get attacked and the guys responsible end up in a bloody heap, he'll *know* you were involved. He *can't* know about what you can do. And, Nicholas, I don't know if you've noticed, but I suck at lying."

"I can solve that problem. Everyone already thinks we're together. I'll use that—"

"Psh. The story won't be about me. I'm a nobo—"

He was very gentle, but the pressure of his fingers at the nape of her neck interrupted her statement. The green fire leaping from his eyes helped silence her as well. "I never want to hear you say that again. You are somebody to Jessie, to Dom, to Father John, and to me." He watched tears slip down her cheeks. The pads of his thumbs were too rough to be stroking her soft skin, but he did it anyway to brush away her tears. "Tell me the rest, Vivian."

207

She hiccupped a sob and lurched forward to bury her face against his chest. "I'm so sorry. I should have been paying more attention! It's my fault, all of it."

It took Nicholas a moment to absorb the shock of her body pressed against his. He slowly wrapped his arms around her back.

"I got Jessie to the car and got her in, but when I turned around to go to the driver's side, the blond guy was right there. I tried to run, but I'd lost my shoe and the lot was graveled and I just tripped! Guess that's when my other shoe came off. Then he was grabbing me and turning me over and shouting what he was going to do to me. He ripped at my blouse, and I just froze. I couldn't think of what to do and, you know, Dom's training didn't handle what I was supposed to do when an enraged Viking had me pinned to the ground."

"A what?" He asked against her hair, since she still hadn't moved.

A laughing hiccup escaped her. "Big, tall, mean guy who likes pillaging villages and assaulting women. We have to work on your nick-name giving ability."

"We really don't." He let the humorous moment hang in the air before returning to the painful subject. "You told us that you weren't sexually assaulted."

"I wasn't."

"Vivian, a man pinning you to the ground and tearing your blouse open counts as sexual assault."

"Fine," she huffed. "But I got away before anything... worse... happened. My spare key fob was still in my hand, and I must have accidentally hit the alarm button. I guess he was afraid someone would come running. He jumped up and ran away. I crawled to the car door—which *hurt*—and got in. Drove home. Called Dom on the way. That's it. Promise."

She stepped back, swiped at her damp cheeks with the back of her hand. "See? I'm not so very heroic after all."

His chin dipped and his right eyebrow crooked upward. It was an expression of contemptuous disagreement that Vivian knew all too well. She swiveled her head to watch him as he stepped neatly around the side of the bed. With a grand sweep of his arm, he pulled the covers back. She slipped out of the leather jacket. Handing it to him, she paused beside the bed.

"You tucking me into bed is becoming a habit."

Nicholas's brows lowered. He tipped his chin down and leaned his upper body toward her. "One I'm rather enjoying." He traced her cheekbone with the backs of his fingers. "Get some sleep."

Dom found Nicholas bent forward, braced with one arm against the wall outside Jessie's room.

"Well?"

Without looking up, Nicholas asked, "You knew she was holding back?"

Dom snorted. "I picked enough gravel out of her knee to pave a bonsai garden. The blouse?"

"I'd rather not tell you."

Dom folded his arms and glared. "Why?"

"Because if you knew, you'd be as mad as I am right now. I'm not sure the furniture or walls can take the combined assault."

"Fair enough." Dom pulled out his phone, checked his messages and the app showing the security deployment around the mansion. "Think you can sleep?"

"No." Nicholas straightened. "I'll take first watch. Get some sleep; I'll wake you up in a few hours. Dom?"

"Yeah?"

"I want these guys."

"We'll get them."

"I don't plan on being merciful."

Dominick Fehr's dark eyes zeroed in on Nicholas Reed. "Neither do I."

The first thing Vivian noticed when she woke up was the quiet. Her apartment's location meant she lived with the constant cacophony of city life. Traffic noises, the elevator, other tenants traversing the hallways, and myriad other urban sounds formed a background of white noise that permeated her home life. Her workspace at Reed Investments was filled with servers and computers, all with fans running. So, the stillness of the morning weighed upon her in a physical sense.

The second thing she noticed was that she hurt. Not just her hand—she'd grown shockingly used to the dull ache of her broken finger. No, this was an entire-body ache that elicited both a groan and a whimper. She tried to shift her position, but it didn't help the pain. Then she realized why everything was so different. She was in the Reeds' mansion. That sparked memories of the previous night, which explained her pain.

Vivian opened her eyes to peer around the guest room. She'd noted the expensive décor before, but in daylight it was more intimidating. There was something about the muted color choices, heavy wood trim, thick-legged chairs, and fresh flowers that made her feel very out of place. Honestly, fresh flowers? Had those been there the night before? She really didn't want to think about the implications if the tasteful arrangement had appeared while she was sleeping.

Sleeping... in the Reed mansion... in Jessie Reed's clothes... down the hall from Nicholas Reed...who had tucked her into bed *again*.

"Crapsicles." With that dry assessment, Vivian flung the covers back and stepped from the bed.

Or, she would have, had the soles of her feet not let her know—with great alacrity and ferocity—just how badly torn they were. As it was, she stumbled and whimpered her way from the bed to the door. She paused to look down at her T-shirt, a muted gray cotton emblazoned with the hot pink words "Drama Queen", and her loose-fitting shorts. Her blue eyes flitted to the table where her ruined clothes from the previous night should have been. They were gone. Obviously, someone had been in her room while she slept. That drew a frown.

All Vivian really wanted to do was flee before she had to deal with any of the residents or the emotions they evoked. However, she didn't have her purse, car keys, clothes, shoes, or phone. If she was going to escape this benevolent incarceration, she'd need help.

Limping along the hallway, she found her way to the main staircase. A well-built man in a suit looked up at her. He nodded smartly then shifted his focus back to the door and the downstairs hallway. From his dress, stance, and deportment, he was obviously one of Fehr's security team. Sadly, she couldn't remember his name.

His gaze flicked back to her when she finally made it down the stairs and stopped a few feet away. "Good morning, ma'am."

"Uh, hi. Um, I came in late last night, actually it was morning, but not, you know, sun-up morning, just

211

after mid-night morning. Anyway, I kind of need my keys and... stuff... back."

"Sorry ma'am, you'll have to ask Mr. Fehr about that."

"Of course. Yeah Dom—I mean Mr. Fehr—will know what I need. I mean, with the keys and all not..." She sighed. "How do I find him?"

Completely unfazed by her random conversational style, the man pointed to a connecting hallway. "Down that way, fifth door on your left. That's the kitchen. He should be there getting coffee."

"Fifth door?" Vivian muttered to herself as she limped along. "Who has hallways long enough for five doors? Well, Nicholas freaking Reed, of course." She whimpered again as the throbbing in her feet increased. Then she had to stop and glance behind her to re-count the doorways. She was still muttering in an irritated voice when she stopped in the kitchen doorway. Across an expansive island, Dom was just lifting a cup of coffee to his mouth. Vivian smiled at him, happy to see a familiar face. Before she could speak, though, the security consultant nodded brusquely.

"Good morning, Miss Richards. Would you like some coffee?" Dom's tone was formal. His eyes cut sharply to the side while he was speaking.

Vivian wasn't that blonde, as she often reminded the men in her life, so she clamped her mouth shut and walked fully into the room. Once there she looked to her right, around the edge of a commercial-grade refrigerator, and saw...

"Father John?"

The priest, dressed in his usual clerical garb, chuckled. "Vivian, I do believe this family will be forever in your debt."

"Does it put us on a hugging basis? I mean because you're still my priest and so very proper and there's Dom, he gets shocked easily. I mean, in my limited experience he seems to, anyway. Also, I'm standing here barefoot wearing your niece's clothes and I haven't even looked in a mirror—"

Dom knew it was only a matter of time before Vivian's verbal train careened off the rails into full-blown, panic induced, catastrophe. He interrupted her by shoving a steaming mug of coffee under her nose. "Drink this."

Dom wasn't entirely sure how John Anson always knew when his relatives were in trouble. He'd briefly entertained the idea of divine intervention, since the ability to show up precisely when needed was so uncanny. Whatever the manner of his knowing, though, the priest's presence was welcome. Father John seemed to be the only person on Earth to whom Jessie Reed would listen. Dom had been forced by necessity to give John the bare-bones story of Jessie and Vivian's narrow escape the night before. He'd known that one look at Vivian's visibly bruised arms would raise uncomfortable questions.

"I should have warned you that my niece gets in far more trouble than her brothers." Father John sipped his coffee. "I was surprised to hear of your... *relationship*... with Nicholas." The priest put just enough emphasis on the word to convey polite skepticism.

Vivian glowered over the rim of her mug. "Oh, that stupid article! I swear I should just give an interview and explain how ridiculous this whole thing is!"

Both men rolled their eyes. Whether it was in agreement with her plan of action or at her naïveté, they did not say.

Vivian glanced around. "How is Jessie? I'd like to see her before I leave, but I don't want to wake her. Though, maybe she doesn't want to see me. I can understand not wanting any reminders of that experience."

"I saw her about an hour ago. She was up and talking to Nicholas. I seriously doubt you'll be allowed to leave without seeing her." Dom's tone and expression, more than his words, made it crystal-clear to Vivian that she wasn't going anywhere until Nicholas deemed it safe.

"It seems you made quite an impression," Father John commented.

"That she did." Dom mock-toasted her with his coffee. "What was the word Jessie used…"

"Demented?" Vivian ran through a list of emotive words. "Deranged? Incoherent with fear? Wait, that was three words."

"Ferocious," said a deep voice from directly behind her. "The exact word Jessie used was ferocious."

CHAPTER THIRTY-ONE

Nicholas Reed stepped to one side of Vivian and smiled warmly at the men in the room. "Good morning, Uncle. Can you excuse me for a just a minute? Jessie's got me running errands for her." He plucked the coffee mug from Vivian's hands and steered her—via the presence of a warm hand splayed across her lower back—out the door.

"I was drinking that!"

"No you weren't. You were gushing over John and being self-deprecating."

She made a disgruntled noise.

"How did you sleep?"

"Fine. Great really."

He stopped and looked down at her feet as she tried to limp at his pace. When he stepped closer, she startled him by pushing him away.

"Oh no you don't, Mr. Reed. You cannot pick me up and carry me around your mansion."

His eyebrow quirked. "I'm certain I can. I seem to recall..."

"Nicholas," Vivian hissed. "Remember how this whole thing started? If we're ever going to convince the press—and everyone you know—that you're not some abusive boyfriend slash pervy boss, you're going to have to stop being so—"

"Concerned? Helpful?"

"Obnoxiously protective! I can walk. Maybe not as quickly as you can—or as quickly as you'd like, because you like to do everything fast except talk—but I got down here just fine and I'm pretty sure—what?"

He repeated, "That wasn't how all of this started. This whole mess started because you couldn't control your temper." Nicholas grinned at her outraged expression. "Also, because I was being a grumpy ass. Now you're yelling at me for being nice."

"I wasn't yelling," she mumbled. She looked contritely up at him. "Sorry. As a compromise, maybe you could help with the stairs?" She regretted that concession when they reached the base of the wide staircase. Nicholas didn't give her any warning before he scooped her up. "I meant I could lean on your arm!"

Eyes twinkling, he looked down at her. "Keep complaining and I'll carry you right into Jessie's room."

"You... I can't believe you'd... gah!" She fumed quietly and tried not to think about the ridges of muscle in the arms holding her so easily, or the hard chest her side was pressed against. She most definitely did not think about how soft the hair was at his nape, or how nice it would feel to run her fingers through it.

She was so busy not thinking about such things that it took her a moment to focus when Nicholas set her back on her feet. "Oh, um, thanks."

"No problem. Text me when you're ready to be carried back to your room."

Her eyes narrowed. "Firstly, no. I've had quite enough of being carted around like your personal sack of potatoes. Eh—hush!" She wagged her finger in his face. "Secondly, I cannot text you because you—or Dom, and frankly I'm not sure I care which one of you is behind it because you're both over-reacting and being stupidly possessive, but you're in front of me now so you get blamed. Blamed for taking my phone. And my purse, car keys, clothes—"

"You were in no condition to drive last night—"

"Fine! I get that. But I'm fine to drive now and I really just want to go—"

"We're not being ridiculous. You were attacked last night! The valet at the club still has your keys." Nicholas nodded briefly to emphasize his point. "You'd forgotten about that, hadn't you?"

"I'm not stupid enough to leave my apartment key on the ring when I hand the keys over to the valet!"

"Only because Dom and I drilled it into your head over and over again!"

"That's crap, Nicholas! I can take care of myself! You aren't responsible for me!"

"Yes. I. Am!" He roared his response while stepping closer to her. His right hand slapped, open palm, against the wall behind her. "Do you have any idea how much you mean to me? To the team?"

"Well, which is it, Nicholas? You or the team?"

"I'm trying, Vivian. I'm trying to listen... to be the person you deserve..." He trailed off, thoroughly miserable.

Vivian raised her hand again, this time to touch his cheek. She couldn't stay mad at him, not when he looked so lost. Before she could do or say anything, though, the door to Jessie's room opened.

"Are you two sure you're not a couple? `cuz, I'm hearing a pretty intense argument here. You might want to take it somewhere private, though. Talk about the gossip..."

Nicholas glared at his sister. She smirked back. With a defiant flip of her head, she turned away from her brother and pulled Vivian into the room. The door shut in Nicholas's face.

Behind the door, Vivian's shoulders slumped. "You're not helping, Jessie."

"Well I guess that depends on what you think I'm trying to do." Despite the mischievous nature of her quip, the young brunette looked pale and tired. "Whoa, you look as awful as I feel."

"Thanks."

"Come sit down. Nicholas will never forgive me if you fall over and he's not here to catch you."

Vivian took a seat on the corner of Jessie's bed while simultaneously shaking her head. "You have a very weird idea of my relationship with Nicholas."

"So there is something there!" Jessie clasped her hands in front of her and hopped onto the bed. "I knew it!"

"Friendship, Jessie. I'm not even sure that's what it is in Nicholas's case. Exasperation seems to be his primary emotion where I'm concerned."

"Ha!"

Vivian winced at Jessie's shout. She rubbed her forehead. "I guess you aren't suffering from any hangover like effects?"

Jessie shrugged her thin shoulders. She wore a pale grey T and comfortable jeans. Her hair was pulled up in a sloppy ponytail and she wore no makeup, but she still looked every inch the billionaire's daughter. "I had a headache when I woke up, but nothing an espresso and two aspirin wouldn't cure. I'm really hazy on details, though. I kind of remember you kicking some serious ass, but... Hey! You're not secretly a crime-fighting superhero, are you?"

"What?" Vivian's shriek of dismay hurt her own head. She glanced frantically at the door, afraid Nicholas or Dom would come running at the noise. "That's ridiculous," she hissed. "All I did was fall down, repeatedly."

"Well," Jessie talked right over Vivian's argument, "you do keep showing up in dangerous situations. You were there when Lee was shot."

"Yeah, and what do those two incidents have in common? Reeds being present. Trouble follows *you* and I keep, somehow, getting sucked into it."

Jessie's nose wrinkled. "But last night... those guys..." She rubbed her forehead. "Is it just my messed-up memory or did they seem to know who you were?"

"They did. They also really didn't seem to be the type to be reading social media gossip. Have you ever seen them before?"

"No. Did they tell us their names?"

"They didn't say."

"Did we get any useful recordings?"

Vivian shook her head, which was a mistake. She moaned again. "I don't know. Dom commandeered my phone." Acknowledging Jessie's look of horror, she continued, "Oh yes, Nicholas and Dom know."

"Pissed?"

"Volcanic."

Jessie pursed her lips. "I'll handle them. After all, it was my bright idea."

"This is so unfair. You get roofied and I'm the one with a headache."

"Maybe you got a weaker dose? It'd be weird for them to drug just one of us."

"I don't know, but I wish I'd finished my coffee. Oh, by the way, your uncle is here."

"John's here?" Jessie squealed with joy as she vaulted from the bed. "Where?"

Vivian held her head in both hands. "Downstairs, in the kitchen, I think. Pretty sure he..." She trailed off, realizing that Jessie had already sprinted from the room.

"And I still don't have my keys or phone." Grumbling about over-protective men and bad life choices, Vivian limped out of Jessie's room.

219

In the kitchen, Father John eyed his nephew with equal measures of exasperation and pride. "Your sister and her—your—friend were assaulted last night, but you want to go into the office? Jessie needs to stay in and rest."

Nicholas nodded. "That's why you're here. I need your help with her. You know you're the only one she listens—"

The rest of Nicholas's statement was truncated by a shrieking dervish who vaulted across the room and into John's arms. "You're here! I'm so glad you're here and stop talking about whatever serious shit you're always going on about when Nick's around."

The priest sternly rebuked her for her language even as he hugged her tightly. "I'll stay as long as Nicholas—and you—need my help." He kissed the top of her head—which action Nicholas noted and realized that it was indeed similar to how he'd kissed Vivian—and soothed her hair. "Good morning, Jessie. I see you're showing no ill effects from last night's adventures?"

"Pft." Jessie's slim fingers waggled in the air. "I was more of a stoned-out bystander. Unintentionally stoned," she added. "Vivian was awesome. Did you hear what she did? It was so cool. Well, the parts I remember, which isn't a lot really."

"Jessie? Did you leave Vivian in your room?"

"Huh? Oh, yeah, possibly. Sorry. You should really take her home, Nick. Although... there are probably paparazzi at her door."

Eyes narrowed, Nicholas retorted, "Jessie, you brat, why couldn't you just have gone to *your* club? If you've caused her any more pain..."

"Who?" Vivian limped back into the kitchen. "Oh, hi again, Father. Why are you all still standing here in the kitchen? I'm pretty sure there are chairs in this house. I

220

sat in at least two of them last night. Nice chairs. Unless you're moving them to a third-floor apartment in a building with no elevator, that is. Which, why would you be? I need coffee."

Dom poured another cup. He handed it to Nicholas who handed it to Vivian. As he did so, he stepped in front of her, blocking her from John's and Jessie's line of sight. "I'm going to take you home, OK?" He frowned when she looked around him to glare at Jessie. "What?"

"Drama."

"What?" He repeated the question, sure he was missing something vital.

"Never mind."

He smiled at her. It was the special smile he only shared with her. The moment ended when he saw the bruises on her arms. "We need to find you something less revealing to wear. Dom?"

"On it. Miss Reed, you wouldn't happen to have a sweater or hoodie Miss Richards could borrow?"

"Jessie, stop suffocating John. He's going to stay here with you—plus *extra* security—until I get back. You will not leave this house, understood?"

"You can't..."

"Jessie." John and Nicholas both said, in identical warning tones.

"Fine."

"Uncle, a moment, please?"

Father John took and squeezed Vivian's left hand before following Nicholas from the room. Jessie and Dom went to get more clothing for Vivian. She stood in the quiet kitchen, sipping her coffee and ruminating on the weird turn her life had taken.

"Vivian?"

"Mm? Oh sorry, Dom, just thinking."

"You OK?" His dark brown eyes searched her face. She smiled up at him, placed the empty mug on the marble countertop, and wrapped her arms around his waist. She felt more than heard his chuckle. "I guess this means yes?"

"I never said thank you."

"I'm pretty sure you did." He gently disentangled himself. "Jessie didn't have much in the way of concealing clothing, unless you wanted to wear one of her old school blazers. But I found this—" He held up a Seattle Sounders cap. "—and this." He had a long coat draped over his arm. "Also, your feet are only one size smaller than Jessie's, so, shoes!"

She giggled.

"What?"

"You're such a guy." When he looked confused, she grinned. "Only a guy would think to combine these boots with this coat and a baseball cap."

Dom crossed his arms over his chest. "Drama Queen," he muttered. It was an obvious reference to both the logo on her borrowed shirt and her behavior.

"Only by association," she shot back. She slipped on the borrowed items.

Nicholas walked back into the room. "I thought I told you to sit down?"

"And I thought I told you I wasn't your prize spaniel and that I didn't respond to sit-stay commands."

Nicholas looked at Dom. "Remember when she didn't argue with everything I said?"

Dom rubbed his chin. "No."

CHAPTER THIRTY-TWO

While Dom brought the car around, Nicholas gave Vivian a once-over. "Nice boots."

"Thanks."

"Here's your purse, with keys, phone, and whatever else you have in there. How can something so tiny hold so much?"

"Woman magic."

Nicholas looked at her blankly.

"Never mind."

"You don't have to go," Nicholas suddenly blurted. He looked uncertain and uneasy. It was, Vivian thought, one of his more innocent expressions.

"I need to. I need a shower, my bed, and some alone time to sort through all the thoughts in my head. It's not your house; it's me."

"Oh, if I had a dollar for every time a girl had used that line on me," Nicholas quipped. His playboy grin resurfaced. He motioned toward the front door.

Vivian smiled up at him. "You'd be a billionaire?"

"Oh wait..." they both said simultaneously.

Vivian frowned at the black Mercedes and the man holding open the rear passenger door. "This is the opposite of subtle. Remember our plan? The very clever plan? The one where we didn't give-in to press speculation about non-existent abuse and non-existent relationships?"

"That was your plan. I have my own." Nicholas rubbed the bridge of his nose. "Get in the car, please. I'll explain on the way."

She muttered something about grumpy bosses and glared at Dom when he chuckled. In an obvious bid to keep her from haranguing him, Nicholas started talking the moment he slid onto the seat beside her.

"Too many people saw you out with Jessie last night. The paparazzi now have your name and are scouring the Internet for every picture and article ever written about you. They'll be camped outside your apartment."

"I realize that, but this will all go away much faster if we don't give them photo opportunities. You escorting me to my front door in a grand walk of shame is a great example of what we should *not* be doing."

"Or you and Jessie can stand up in front of the press and tell them exactly what happened last night."

"No! Big tall glass of nope. No. Not going—"

He reached over and lightly grasped her left hand. "Vivian, remember what you told me in the hospital? About how sad it was that so many women in this city couldn't feel safe in their own homes? I, we, cannot stop every crime in this city. I've told you that before. Remember what you said?"

She ducked her head and bit her lip. "That doesn't mean we shouldn't try to stop some of them."

"Exactly." His fingers squeezed gently around hers. "We can't stop every instance of domestic abuse or date rape, but we can make a stand. We can encourage others to fight with us. There are twenty-six women missing from our city. You and Jessie might well have made that number twenty-eight. Tell the press *that*. Let *that* be the story."

Dom, from the front seat, added, "There's no way you and Jessie were the first women those two assholes assaulted. You know they'll try again. You need to go to the police and then to the press."

"What if it wasn't just a random assault? What if they were targeting Jessie, or me?"

Nicholas's lips pressed into a thin line. He didn't respond, but Dom did.

"That's why we'll keep investigating. If this wasn't a random attack, then we'll deal with it in-house."

"What if the police get involved and then those assholes disappear?"

"The SPD is welcome to catch the guys on their own, if they can beat me to them," Nicholas growled.

Those words left them in silent contemplation. Dom watched the road and the cars around them. Nicholas stared out the window, wishing he felt more secure leaving the matter to police. Sadly, the justice system all too often failed the victims of assault and rape. Vivian toyed with a loose thread on the left sleeve of her borrowed coat. She noted that Nicholas still held her hand. His thumb stroked over her knuckles in an absent-minded, soothing, gesture.

She suddenly jolted. "Oh my gosh! I'm supposed to be at work in an hour! Where's my phone? I've got to call and apologize for being late. We have that off-site data storage firm coming in today and—"

Nicholas reached over and plucked her phone from her hand. "Vivian, I already rescheduled that meeting and explained to the staff that you are ill."

"I'm not..." She trailed off when he raised an eyebrow. "Fine." She looked out the window, trying to settle her nerves. When she swung her head back around, there was a challenging glint to her blue eyes. "You don't let Dom take a day off when he's been shot, or stabbed, or beaten. Are you coddling me, Mr. Reed?"

Nicholas rolled his eyes. "Dom, would you like a day off next time you get an owie?"

The man in the front seat chuckled. "Don't hit him, Vivian. Your hand needs to heal first."

"I don't know why I put up with you teasing me."

"Two words," Nicholas whispered as he leaned in close. He stared right into her face and carefully enunciated each word in a low, husky voice. "Shirtless workouts." When he leaned back to watch her blush spread across her cheekbones, there was a satisfied smirk on his face.

They reached the parking garage beside Vivian's building with Vivian still flustered, Nicholas still holding her hand, and Dom checking on them via the rear-view mirror. The car slowed next to the elevator entrance. Dom looked around, eyes narrowed.

"I don't like your parking situation, Vivian. There's not enough security. Anyone can get in or out of here. Is there even a code for the elevator?"

Nicholas turned his head and looked at her.

Vivian snatched her purse from the seat. "You're both ridiculous. We can't all live in castles." She reached for the door handle, but Nicholas stopped her.

"Dom, wait with the car? I'll be back in a few." He marched quickly around the vehicle to open Vivian's door for her. Pointedly ignoring her dirty look, he splayed his hand across her lower back while they walked to the elevator. There wasn't any sort of key or security code for the elevator—a fact Nicholas made note of for future arguments. Once they were inside the elevator, he turned his head to look down at her. The brim of the baseball cap hid her eyes.

"That hat looks ridiculous." He snatched it off then stood, spellbound, as her hair tumbled down her shoulders.

"I think Dom was going for anonymity?"

Nicholas barely heard her. He was fighting the urge to run his hands through that glorious golden hair. He'd always been attracted to her on some level, but this... urgency... was new. He struggled with the need to touch her.

"What?" Her concerned question brought him back to Earth.

"Hm?"

"What did I do now? You're looking at me..."

"Relax. I'm not going to eat you."

They both blinked, stunned at the words that had come out of Nicholas's mouth. The elevator bell dinged, announcing Vivian's floor.

"Uh, show time, I guess." She glanced up at him, nerves making her frantic once more. "What should I say? We never went over what I'm supposed to say, and there's sure to be someone outside my door. You said it yourself that there would be. I have no idea what to do in these situations!"

Nicholas brushed the hair back off her shoulders and tipped her chin up with his knuckles. "Say whatever you want or say nothing at all. I'll back you up, whatever decision you make."

"OK." She took a deep breath before turning and exiting the elevator. As soon as she saw the five photographers jammed in the narrow hallway outside of her apartment, she squeaked in alarm. Nicholas's hand against her back, pushing her forward, was the only thing that kept her from fleeing.

The paparazzi started shouting questions all at once. The cameras flashed and Vivian blinked. The sudden cavalcade of light and sound made her headache come rushing back. She didn't want to deal with this right now. She wanted peace and quiet.

"Miss Richards does not have a statement at this time. If you'll be so kind as to let us through, she'll grant interviews when she's ready." Nicholas looked and spoke like the businessman that was his public persona.

"What about you, Mr. Reed? What's your relationship with Ms. Richards? What kind of statement will she be giving? Do you two have an announcement to make?"

"Miss Richards is a valued member of my team at Reed Investments. She's also my friend. Please excuse us." He shut the door in their faces.

Vivian was already stripping out of her borrowed coat and boots. She tried to hand them back to her boss, but he shook his head. "I can't very well carry your clothing back down the hallway past those reporters."

"Oh, right. Sorry. Not thinking. I'm new at this."

"Just leave them here. You can return them later, once the attention has died down." He glanced around. "I'm trying to find a polite way to ask this, but..."

She'd already noticed his barely contained energy and quickly moving eyes. "Yes, you can check my apartment for locked windows. Be sure to look for monsters under the bed." That comment earned her another tight-lipped look.

By the time he'd finished prowling around, Vivian was in the tiny kitchen. She'd gulped down two aspirin and was contemplating which she wanted more: a shower or sleep.

"Everything's secure," Nicholas stated unnecessarily. He noticed how tired she looked. "Do you want me to stay?"

She smiled. "Thanks, but I really just want a shower and a really long nap. I won't be able to relax if you're out here on the couch." She winced at his brief, stricken, expression. "That's not what I meant. I'd just be worried about you being uncomfortable and thinking about what you could be doing instead of babysitting me and... You know not to take anything I say seriously, right?"

He shook his head as he crossed the floor to her. "The opposite, actually. You have an amazing capacity for truth. I love that about you. Please don't ever stop."

"Didn't my amazing capacity for blurting out uncomfortable truths get us in this mess?"

"Maybe we should stop seeing it as a mess and start appreciating the opportunity. Vivian... I can't ever thank you. You've saved my family, each of us—first Lee, now Jessie, and even me. You keep saving me, even when I don't deserve it. I'm supposed to be the savior."

She placed her undamaged hand gently on his forearm. "Nicholas. You don't have to save everyone. You have friends. Friends help each other."

"Even when we're being awfully hard to like?"

"Especially then." She hugged him quickly but pulled away when his chin dipped toward her hairline. "You've got to stop doing that."

"What?"

"You know what. Kissing me on my forehead. The big brother kiss. You're making a habit out of it. It's sweet and I love it, I mean... never mind. But you are going to forget and do it in front of someone, and then we'll have even more explaining to do."

"You're right, I'm sorry. I'm going to let you get some rest. Call me or Dom when you're ready to go out again, please. You don't have a car," he reminded her.

She nodded. He stepped back but lifted her splinted hand to his lips. Holding her gaze, he brushed his lips across her bound knuckles. "When this hand is better, we're going to talk about acceptable public displays of affection." He squeezed her fingers gently. "Lock the door behind me."

Nicholas left her standing there, mouth slightly parted and eyes glazed over with both exhaustion and emotion.

CHAPTER THIRTY-THREE

Detective Kwon sat perched on the edge of a sofa worth more than his annual salary. He flipped his paper notepad closed and turned off the record function on his phone. His features hid none of his contempt for the people in front of him. He resented being summoned to conduct an interview. *Normal* people came to the police station. They came to him for help. They did not arrange meetings in expensively furnished rooms with lawyers and priests flanking them. *Honestly*, he thought, *a priest*?

"And you? Where were you during all of this?" Kwon's question was directed at Nicholas. His tone was, as usual, scornful.

"Meeting with my uncle. I knew Vivian would be with Jessie. I trust them both, implicitly."

"A trust well earned, it would seem," interjected Father John. "Detective, if you have no further questions, the ladies need to prepare for their press conference."

"Putting out descriptions of your attackers could be interpreted as obstructing justice and encouraging vigilantism."

"Detective, your department puts out descriptions of wanted persons every day. We're merely assisting you in your efforts by informing the public. This family and this company attract a lot of media attention. We'd like to use that for good, finally." Nicholas's tone was as conciliatory and reasonable as he could make it.

"Fine. I suggest you ladies stay close to home—just in case these individuals seek revenge for becoming Seattle's Most Wanted."

"We won't let them out of our sight," Nicholas said.

While Nicholas and the lawyer, Mr. Garvey, walked the detective to the door, Jessie went to touch-up her makeup. Dom joined Vivian in the kitchen. She sipped water while tapping her nails against the counter. She'd taken the time to repaint them; her colorful polish had been horribly chipped during the previous night's struggles.

"How you holding up?"

Her nose wrinkled. "Fine." After a pause, she continued, "I'm going to get tired of people asking me that, aren't I?"

"Probably." He cocked his head, listening to the sounds from other rooms. "Ready for round two?"

"Oh sure." She gulped her water down. "How do I look?"

"Ferocious." Dom motioned toward the door while smiling down at her.

"Not sure that was the look I was going for."

"It works for you, trust me."

Two hours later, Vivian leaned against the glass wall of the VIP balcony in Willow. She hadn't wanted to come to Jessie's club. The last thing her aching body needed was being crushed in a crowd or assaulted by pounding music. But, Nicholas insisted he had a hunch, and, as usually happened, he'd been right. Within fifteen minutes of Jessie and Vivian's arrival, women were quietly asking to speak to them in private. The number of ladies sharing similar stories of assault was heartbreaking. Most of them had not been as fortunate as Jessie and Vivian.

"Here," said a deep voice right behind her.

Vivian jumped before a familiar hand squeezed her shoulder.

"Sorry. I shouldn't sneak up on you."

She looked over her shoulder at Nicholas. "You can't help it." She took the drink he offered her.

"Sip it," he tried to warn her. His pupils expanded when she slammed back half of the whiskey. "Jessie's new bartender makes them strong."

"I like them strong."

Nicholas stepped closer. He watched her, awaiting her babbled apology for the double entendre. His eyebrows reached for his hairline when she stared back defiantly, not retracting a single word.

"Ready to get out of here?"

"Can we? You were right, of course. There's been so many..." Vivian hunched her shoulders and gripped the tumbler. "I don't want to leave Jessie alone to deal with anyone else coming up here."

"She's going down closer to the bar. Dom will stay with her. I'll take you home."

Her blue eyes shone with intensity. "I don't want to go home yet."

His answering smile was almost predatory. "I didn't think you would."

Nicholas escorted Vivian down the stairs. They made their way across the floor toward the bar. Even in her most comfortable pumps, Vivian's feet were still sore. People barely moved out of their way. Nicholas's social smile was plastered to his face, but he didn't invite conversation. Still, the press of bodies wrought havoc on Vivian's nerves. By the time they reached the bar, she was as close as she could comfortably get to Nicholas's side. He'd moved from having a hand on her lower back to an arm completely wrapped around her waist.

Nicholas nodded at Dom. He narrowed his eyes at Jessie, who was openly flirting with a young man at the end of the bar. "I'm taking Vivian home. Mr. Fehr, can you please make sure my sister is escorted home?"

Jessie rolled her eyes. Dom nodded. "Absolutely, Mr. Reed."

Jessie stopped flirting long enough to give Vivian an exuberant hug. "Thanks for coming. This couldn't have been easy. We need to have a girls' night that is just us, for fun." She watched Vivian nod. "Nick, you make sure she gets home safely. If you need to stay at her place, we'll all understand."

Nicholas's arm flexed around Vivian. "Jessie?"

"Yes?"

"Shut up."

He steered them to the door and his car. Once at the Reed building and in the workshop, Nicholas helped Vivian slide her arms into her cardigan and pulled her chair out for her.

"You're going to look through the Willow security feeds to see if you can identify those two?"

"Yup."

"Need any help?"

She chuckled. "No, Nicholas, this is my thing. Go work out."

Already removing his suit coat, he stilled. "You're sure?"

"Positive."

"OK." He started working on the buttons of his shirt. Nimble fingers stopped, though, when he saw her watching. "Aren't you supposed to be staring at the monitor?"

She jumped and blushed. Her loosely piled hair slipped a bit when she jerked her head in indignation. "Well if you don't want an audience, Nicholas, don't put on a show!" With a huff, she turned around in her chair.

Time slipped away from them both. Vivian pored through endless hours of security footage from Willow. Frustrated with her fruitless efforts, she turned to hacking the feed from 757. Or more precisely, she *tried* to hack the feed from 757. The club only had one wireless port that, despite sitting behind a very secure password and impressive firewall, yielded no valuable information. Her failure only slightly mitigated the guilt Vivian felt at going against her "no hacking" resolution.

Across the basement, Nicholas worked off some of his pent-up rage and frustration. He hadn't changed his mind: he still wanted to break the hands and knees of the men who'd dared to hurt his sister and friend. Dom had been the one to suggest letting Vivian and Jessie share their story with the public. He thought, and Nicholas begrudgingly agreed, that the two women would feel less victimized if they played a role in their attackers' capture. Nicholas had known Vivian would handle the police inquiry and her computer-based searches with aplomb. The more public role was intended for Jessie. Unfortunately, the press had other ideas. Snippets from the press conferences played through Nicholas's head as he punched a hanging bag.

"Ms. Richards, isn't it true that you're sleeping with Nicholas Reed?"

Nicholas winced again, remembering her eyes meeting his as she laughed. "Do I look like the type of girl Nicholas Reed sleeps with?"

Several of the reporters had smirked, causing Nicholas's muscles to knot.

"How did you injure your hand, Ms. Richards?"

"I tried to learn a self-defense move and hit the punching bag incorrectly."

"Why do you need self-defense?"

Nicholas remembered that part with amusement. The reporter had opened himself up for the brunt of Vivian's withering scorn.

"That should be obvious. Every woman in this city—sadly—needs to learn basic self-defense."

Unfortunately, most of the questions had been less about the necessity of stopping future assaults and more about salacious gossip.

"You should save some of that for Blondie and Limpy." Dom's words interrupted Nicholas's reverie.

Nicholas grabbed a towel. He swiped at the sweat on his face and shoulders. "We have to find them first."

"We will. Jessie's back at the house."

Dom tossed his suit jacket over his shoulder as he walked away. He leaned against Vivian's workstation. "You should give it up for the night."

She looked up at him. Her exhaustion and frustration were clear.

"Well, at least set up one of those ping programs and let the searches run while you sleep."

She still didn't move.

He leaned closer. "Nicholas won't leave as long as you are here. He barely slept last night. Do you really want him going after these guys when he's tired?"

"I know what you're doing."

Dom shrugged. "You're the genius; I'm just the hired help."

"Whatever. Fine. I could probably sleep here. Unless he's going to keep beating things with sticks. I don't want to listen to that all night."

"So, when you dream about him, it's quiet?" He asked in a teasing tone while he helped her to her feet.

"I don't... shh! You're worse than Jessie."

"No, I'm really not. Trust me, she's already planning your wedding." He caught sight of Vivian's mortified expression. "Relax. I'm just teasing." He held out her coat. "Seriously, though, this adrenaline high you've been running on is going to end—and soon. You've been through *another* traumatic event. You need rest."

She looked up and smiled softly. "Thanks."

Nicholas walked in. He'd showered in the bathroom and was wearing his white oxford shirt and gray slacks with his suit jacket draped over one arm. "Vivian, are you ready to go?"

"Yes."

"Goodnight you two." Dom sauntered up the stairs, whistling "Get Me to the Church on Time".

Vivian groaned.

Nicholas tilted his head. "I don't think I've heard him whistle before."

"You won't hear it again, because I'm going to kill him tomorrow."

"O...k..."

"I mean it. I'd do it right now, but I'm too tired. Maybe you can do it for me?"

Nicholas laughed. "Maybe. I want to get you in bed first."

Her head snapped up.

He squeezed his eyes shut. "I really just said that."

"You did. Wow, twice in one day. Maybe my foot-in-mouth disease is contagious."

Nicholas groaned.

As they pulled out of the garage, Vivian said, "You could just take me to your place."

Nicholas's hands slid over the Italian leather steering wheel while his head turned toward her.

"So I can get my car, I mean. Obviously."

His look continued to tell her that it was not obvious. He turned to watch the road, again, his lips pressed together in a frown. "No. Dom can bring it to you tomorrow when he picks you up for work."

"Fine."

"Try not to kill him when he shows up."

She harrumphed. "If you had any idea what he'd been teasing me about, you'd fire him for sure."

"Oh?" Nicholas's amusement and curiosity increased as he noticed Vivian blush. "What was he teasing you about?"

"Nothing. Ignore me. I'm really tired. Very, very, tired. Just need my bed."

CHAPTER THIRTY-FOUR

Nicholas was still chuckling to himself when he pulled the car into a visitor parking space. Vivian stopped him before he could escort her into the elevator.

"Thanks for the ride. I'm fine from here, really. I'll see you tomorrow in the office."

Tired and exasperated, Nicholas barked, "Vivian! I'm walking you into your apartment. Let's go."

"This is totally unnecessary."

Nicholas rubbed a hand over his face. He glanced at his watch and winced at the time. "Yes, your constant stubbornness is unnecessary. I refuse to have this argument with you every time I'm concerned for your safety."

Vivian harrumphed again and crossed her arms over her chest. She kept her aggravated silence even when they reached the inside of the apartment. While she stripped out of her shoes and plugged her phone into the charger, Nicholas prowled around. When he didn't immediately return from her bedroom, Vivian threw up her hands in frustration.

"Nicholas, we both really need sleep. If you insist upon making sure the windows are locked, fine. Just do it and... what?" She backed away, eyes wide at the fury on Nicholas's face.

"Get your things, we're leaving."

"What? Nicholas, move." She tried to push him away from her bedroom door. He blocked the way, preventing her from seeing what had him so upset. Pushing against his chest was pointless. She might as well have been bench-pressing a Giant Sequoia. "This is my apartment, mister. Move it!"

He did move, but it was to step closer to her, backing her further against the wall. "You are not staying here." Each word was a staccato burst growled out from a dark place inside of him.

"Oh for crying out-loud." Vivian ducked under his arm. She only made it a step into the doorway before she stopped.

Her room was just as she'd left it—immaculate—save for one horrible detail. A printed picture from a gossip site was tacked to her pillow with a black-handled knife. The blade was completely embedded in her pillow, leaving only the hilt showing. Beneath the grip, Vivian's pictured forehead had been neatly punctured.

"Well hell," she muttered.

"Vivian..." Nicholas trailed off and stared in shock. Vivian wasn't a weak-willed, simpering woman who cried at the slightest bit of drama. He knew that. But since she'd met him, she'd had a gun pointed at her head, interrupted a violent attack, seen a friend shot and another man killed, broken her hand on her boss's face, been harassed by the press, assaulted at a club, and saved his sister. Everyone had his—or her—limits, and surely Vivian was due for a few tears? Instead, she marched toward the bed while yanking her hair into a ponytail and cursing under her breath. He lunged forward to stop her before she gripped the knife. With one arm around her waist, he pulled her back from the bed.

She wriggled in his grasp, a ball of fury ready to take vengeance on the nearest symbol of her tormentors. "Let me go, Nicholas! This is my home and my bed. I'll be damned if these cowards are going to chase me away. Oh, they have no idea who they are messing with!"

"Vivian." He dropped his head and his voice to whisper in her ear. "Hey. Stop for a second to use that big brain of yours. This is a crime scene. You can't mess it up before SPD has the crime lab people take pictures and prints."

Vivian stopped struggling, although she remained tense. It was hard to relax with Nicholas breathing on her neck, his body pressed against her back. "We can't call SPD at this hour, Nicholas. I'm tired. You're tired. Neither one of us has slept well in days. If they show up here—"

"It will take hours. I know. That's why I asked you to pack a bag. I'll take you back to my place. We can call the cops in the morning."

"You didn't ask; you ordered me to get my things."

He huffed out a sigh against her neck. "Sorry. I went into protector mode." His arms squeezed her lightly. "If I let you go, are you going to punch me again for being an arrogant, controlling, ass?"

"No. I'm too tired and you still haven't shown me how to punch people without hurting myself."

"I'm not sure I want to. Hitting people is no way to solve problems, Miss Richards."

"Ha!" She pulled out of his grasp. Her anger had cooled enough to allow logic to take over. Nicholas was right; she couldn't just yank the knife out of her pillow and go to sleep. They also didn't need to waste precious time waiting for the police to show up. The crime scene could wait until the morning. The only thing she was in imminent danger of, at the moment, was falling asleep on her feet.

Having quickly packed toiletries and clothing to wear to the office the next day, Vivian walked to the front door. Nicholas was waiting there, trying to look relaxed. "Take me back to your place, Mr. Reed." She smirked at him. "Yes, I know, you've heard that line a billion times."

By the time they'd driven back across the lake to the Reed mansion, neither felt like quips or sexual innuendos. They were both truly exhausted. Vivian limped up the grand staircase while Nicholas carried her bag. He showed her to the same room she'd occupied the previous night. It felt like a lifetime ago; so much had happened in just a few hours.

"Sleep well. I'm right down the hall if you need anything."

"Thanks." She covered her mouth with her hand, trying to mask a huge yawn. "Hey, can the staff maybe not drop off fresh flowers in the morning? Which is in a few hours, of course. It's kind of creepy knowing some stranger is walking around in the room while I'm asleep."

Nicholas smiled. "I put the flowers there, Vivian."

Vivian rolled over and automatically reached for her phone. The elegant little bedside table did not yield the device, though. Instead, there was a neatly folded note. Inside, Nicholas had scrawled:

Took your phone so it wouldn't disturb you. Come yell at me when you're awake.

She muttered about presumptuous, over-protective men the entire time she showered and dressed. A glance at the clock told her it was only 7 a.m. She was surprised she'd only slept for five hours. Before she pulled on her strappy blue heels, Vivian checked her makeup in the mirror. Her white silk A-line dress was decorated with large navy polka dots. She'd forgotten to pack her deep wine lipstick. The only shade in her purse was bright pink, which would look ridiculous. *Maybe*, she thought, *I can sneak into my bathroom and grab it before Detective Kwon declares my entire apartment a crime scene. Yeah, sure.*

Her eyes narrowed when they fell, again, on Nicholas's note. She knew he was right next door. Still in her stocking feet, she snatched up the note and marched to his room. In her defense, she did stop to listen for movement in the room before opening the door. Hearing him moving around, though, she pushed open the door and stormed in.

"Listen, mister, the flowers were nice but this note leaving is just cree—oh."

"Vivian!" An aggrieved Nicholas sprang across the room, pulled her fully inside, and closed the door behind her. He was exasperated, shocked, and shirtless.

As a testament to how used to him she'd become, Vivian noticed the shirtless part last. "Oh for crying out loud, Nicholas. I've seen you half naked before."

"And how are you going to explain that to Jessie or, God forbid, my mother?"

"Oh. Um, you have a very loose office dress code?"

He huffed in annoyance. Turning away, he picked up the shirt he'd dropped on the end of the bed when she entered.

"If you didn't want to explain me in your room, why'd you leave that note? Stop. You can't wear that one. It has a bloodstain on the sleeve."

He stripped out of the shirt and examined the sleeves. Finding the offending stain, he raised an eyebrow at her. Wordlessly acknowledging her powers of perception, and fashion sense, he motioned toward his closet. Vivian flipped through his shirt selection while he leaned against the doorframe separating the walk-in closet from his bedroom.

"I need a closet this size. This is obscene, Nicholas, especially for a man."

Chuckling, he said, "I never managed to fill it, even in my partying days. You should see Jessie's." He took the shirt she handed him. "You might as well pick out my tie, too."

"Nicholas Reed's personal IT chick and fashion adviser. I'm moving up in the world."

"Is that your way of saying you want a raise?"

She handed him a pale green silk tie. "Just my phone, thank you. I'll take my car back to the apartment and meet whoever SPD sends over to file the report. Then I have... *work*... to do in the office."

He stopped buttoning his shirt and cursed softly. "I forgot—I have an early conference call with some Cheyenne executives. I thought we'd be finished by the time you were awake and ready to go." He stepped closer. "Why didn't you sleep longer? You were so tired."

She smiled up at him. "You're not the only one who cannot sleep more than five hours a night." Her shoulders shrugged. "I have a lot on my mind. Now—" She gently patted his bicep. "—stop worrying about me. You need to focus on work right now."

"I need to—"

"No," she cut him off. "You do not need to protect me every moment of every day."

Nicholas suddenly loomed over her, eliminating the minuscule amount of space between their bodies. "I don't want you hurt, again."

"You can't stop every hurt life throws my way. Besides, I've gotten pretty good at taking care of myself."

"But you shouldn't have to face it all alone. You deserve to be happy."

"Stop it, Nicholas. You don't get to lecture me about personal happiness—or trying to save the world on my own. I help people—Lee, Evan, you, the homeless—because it returns a little light to the city. My parents were ripped out of this world. They were *good* people. Other good people saved me when I was at my lowest. Yes, I wanted to find my parents' killers, but not for revenge. I wanted to keep others from feeling that darkness of lost hope closing in around them. This city, your family, Dom and I, we don't need an avenging angel. We also don't need you to just be a protector."

She pressed her palm over his mouth when he tried to interrupt her. She ignored his irritated expression. "You want to lecture me about not finding happiness? If you save all of us at the expense of losing yourself to the darkness, it's no better than if you died to save us. We need you to *live* Nicholas, in every sense of the word. Find someone who makes you happy, who brings light into your life."

Vivian dropped her hand. She wasn't sure who was more shocked: her for getting all of that out without babbling off on a tangent, or Nicholas for the passion with which she'd said it.

"So smart." He brushed a tendril of hair from her cheek, tucking it behind her ear. "So perceptive." His hand moved to tease the nape of her neck. She couldn't help the soft purr-like sound that escaped her throat. His other hand stroked over her hip. His forehead lowered to press against hers. "So remarkably clueless." His chuckle brushed over her lips when she jerked at his insult. "I don't need to go anywhere to find happiness. Vivian Richards, you're all the happiness I need or could ever want."

"Me?"

"You."

She took a shuddering breath. "You said I was exasperating."

"Oh, you are. And also fascinating, brave, ferocious, beautiful, and wickedly smart." Watching her eyes move over his face, feeling her tense, Nicholas tugged her closer. He smiled. "You said no more big-brother pecks on the forehead. Does that include all kisses?"

"Uh, I said that? Was I awake? Drinking? Why do you take anything I say seriously? I cannot imagine why—"

His lips were curved into a smile right up until they pressed against hers.

Nicholas Reed, Vivian discovered, kissed like he did so many other things—with intense passion and singular focus. He twisted his fingers in her hair as his lips teased hers. When she twined her arms around him, he moved both hands to cup her face. They nipped and tasted until Vivian was out of breath. Nicholas pulled her head to his chest while hugging her tightly with his free arm.

"I really wish I hadn't scheduled that meeting," he groused against her hairline.

"You have such odd pillow talk. Uh, not that this is pillow talk, or could lead to pillow talk. Oh wow, who knew that kissing you would only increase the idiotic things coming out of my mouth?"

"I adore your mouth." His chest expanded beneath her head. Regret tingeing every movement, he gently pried her fingers from his shoulders. "I have to go."

"I know, sorry. Just..."

"Hey." He reached out to grab her left hand. Squeezing her fingers, he said, "Talk to me."

"Yeah." Her voice squeaked slightly. "Sorry, yeah. Got to stop saying sorry... because I'm not. At all."

"Good." He adjusted his tie but caught her eye in the mirror. "Any stray bloodstains, or lipstick, I should be aware of?"

Her laughter made his smile expand. "No, you're good. I didn't have a chance to grab the right shade, so I don't have any on yet. Lipstick, I mean, not blood. Obviously."

"Mm." The backs of his fingers brushed over her jawline. "Oops."

"Oops?"

"Stubble burn. My turn to say sorry."

She looked up at him, blue eyes wide with challenge. "Totally worth it. I'll repair my makeup before meeting Dom." Nodding, she added, "Yes, I'll take Dom along. If you think you can spare him?"

"Just return him in one piece. See you soon." He dropped a quick kiss on her lips before leaving.

Vivian was left standing in Nicholas Reed's bedroom. She stared around her, wondering if she was having a particularly vivid dream. One glance at herself in the full-length mirror cured any doubts. Her cheeks were flushed. She didn't need lipstick to make her lips look bruised or plump. Her pale, sensitive, skin, the bane of her adolescent romances, still showed the slight imprint of Nicholas's attention to her throat.

A noise from down the hall startled her. She snatched her phone from Nicholas's desk and slipped out the door.

CHAPTER THIRTY-FIVE

Dom watched Vivian closely during her interview with Detective Suisse. The SPD crime scene unit crawled through her apartment, searching for fingerprints and how her attacker had gained access. When she volunteered that Nicholas's prints would definitely show up, Suisse scowled. He made a sharp crack about having her boss in her bedroom. Dom expected a scathing retort from Vivian. Her stammering blush raised his curiosity.

Later, back at the Reed house, Dom observed with bemusement Nicholas's exceptionally good mood. He was smiling at everyone. It was kind of creepy.

"Man, what is it with you today?"

Nicholas grinned. "Mm?"

"If I didn't know you better, I'd say you're happy."

"Why is that so hard to believe?"

Dom folded his arms over his chest and stared, stone-faced, at his friend.

Nicholas punched him, lightly, on the arm, still grinning. "Lighten up, Dom. It's a great day."

"I watched SPD pull a nine-inch knife out of Vivian's pillow this morning. Remind me again what's so great about today?"

That comment sobered Nicholas. He sighed and rubbed his jaw. "Did they get any leads?"

"No. They also couldn't find out how the guy got in. Which made Vivian, and I'm quoting here, 'highly disturbed'."

"We've got to find these guys."

"What's your plan until then?"

Nicholas's deadly focus showed on his face. "She stays with one of us at all times."

He knew the answer, but Dom asked the question just to see Nicholas's reaction. "Jessie or Vivian?"

"Both," Nicholas snapped.

Vivian drove herself to Willow that evening. When she came in through the VIP entrance, Dom intercepted her. He pointed her toward the club office.

"He wants to see you. He's been antsy since you left by yourself."

Vivian rolled her eyes. "And how many traffic laws, or laws of physics, did you break to beat me over here? I left before you two did!"

Dom looked down at her. "And you give us crap about being bad liars..."

"I wasn't lying." She tossed her head. "I merely omitted certain relevant details regarding my itinerary."

"Please don't go out by yourself again. Not until we catch these bastards. I know your first instinct is to argue with Nicholas when he's in 'Savior of the City' mode, so I'm asking. Just as a friend."

She nodded her agreement, but not before blushing at the mention of Nicholas's name. Dom's eyes narrowed as he watched her trot up the stairs to the club office. Nicholas and Vivian both acting oddly on the same day...

"Hi," Vivian said as she pushed the door closed. She clasped her hands in front of her, twisting her rings nervously. "Dom said you were up here and wanted to see me. I'm not really dressed for clubbing, so I thought I'd just check in with Jessie then—"

The minute the door clicked shut, Nicholas was out of his chair and striding across the small room. He stopped just out of arm's reach. "I want to kiss you again," he blurted.

"Oh."

"I shouldn't have this morning."

Her face fell.

He rushed to explain. "You were just attacked. Violently. The last thing you need is me pawing at you. But I want to make it clear that if you want to—"

Nicholas, interrupted mid-sentence, had his mouth open when she rose on her tip toes and ran her tongue across his bottom lip. He curled one hand around her nape and tugged her close. His lips sealed over hers. The hand at her waist moved to her lower back, pulling her flush against his body. When she raised one knee to drag her foot against his calf, Nicholas growled his approval. She scraped her nails down his bicep.

The splint on her right hand prevented her from rubbing his jawline. She hissed in frustration. Kissing along her neck, Nicholas made soothing noises.

"Stupid hand."

"Mm."

Kisses feathered over her lips to trace down the opposite side of her neck.

"Broken on your stupid hard head."

Chuckles bubbled from his lips. "Beautiful, stupid, jaw, remember?"

"Doubly stupid."

He pulled his head back to look down at her.

"What?"

"Would you prefer I stop kissing you?"

"I'm going to stop talking now."

Nicholas murmured, "Excellent." He picked her up and carried her, with ease, to the nearby desk. Her tight knee-length dress prevented him from stepping between her legs. "I no longer like this dress," he growled.

"Well, you could always bleed on it and ruin it."

"You think you're very funny, don't you?"

She nodded vigorously. "I know I am. You're always laughing at me."

"Not *at* you, Vivian. B*ecause* of you."

"Pft. No serious talk. No more talk at all." Vivian pushed him into the desk chair. Eyes glinting, she settled sideways onto his lap. Her good hand brushed along his jaw while her splinted hand's fingertips toyed with his tie. Her tongue traced over his lips until they parted. When she sucked his tongue into her mouth, his hand on her hip clenched. Vivian shifted on his lap. Nicholas murmured his approval even as he sucked on her earlobe.

They traded kisses and touches, lost in each other. The club, their friends, and the city were forgotten for a few blissful moments. When Jessie rattled the office doorknob and then loudly demanded to know why they'd locked her out of her own office, Vivian buried her head in Nicholas's neck. The harder she tried to stifle her giggles, the more she squirmed. He picked her up and stood. He had to steady Vivian with a hand under her elbow—not that he felt very steady, either. It took several deep breaths, while looking at anything but the woman beside him, before he could speak.

"So, how was your day?"

Vivian collapsed into more giggles. She found refuge in the chair they'd just vacated while Nicholas paced—and adjusted his clothing.

"Why'd you want to come over here?"

"I thought it would be a good idea to be seen with Jessie, again. This time, for Detective Kwon's benefit."

His expression quizzical, he asked, "Is he here?"

"No, but he always seems to know where one of us has been." She frowned. "Isn't that kind of weird?"

"It is. So, an hour being seen in the club, and then we can go do work?"

"You're staying?"

"Oh yes." Despite being on the other side of the office from her, the look Nicholas gave Vivian set her skin on fire. "I've decided on a new approach for our press problem."

"Uh…"

He nodded. "I propose a united front. Let anyone who thinks of messing with us know that if they attack one, we *all* respond." Offering a hand, he pulled her to her feet, but kept his distance. "If that is all right with you?"

"And if I say no?"

"Then we think of something else. Together." His expression mirrored the sincerity of his words. Vivian understood that he was abandoning his autocrat role and giving her a choice. She nodded. Then, with a seductive smile, she slid past him and walked out of the office.

Half an hour later, Nicholas leaned against the rail of loft, watching the human spectacle below him. Vivian had ducked into the ladies' room.

"Well, this has officially passed from creepy to downright unsettling."

Nicholas's eyebrow quirked upward.

Dom crossed his arms over his chest. He glared at his friend. "Jessie has spent the past five minutes trying to locate that man's tonsils with her tongue, and you're up here smiling."

Despite his good mood, Nicholas's expression soured. His head swiveled toward the back of the bar. "Oh good, I haven't hit anything today…" He pushed away from the railing, ready to physically separate his sister from her latest boy-toy.

Dom started to follow the younger man. "Hey, you're not actually going to beat that guy, right?"

Vivian stepped in front of Nicholas. "Can we get out of here now?"

His posture instantly relaxed. "Absolutely. Office?"

"Yes, please." As they ducked through the back hallway, she asked "Who were you going to beat up?"

"What? Oh, nobody important."

"Seriously disturbing," muttered Dom.

When they reached the basement workshop, Vivian plopped down in front of the computers. She tapped keys and scrolled through video footage for several minutes. Nicholas cleared his throat to get her attention. She twirled around in her chair, then crossed her legs, slowly, while making direct eye contact with him. Dom heard him swallow. The sudden realization of what exactly was going on slammed into the security chief's head like an artillery barrage. Before he could comment, though, Nicholas started talking.

"Vivian, you've heard Dom mention his girlfriend, Hannah, right?"

"Yes, but I haven't met her yet." She looked quizzically at Dom. "Why is that?"

"I try to keep my private life separate from what we do here. Also, you've been busy."

Nicholas, expression aggrieved, continued. "Hannah is the COO of a charity set up through one of my family trusts. I own an apartment building not far from here. We, the charity that is, provide affordable housing to crime victims."

Dom could see Vivian tense. Her left hand gripped the arm rest of her chair while her eyes darted to the door.

"Hannah's story is her own to tell, but she is intimately aware of what it's like to feel unsafe in one's own home. She lives in the building, screens tenants, and manages the charity for Nicholas. I'd like you to meet her."

"I'd like you to consider living there," Nicholas interjected.

Vivian shook her head vehemently. "No. I have a paying job. I have a place to live—"

"Not a safe one."

Her head snapped sideways. "*If* I decide to move, it will be *my* decision. Got it? And it will not be into an apartment paid for by you."

"He doesn't pay for it, Vivian. Tenants work out an agreement with Hannah based on their income. There's a one-bedroom on the fifth floor that is sitting vacant right now. The building has a doorman, security cameras, and secure parking."

Nicholas crouched beside her chair. Moving slowly, he reached out and gently stroked the fingers of her right hand where they protruded from the splint. "Please consider it. For me?"

"You two aren't letting me go back to my apartment, are you?"

Nicholas, trying very hard not to be domineering, managed a weak smile. Dom went for full grizzly mode. He folded his massive arms across his chest, looked down his nose at her and intoned, "Over my dead body."

CHAPTER THIRTY-SIX

The next week passed in a blur for Vivian. Even as her bruises started to fade and the cuts on her feet and knees slowly healed, the emotional trauma had her fighting panic attacks and nightmares. While she had no intention of admitting it to either Dom or Nicholas, the idea of going back to her apartment left her in a cold sweat.

Hannah, a beautiful, olive-skinned, dark-haired woman, instantly set Vivian's frayed nerves at ease. After hearing what Nicholas and Dom had told her about the building, Hannah rolled her eyes.

"And this is why *I* run the charity. Those two constantly either over or under sell what we do here. This building is meant to be a refuge for battered wives, mothers whose children have been injured by gang violence, sex trafficking victims, or those the Triad have threatened. We currently have apartments on ten floors. The basement garage has two levels, both gated. We have full-time on-site security trained by Dom and paid for by one of the Reed holding companies. I have both a one-bedroom and a two-bedroom currently available."

"I don't need two bedrooms."

Hannah gave her a shrewd look. "What if your younger brother comes for a visit?"

"Fine, I can't *afford* two bedrooms. Not in this neighborhood."

"We charge twenty-five percent of your *net* monthly income."

"How do you know how much I make?"

"I don't. That is the formula we apply to all tenants."

Flustered, Vivian blurted, "But there's no way you can pay the property taxes, much less upkeep, if you're only charging that!"

"And yet, we do." Hannah sipped her tea. "So, do you want to see the two-bedroom?"

Feeling wantonly extravagant, Vivian moved in the next day. Father John brought Evan by to help her put her bedstead back together. Johann, Frank, and Dave, from the Reed Investments security team, helped carry her meager belongings. Nicholas wandered in, leaning on his cane more than usual, well after dinnertime.

"I grabbed Ezell's chicken. Sorry, not up to cooking tonight."

Vivian took the food from him and led him to her battered couch. "This is perfect. Sorry about the furniture."

"You can buy more, make this place feel like your home. Maybe I should give you a raise." At her horrified expression, he chuckled. "Fine, not yet. Aren't you technically still a probationary hire?"

She stuck her tongue out at him. "You just try to fire me, Mr. Reed. I'll crash your whole system on my way out the door."

Nicholas grinned but leaned his head back and closed his eyes.

"No luck finding them?"

"Not yet." He sat up. "I feel better knowing you're here where they have to go through hardened security to get to you."

They ate slowly. Vivian told him funny incidents from the day. He gave her a broad over-view of his physical altercation with three Triad members. When she came back to the couch with a bottle of wine, Nicholas shook his head.

"Not tonight." He pulled her down onto his lap and kissed her slowly. One hand splayed over her lower back while the other twisted in the hair at her nape. His stubble lightly abraded her cheeks and throat. When Vivian's fingers moved to the buttons his shirt, Nicholas pulled back and rested his forehead on hers.

"I can't stay." One rough-padded thumb dragged over her lips. "My hip is rebelling, again. I need a treatment and sleep."

Ardor cooled by concern, Vivian walked him to the door. He pulled her close, kissed her one last time, and whispered, "Sleep well. I'll see you tomorrow."

Two nights later, Dom and Nicholas descended the workshop stairs to find Vivian tapping at keys on her workstation. She pivoted to face them.

"So, don't be mad. OK, that's just silly, I know if I even start a sentence that way, of course you'll be mad. Maybe be less mad, then? I was perfectly safe the whole time and Mr. Ramirez helped with the hook-up, so it's not like I went out courting the city's underworld for contacts or anything. Hmm... that sounded better in my head, as usual."

"Vi-vi-an."

"Right, sorry. I ran an errand before I came down here tonight."

Dom frowned while Nicholas tilted his head to one side and pressed his lips together in a patently indulgent look.

"I dropped some tech off with Mr. Ramirez, and he installed it on the roof of 757."

Both men stared at her.

She sighed. "Because we can't get any good feeds from their internal cameras? The tech tapped the line and now I can see everything." She emphasized her point with both hands. "Everything. If they sneeze, I'll see it. As soon as we see them do something illegal, the cops can move in and arrest them."

This time it was Dom who said her name, albeit in a gentler tone. "Vivian." His brown eyes looked sad. "The police can't use anything from a warrant-less tap. You know that."

"Of course, I know that. *But*, when they do something illegal, we'll hear their plans and Nicholas can intercept them. If they're turned over to the police when caught in an illegal act, it doesn't matter about the tap." Vivian huffed in annoyance. "Honestly, I wish you two would have more faith in me."

They both mumbled apologies. She beamed. "Thank you. You'd better get going."

"Huh?"

"They, the guys from the club, are there again. In fact, they are in the club office."

"Wait," Nicholas said even as he changed his shirt. "How are you seeing this? Wouldn't the router access just give you information on the computers?"

She snorted. "Only if I was a noob. I hacked *everything*. I used the router access to infiltrate their security system and recorded everything from the cameras. I also turned on the wireless feature of the router through which I Bluetooth-jacked their phones and the club's audio system." Her teeth caught at her bottom lip. "I had to go back and scrub all of the music from the feed, though. Should have anticipated that. Next time, I guess. So, yeah, I can read, hear, and see, everything going on in that hell hole. By the way,

Broken-nose is Jerry and the Viking-looking one is Tom."

Dom laughed heartily. "You're kidding, right?"

"I didn't think it was possible for their names to be any more ridiculous than those nicknames," Nicholas muttered as he grabbed his helmet and Kevlar vest. He pulled open a drawer to retrieve a syringe. Seeing Vivian's worried look, he paused. "Don't worry. It's stimulants and anti-inflammatory agents."

She turned away, unable to watch him inject the concoction. Turning back to her computers, she found Dom watching her intently.

"You know, I'm not sure which one of you I should have the talk with," he whispered.

She sputtered, unable to form intelligible words.

"But honestly, we both know that between the two of you, Nicholas is the more emotionally fragile."

Vivian nodded again.

Dom crossed his arms. He glared down at her. "So, don't you dare hurt that boy, you hear me?"

She rose and flung her arms around the big man in front of her. "You're a good friend, Dom."

He laughed. "Yeah, well, one other thing. I don't want to ever walk in on you two making out." He shuddered. "I have limits, you know."

"Uh huh. Sure. Remind me to install new locks on the workshop doors and soundproof the back seat of the car." Vivian laughed long and hard at his look of horror.

Nicholas crossed the room. "Dom, you ready?" Then, to Vivian, he said, "Please stay here. Snatching these two up might spook whoever is giving the orders. Stay here until one of us comes to get you. And I want..." He took a deep breath. "I want to *ask* you to please consider staying at my house tonight."

"Just focus on catching them. Don't worry about me." She stood on her tiptoes but still had to pull his head down to kiss his cheek. "Be careful, please."

CHAPTER THIRTY-SEVEN

As apprehension ops went, scooping up Tom and Jerry proved to be routine. Dom and Nicholas waited in the shadows outside the 757 club's back entrance. Vivian, talking with them via voice-over-internet-protocol earbuds, alerted them as soon as their quarry moved toward the exit. Nicholas, spoiling for a fight, stared down in disbelief at the crumpled form of the attacker Vivian had nick-named Viking.

"One punch? Really?"

Dom, who'd had to tase the broken-nosed goon, grunted. "Stop your bitching and get them in the van."

Working together, they hauled the two men into a black van. Legs secured via corrections-manacles to ring bolts in the floor, arms pulled over their heads and secured to the ceiling, and heads covered with hoods, the two suspects were in custody in under ten minutes. Dom pulled out of the alley, signaled his turn, and stayed exactly at the speed limit all the way to the heliport.

"I know you're jacked up on that mixture and I *know* we want to make these assholes pay for putting hands on Jessie and Vivian. But, man, you've got to be careful. We need them to talk. If it turns out they're just the regular flavor of would-be-rapists, we've got to remand them to the locals. We can't be doing that if their faces look like cottage cheese."

"I'm aware, Dom." Nicholas stared out the window at the nearly deserted streets. "How long is the flight out to the freighter?" Out in the darkness of the Pacific, well beyond the territorial waters of the United States, a Panamanian-flagged freighter steamed in large, lazy, loops. US and Canadian Coast Guard officials thought the freighter housed state-of-the-art under-sea mapping equipment that monitored the motion of the Juan de Fuca Plate. It actually did, but the main purpose of the ship was much grimmer. Cheyenne Consortium used it as a floating detention center. The ship also occasionally hosted people the CIA very much wanted to speak with—unencumbered by certain civil-rights statutes.

"I think she's at the top of her loop tonight, so about two hours. May be a bit more."

"I don't want to leave Vivian alone that long. I really don't want her going home, either."

"Call her and ask her to wait for me. I'll take her to the house."

"You're sure?"

"Do you think it's a good idea for you to be around her right now?"

Nicholas knew what his friend meant, but the question still chafed. He was too keyed up, his senses too hyper-aware. Being near Vivian in that state would likely end up with him pushing her too far, too fast. "No. Plus she's likely to argue about having to go back to the house instead of her new apartment. Better you be the one to tell her. She likes you."

"Not as much as she likes you," Dom muttered under his breath.

They pulled up to the private heliport. Two more armed men, similarly dressed in body armor and motorcycle helmets, helped move the prisoners to the waiting A109S helicopter. Both Tom and Jerry were given mild sedatives, secured to seats with zip-ties, and outfitted with ear protection. Due to the possible side effects of the sedative, they were also fitted with pulse-ox meters. The additional security team took seats behind the two prisoners. Dom checked with the pilots to make sure they had everything they needed.

Nicholas stepped away to call Vivian.

"Any problems?"

"None at all, thanks to your excellent information. We have them loaded on a chopper. Listen, I—"

"You're going with them. To question them. So, you won't be home tonight."

Thrown off-balance by her response, Nicholas stopped pacing. "You're not going to argue with me?"

"Would it change your mind about letting me go home to sleep in my own bed?"

"No."

"Would it make you angry and distract you from the important work you need to do now?"

"Who are you and what have you done with Vivian Richards?"

She laughed. The sound coming through his phone made Nicholas grin like a child on Christmas morning. "I'll see you tomorrow?"

"Count on it."

"Be safe."

"You too." He ended the call. Walking back to the chopper, he took several deep breaths.

"Good to go?"

"Yup." Nicholas slapped one hand against Dom's shoulder. "See you tomorrow."

Dom watched until the helicopter's lights disappeared to the south-west. Once he'd picked up Vivian from the Reed building, he asked, "Have you eaten? I'm starving."

"Hm, no, I seem to have skipped dinner. It's been a weird day."

"It's been a weird year, so far." They exchanged wry looks at the truth of that statement.

"Can we swing by my place? I need to grab some clothes."

"Yup."

Side-trip completed, Vivian climbed back in the van. "So, I did some digging while I was alone tonight."

"Oh?"

"The intake nurse at the hospital—the one that Nicholas took me to when his stupid head broke my hand—"

"Is that how we're telling the story now?"

"Hush. Anyway, that intake nurse is Detective Suisse's cousin. That seems like an odd coincidence. Especially if our assumption about someone in the hospital leaking my name to the press is correct."

Dom agreed. "That—combined with Kwon and Suisse being tasked with investigating the break-in last Fall, Lee's shooting, *and* the assault on you and Jessie—does sound like a few too many coincidences.

"But is it odd? I mean, they all were violent crimes."

"Here, use the app and order Chinese food for us. The address and card are already saved. That way we won't have to wait when we get to the house." He handed Vivian his phone while he drove. "Now, yes, those were all violent crimes, but SPD has more than two major crime detectives. The only reason to have the same pair on all three cases would be if the cases were related."

She turned her head to look at him. The regularly spaced lights of the bridge created a flashing effect within the van. "Which they are."

"Are they? We know Lee instigated the robbery attempt. The guys he hired aren't even tangentially connected to the Triads. We checked."

Vivian frowned as she considered his point. "OK, but Lee's questions about his father led to the Triad trying to kidnap him. That's an obvious connection between the two incidents: Lee."

"But the detectives don't know that. Those two knuckleheads who broke in don't even know it was Lee who hired them. And how does the assault on you and Jessie factor in? Once Lee was unavailable, the Triad switched to Jessie?"

"It does seem unlikely that the Triad is backing Tom and Jerry. They weren't very... I don't know, is skilled the right word? Are there skilled rapists?"

"Sadly, yes."

They both contemplated that disgusting fact in silence. Vivian turned the coincidences over and over in her head.

"There is one other thing that all three cases have in common—and it's an obvious link the detectives will have noticed." Growing horror at the realization of what she was saying caused her to nearly whisper the word. "Me. I'm the link."

Dom pulled the van into the garage connected to the guest-house-turned-security-headquarters. As he led the way into his kitchen, he looked down at Vivian. "I don't think you're wrong. Actually, I'm terrified that you're right. But before we jump to conclusions, let's see what Nicholas learns from those two assholes we picked up tonight."

"Fine, but I'm going to dig deeper into those two detectives."

"I would expect nothing less."

Detective Kwon read the forensics report twice before calling the crime scene unit directly.

265

"The only fingerprints on the knife belonged to Detective Suisse? How is that possible?"

"It has to have been cross contamination. I didn't see him touch the knife at the Richards scene before I fingerprinted it, but he must have."

"The print was on the blade?"

"Yeah. The handle had only smudged, un-usable prints. Like the perpetrator wiped it down."

"So it's possible that Detective Suisse touched the blade after you'd printed then removed the knife from Ms. Richards's pillow."

"I guess it's possible... The print was right where the hilt met the blade."

"He wasn't wearing gloves?"

"I... I'm sorry. I don't remember."

Kwon hung up, feeling frustrated. He'd been frustrated for months, it seemed. After the attack on Vivian Richards and Jessie Reed, he'd looked into the missing women they'd mentioned. The women shared only gender and general age-range as characteristics. They'd come from different neighborhoods in Seattle and the surrounding cities. Two were open lesbians; four had a record of past drug use. None of them had used phones or credit cards after the nights they disappeared. No bodies, or obvious crime scenes, had been found. The detective wondered how two young civilians managed to find the pattern of abductions before the police had.

He also wondered how the Triads, the Reed family businesses, and the trouble-attracting Vivian Richards, factored into this latest mystery.

CHAPTER THIRTY-EIGHT

Nicholas pushed the man named Tom back into the tiny cell in the hold of the freighter. He slammed and bolted the door before walking to the next cell. When he yanked the door open, it came off the hinges. He stood there holding the heavy steel door in one hand, glaring at Jerry. The criminal's pupils dilated to the size of dinner plates. He scrambled into the farthest corner. Nicholas thrust his arm out and flung the door down the passageway. Then he stepped over the raised door jamb, picked Jerry up by his collar, and dragged him down the hall.

As soon as Nicholas turned the corner, three Cheyenne employees picked up the door and placed it back on its hinges. This time, they actually attached the pins holding it in place. Nicholas's little bit of theater had them all grinning.

"You know who I am?"

"How... How'd you do that, man. You some 'roid freak?"

"That's the question you want to ask me?" Nicholas, having secured Jerry's wrist and leg shackles to a table, leaned against the bulkhead. He purposely kept his voice at a low growl without yelling. The stimulant mixture he'd injected prior to scooping up the pair of stupidly named offenders had started to wear off. His anger, though, hadn't abated much. All he had to do was remember his drugged sister, or Vivian's torn blouse, and the urge to dismember someone came flooding back.

"No..."

"Do you *know* who I am?"

"Yeah, man. You're the Reed."

The Reed had been his father's title among the criminal element. It had served as a nominal shield against retribution—and a reminder of Clark Reed's own brutality—right up until the day that name meant nothing. That was the day the Triad gunned him down.

"So, knowing who I am, *what* I am, you still roofied my sister and tried to rape her?"

"What? No! No way! We weren't gonna rape no one. Soon as we realized she was your sister, we was gonna let her go."

"Tom said differently."

"Well that blonde got him all riled up, didn't she?"

Nicholas pushed with his shoulders so that he was standing straight instead of leaning. The motion, as small as it was, had Jerry babbling again.

"I didn't ha' nothing to do with it! I said to let 'em go. They wasn't worth the trouble. She broke my nose, man."

"You bruised her arms. Your partner tore her blouse open. *You put your hands on my woman.*"

With each clipped, staccato, syllable, Jerry sank lower into his chair. Nicholas rubbed his thumbs into his palms and flexed his hands while staring the man down.

"We... we didn't know she was your woman. We was told to grab Vivian Richards. He texted us a picture, told us where she'd be."

"He gave you her name?"

"Yeah."

"He told you where she'd be?"

"Yeah. Well, no. He told us where she worked and where she lived. We followed her car."

"What was your plan?"

Jerry nearly folded himself in half trying to slink down under the table. His hands, manacled to the tabletop, prevented that escape.

"What...was...your...plan."

"We was to snatch her up and make it look like she'd left town. No mess."

Icy fury chased cold dread through Nicholas's veins. If Vivian hadn't fought back...

"Who's he?"

"What?"

"Who is *he?* Who hired you?"

"I don't know! Ain't never met him. He texts, we do the job, we get paid."

"How?"

"How does he text? On a phone, I guess."

Nicholas rubbed two fingers between his eyebrows. "No, you damn idiot, how did you get paid?"

"On the phone, man. Really! He paid us via PayPal."

"You got paid for kidnapping and attempted rape via PayPal? How fucking stupid are you two?"

"We wasn't gonna rape her!"

"Which one of you put the knife in her pillow?"

Jerry's naturally stupid expression blanked even further. "What?"

"The knife. In her pillow. Which one of you broke into her apartment and how?"

"What the hell, man? I just told you, we cut our losses. We haven't been anywhere near either of them since that night at the club. I don't know nothin' about a knife or a pillow or whatever."

Unsure that he could contain his temper any longer, Nicholas walked out of the interrogation room. He jerked his head toward the room as he passed the guards stationed outside. "Move the filth back to his hole, please."

"Right away, Mr. Reed."

"Oh, and let Captain Delozier know that I'm hitting the rack for a few hours."

"Will do."

Nicholas climbed several ladders before reaching the broad open deck of the freighter. The sun clawed its way above the horizon, ducking in and out of gray clouds. A stiff breeze blew across the deck from the north-west. Nicholas turned his face into the wind. He tasted the salt spray, let it sting his eyes and nostrils. Feeling calmer, more centered, he ducked back inside and found his assigned cabin. He expected sleep to come quickly. Instead, while lying on the thin mattress, staring at the ceiling, he thought about Vivian.

There had always been, he thought, some level of attraction. He'd easily ignored it when she was just the irksome blonde IT girl. Seeing her on Lee's arm at the Christmas party, though... Nicholas didn't want to call the feeling that memory evoked *jealousy,* but he also couldn't think of a better word. Since she'd learned of his abilities, and particularly since Lee had been shot, Vivian had become an intrinsic feature of his life. He constantly needed to know what she was doing and where she was going, but it was more than just protective urges. The need extended to knowing her thoughts, to making her laugh. Or making her blush...

When sleep finally dragged him down, Nicholas was smiling.

Johann was not Catholic. He informed Vivian that he wasn't even particularly religious. So, he accompanied her into the church but stood in the narthex during the service. Vivian tried to assure him that she'd be fine and didn't need a bodyguard. The young man shook his head.

"Vivian, Mr. Reed scares me way more than you do. Seeing as how that's his uncle the priest standing right there, I'm not letting you out of my sight."

Finding him standing there after the service, she threw hands in the air. "Fine! But you're about to learn the first rule of St. Simeon's: idle hands are put to work. I hope you're good with a potato peeler."

The driver and bodyguard cheerfully accepted all the tasks Vivian, and Sister Martha, assigned him. Evan started shadowing Johann and peppering him with questions about cars. Throughout the rest of the afternoon and into the evening shift at the soup kitchen, Johann never ceased to be cheerfully polite. He, Vivian, and Evan were mopping floors when Nicholas sauntered in the side door. Seeing his boss, the driver nodded in greeting, then said to Evan, "Why don't you show me that robot you're building, before I leave?"

"Good night, Johann. Thank you for keeping her safe."

Once they were alone, Nicholas leaned against the doorframe. He watched Vivian mop the final two rows of tiles, then wring out her mop. When she started to lift the mop bucket to empty it into the washing sink, Nicholas walked over and hefted it with one hand. The dirty water disposed of, he sat the bucket back on the floor. Vivian placed her mop in it, washed her hands, then stepped toward him.

His usually carefully groomed stubble had grown longer than normal. Faint shadows under his eyes and visible tension in his shoulders conveyed his exhaustion. Vivian palmed his cheek. He covered her small hand with his larger, scarred one.

"You look tired," she whispered.

"You look beautiful."

Vivian looked down at her mop-splattered khakis and faded tennis shoes. "If you say so."

Nicholas shook his head at her self-doubt. He turned his face into her palm and trailed kisses down her wrist. Hearing her gasp, he smiled against her soft skin before stepping back. "Almost done here?"

"Y... yes. To the office?"

"No. I *am* tired. Do you mind staying at my place for another night? I want to hear about your day, then pass out for several hours."

"After you tell Dom and I what you learned."

His eyebrows arched. Without touching her at all, and with several feet of space between them, just a look sent her nerve endings into overdrive. "I can talk to Dom tomorrow. Tonight, *you're* my focus."

She had to swallow twice before she could answer. "Let me get my things."

Nicholas trailed behind her as she gathered her purse and jacket. He heard his uncle approach even before the priest cleared his throat. Reluctantly pivoting from watching Vivian, Nicholas held out his hand.

Father John shook the proffered hand in both of his own. "Missed you at Mass today."

"I was working."

"That much is evident. Will you be taking Vivian home?"

"Yes, to *my* home." Nicholas narrowed his eyes at his uncle. "Don't start with me. She's staying in a guest bedroom."

"Of course she is." He lowered his voice. "Keep an eye on her. She's putting up a brave face, but I think

the enormity of events is starting to catch up to her."
He shook his head at his nephew's questioning look. "I won't go into details. Just take care of her."

"I *am* trying."

Father John's lined face broke into a smile as Vivian walked up to the pair. "Go in peace my children. Get some rest... both of you."

CHAPTER THIRTY-NINE

"What was that all about?" Vivian inquired as they exited the church basement.

"He was meddling, as usual."

Vivian stopped and laughed when she saw a remarkably familiar red Ferrari Spider in the parking lot. "Why, Mr. Reed, did you steal your brother's car?"

"Oh get in." Only once she was wriggling down into the Italian leather seat did he bother to respond. "I didn't steal it. I *borrowed* it. He doesn't need it right now, and I wasn't sure how you felt about motorcycles."

"They scare me."

"You? That's a rare thing indeed."

Vivian didn't respond. She leaned her head against the window. They rode in silence all the way to the house. After parking, Nicholas reached out and took her hand. He led her through the gate and past the pool, just as Lee had done on the night of the Christmas party. Instead of the French doors leading to the ballroom, though, Nicholas took her through another pair of doors farther down the porch.

"My office," he explained in a low voice. "Let me just lock these things in the safe." He released her hand and moved around a wide, glass-topped desk with black metal legs. In the corner, beside the fireplace, stood a tall safe. It needed a numerical combination, a palm scan, and a retina scan to open. Before meeting the Reed family, Vivian would have thought such redundant measures on a home safe to be ridiculous.

"You don't hide it behind... I don't know, a painting?"

"Why bother? My father had a safe hidden by bookshelves. I always though it silly. Anyone who has made it this far isn't going to be fooled by a couple of false shelving units or a hinged painting." He pulled several flash-drives and two cell phones from his pockets. After closing the safe and checking to make sure the locks engaged, he prowled across the floor to her.

"Wine? Food?"

"No, thank you." She fought a yawn. "Let's go upstairs."

He didn't answer her with words. His fingers flexed around hers as he led her up the main hall and staircase. The rest of the house was quiet and only dimly lit. As soon as the door to his bedroom clicked shut behind them, Nicholas cupped her face in his hands. The kisses he laid upon her lips started as gentle barely-there adorations. Then one hand slipped to her jean-clad hip. Vivian clasped the back of his neck with her left hand. Her right-hand fingers brushed against his throat.

All Nicholas felt was the edge of her splint. The reason she had that splint, the reason she had skinned knees, yellowing bruises on her arms, and new nightmare fuel, slammed into his thoughts. He reached up and clasped both of her hands in his as he broke their kiss. Unable to step away from her, though, he leaned his forehead against hers.

"What is it?"

Green eyes flashed behind tawny lashes. "We're both tired. It's been a long week."

"Did you get any sleep at all last night?"

He sighed and shoved his hands in his pockets. "A few hours after dawn. Not enough to make up the deficit I've been accruing."

Vivian tilted her head to one side. "You're hurting more than you're letting on. Do we need to get your... is medicine the right word?"

"No. I just need sleep. But..." He trailed off.

Vivian sensed his tension. "What do you need? Do you need me to go?"

"No. I..." Looking even more stressed and out of sorts, Nicholas ended up shaking his head, unable to say what he needed.

"OK. I'm going to go down the hall to my room—the room where I'm staying, I mean. I brought some clothing over last night. I'll be right back." She kissed his cheek. "Take your boots off, Nicholas."

Ten minutes later, she knocked softly on his door before entering. Nicholas rose from the couch. He'd changed into a pair of loose-fitting basketball shorts and a T-shirt. Vivian also wore a T-shirt but hers was paired with loose pajama pants covered in somersaulting pandas.

"Nice pants."

She rolled her eyes. She sat on the couch and waited till he'd resumed his place. He purposely sat far enough away that he was not touching her. "So, I have a theory." When he didn't say anything in response, she continued. "You haven't been sleeping because you've been worried—about me, about Jessie, about Lee... about everyone in the city, probably. All those treatments and drugs Cheyenne pumps into you probably give you greater stamina than most men." She was glad for the dim lighting; it hid her blushes. "But not even their impressive biochemistry can stop the basic laws of energy transference. You, Nicholas, have run your engine dry and need to recharge. That's hard to do with images of bad guys floating in your head, though. Am I wrong?"

"No."

"Right then. You need sleep. I will stay right here in this room so you won't have to worry. I'm not sure that having me dozing on the couch instead of right next door will somehow be bet—" Her words ended in a slight yelp. At the word *couch*, Nicholas rose, slid one arm under her knees and the other around her shoulder and hefted her into the air. "What are you doing?"

He walked across his bedroom to the California King sleigh bed. Juggling her for a moment, he pulled the sheets back before laying her down. Then, still not saying a word, he walked around to the other side of the bed, crawled under the sheets, and pulled her back to his chest. Spooned against her, with her hair tickling his nose, he finally spoke. "You *are* wrong if you think I could possibly sleep with you on the couch instead of beside me." The heaviness of his arm across her waist shifted as he entwined his fingers with hers. "Goodnight, Vivian."

Vivian woke to the smell of coffee. She sat up in bed— an exceptionally large bed that was most definitely not hers—and brushed her hair out of her face. Nicholas rose from the couch and smiled at her.

"Good morning." He handed her a coffee cup. "I was surprised to learn that we keep soy milk in our fridge. I didn't know if you wanted sugar, though."

"This is fine, thanks." She took a sip, watching him. "Mm. That's really good." Pulling her knees to her chest, she indicated the spot where her legs had just been. "Sit. Stop looming."

"Looming? Really? I just brought you coffee. In bed." Having sat, he leaned forward and dropped his voice. "*My* bed."

Despite the heat that crawled up her cheekbones, Vivian didn't look away. "And a very nice bed it is. Did you actually sleep?"

"The best I've slept in years." Honesty imbued every word of his simple statement. "You?"

"Really well, actually. What time is it?"

"Almost nine, sleepyhead." He patted her foot. "Plenty of time for you to have breakfast and get dressed. Then we can sit down with Dom. I'll fill you in on Tom and Jerry."

As he'd anticipated, the mention of her attackers' names focused her attention on their investigation and work. Nicholas wasn't entirely sure he could have resisted crawling back into bed if she'd suggested it. But, as she slid out of the bed, he couldn't forego stopping her for a kiss.

"Mmph, sorry, coffee morning breath," she muttered.

"Don't care," he responded before placing one more quick kiss on her lips.

Vivian grabbed a pastry from the tray on the coffee table, poked her head out the door to make sure no one else was in the hallway, then slipped out. Nicholas smiled to himself, realizing that she'd forgotten about the security cameras recording every movement in the hall. He certainly wasn't going to remind her.

Dom, dressed in a dark gray suit that would have allowed him to blend in at any Wall Street board meeting, greeted them at the door to the guest house. They sat at the small kitchen table. Vivian sipped another cup of coffee while the men drank water.

"The doc wants me to hook you up to the monitors for a few minutes—or, at least, she did last night. You looked rested, though, so we might be able to hold off. First, tell me what you learned."

"Quick summary line: those two are as stupid as their names. Also, Vivian was the target all along."

Dom and Vivian shared a glance.

Nicholas looked at each of them. "I expected that to be more of a shock."

"We've been busy too. You finish, though."

"Jerry was more forthcoming than Tom. This is not the first time they've *relocated* women from Seattle. They're not with any specific organization. Basically, they're freelance idiots. The plan was to snatch up Vivian and arrange for her to disappear. Jessie was an unexpected complication. As was someone's complete unwillingness to meekly submit to being kidnapped." He winked at Vivian. "The guys on the boat mined the phones we took off Tweedle Dumb and Tweedle Rapey. Would you believe they got paid via PayPal? They were also hired by text. The gurus on the boat tried to track the text back to a name or even a phone. No luck, but I thought Vivian should try."

"If super-secret-spy dudes can't crack it, how am I supposed to?"

Dom answered her. "Because you're smart and don't approach a problem with institutional biases." To Nicholas, he said, "Do you believe them? Any reason to doubt their story?"

"We found the text on Tom's phone, along with a picture of Vivian. They had no reason to lie."

"Did they take all of the missing women? And—" Vivian swallowed. "—are any of the women still alive?"

"They took at least six of them. We found that much on the phones, and the dates of their PayPal transactions match up. As to the fates of the women, we still don't know. They handed them off. We need to follow the trail if we hope to find the women."

"So, what happens to Tom and Jerry now?"

"They enjoy our ship-board hospitality for a few more days. Then we'll bring them back here, where they will be pleading guilty to assault, kidnapping, attempted kidnapping, and attempted rape."

Vivian looked puzzled. "Why would they agree to that? Can the courts actually use any of the evidence you gathered?"

"Technically, no. That's why the guilty pleas are necessary. As to why those idiots would plead guilty, well, because the alternative terrifies them." Seeing her confusion turn to horror, Nicholas quickly explained. "I didn't hurt them. Well, OK, I punched Tom when we first grabbed them. Other than that, though, I didn't harm them at all. They are being fed, have beds, blankets, and toilet facilities. What they fear, though, is that instead of returning them to the US, we'll drop them off in China or North Korea."

"Would you?"

"If I thought they posed a continuing threat to you, yes." Nicholas sipped his water. "Now, what did you two discover?"

Dom told Nicholas what he and Vivian had surmised about her being the link between the cases. Vivian filled in her suspicions about Detective Kwon.

"Dom, who is apparently a magician, retrieved the detective's employment file from SPD. I haven't had a chance to read through it yet, but he said there were no red flags."

"Not that I saw," confirmed the security chief.

"Back up a minute," said Nicholas. "We know it was Triad coming after Lee. Isn't it possible that they are pulling the strings? Having learned of Vivian's involvement with my family, they decided to kill two birds with one stone, so to speak?"

"You just said there's no evidence of Triad involvement with Tom and Jerry." Vivian stood and started to pace. Her heels tapped on the tile floor. "Why would the Triad send their own crews to attack Lee and you but hire two nobodies to take me? Unless they ran out of goons?"

Both men shook their heads. "Unlikely," said Dom. "They have extensive rosters of bruisers, kidnappers, and killers."

"That leads credence to the idea that someone else is behind the attacks on me." She continued to pace.

After watching her walk the length of his small kitchen several times, Dom looked at Nicholas with a raised brow. "How much coffee did you give her?"

"One cup."

"You handed me a second cup when we walked in," Vivian corrected. "What about the men who killed my parents?"

"Huh?"

"You said it was some of your father's men."

"It was. They are either dead or in Federal prison, now. They were the *first* guys we took down when I came back to Seattle."

"But not the Triad, right? Just your run-of-the-mill American bad guys?"

Nicholas's brows drew together. "I'm not sure where you're going with this."

Vivian slashed her un-splinted left hand through the air. "Someone helped cover it all up, though. Someone on San Juan and someone here. Did you ever catch that person?"

"Well, no. We didn't actually know about the cover-up, the claim that negligence caused the fire, or the asset forfeiture."

"It wasn't negligence," Vivian snapped.

Nicholas stepped in front of her to arrest her frantic pacing. "Hey." He gently took both of her hands in his. "We know that. We're here to help, remember?" Eyes twinkling, he quipped, "Me: friend."

She laughed, as he'd intended. "Sorry. But do you understand? There's someone out there trying to hurt me. Again."

CHAPTER FORTY

Suddenly recalling what he'd left off from his previous recounting, Nicholas frowned. "I forgot to mention—both Jerry and Tom deny having anything to do with the break-in at your old apartment."

Vivian stared at him open-mouthed. "But..."

"Vivian," Dom interrupted, "remember how it was just Suisse that took the report at your apartment? I wonder why that was?"

She pulled her hands free and sat back down at the table. "I just assumed a little thing like a threatening note and break-in weren't worth Detective Kwon's time."

"And miss an opportunity to accuse Nicholas of being a mob boss?"

"He does seem really convinced that you're a criminal mastermind."

"Just proving that he doesn't really know me at all."

"Yeah, I mean, of all the Reeds, Jessie is the obvious brains of the operation." Dom said. Then he turned serious. "Do we assume that the person, or persons, who hired Tom and Jerry also hired the individual who broke into Vivian's apartment? Would it be the same person who had someone following her last month?"

"*If* someone was actually following me."

Nicholas's head came up. "Wait. Describe the car you saw that night."

"A dark colored sedan with tinted windows. Completely unremarkable."

Nicholas looked at Dom. "There's one person who we know was following her, way back in November. And he drives a boring unremarkable sedan. Just like a—"

"Cop," said Dom. He nodded his agreement. "That makes sense. We know from their continued questioning that Kwon and Suisse think Vivian's been caught up in our nefarious schemes. They might have been tailing her, hoping her actions would provide a lead."

Vivian picked up her purse. "Tailing me while looking for a break in their case hardly connects them to Tom and Jerry. Which leaves us no closer to finding out who's ordering these attacks. One of you, give me the keys to one of the six vehicles currently on the property."

"You have somewhere to be?"

"Yes and, as usual, I have no car here. I want to compare the phones from Tom and Jerry to those you've been taking off Triad drug runners. I also need to do laundry, catch up on the work you actually pay me to do, and maybe even do some schoolwork."

"Not alone."

She rolled her eyes. "Yes, alone. I, now, live and work in *very* safe buildings. You have trackers on my phone and on every car in the fleet." She cut her eyes toward Dom. "Yes, I know about them." Seeing Nicholas's stubborn expression, Vivian crossed her arms and tapped her foot. "Keys."

Both men appeared unhappy. Nicholas clenched his hands several time before giving the quickest of nods to Dom.

"Take the SUV. It's heavier, has bullet-resistant glass, and a panic button." Dom pulled the keys back as Vivian reached for them. "No joyriding all over town."

She snatched the keys while favoring him with a particularly annoyed look. When Nicholas didn't rise from the table, or even look at her, she stepped toward him. Then she swallowed once and walked out of the guest house.

The silence she left in her wake broke when Nicholas slammed his hand down on the table. "Who's next on our Triad list?"

Dom considered making a comment about the safety of furniture when Nicholas was in love but decided against it. "Let's go to the office. I'll pull together what Vivian's gleaned from our latest searches."

Since their faces, and the faces of every single one of their employees, were well-known to Seattle's criminal element, an undercover drug sting was out of the question. For the past few weeks, a member of the security team had monitored—in person or electronically—known Triad dealers.

Sitting behind his desk in Reed Investments, Nicholas listened to Manny Kekoa's report.

"You're sure this shipment is due tonight?"

Kekoa nodded. "You've completely drained their supply. They are bringing a truck in from Portland and a boat from B.C."

Dom's eyebrows rose. "I thought the routes through the San Juans were locked down."

"They're desperate. That's why leaders are taking delivery personally."

"That's what worries me. This feels like a trap. The leaders stay in the shadows. They never touch the drugs, or money, or girls... or whatever the product is... directly. That's how they stay insulated from implication—and charges."

Nicholas nodded in concurrence with Dom's statements. "But," he said, "trap or not, we can't afford to ignore it. If we can grab even one of the leaders, it would cripple the Triads in Seattle for months, maybe even years."

"Big operation," Kekoa pointed out. "The boat's putting in at a marina north of here. Truck is supposed to go to a warehouse in Shoreline. Lot of ground to cover. And no indication that the kidnapped women are involved in any way."

"We'll need the drone and two five-man teams." Nicholas looked at Dom. "And Vivian."

"Call her. I'll get started on logistics. Oh, and tell her I need that SUV back."

Nicholas crouched on the deck of a small yacht, trying to stay in the shadows. He absently wondered if he knew the owner of the *Witchy Lady*. A chirp in his earbud re-focused his attention.

"The drone is overhead now. I really hope I don't run it into anything. You really should've let me practice with it before tonight."

"Vi-vi-an," hissed Nicholas.

She muttered a curse in response.

Dom, leading the team hitting the warehouse, clicked his mic twice. The signal meant that the truck had arrived. Nicholas didn't have to tell his friend to be careful. Their plan valued the safety of the teams above the capture of any Triad members. Each team, once the heroin shipments arrived, would watch and wait, hoping to confirm the presence of a Triad officer on-site, before moving in. If no leader showed, the team leader—Dom at the warehouse, Nicholas at the marina—would call in a tip to a DEA agent they worked with. The DEA and Seattle police could apprehend the drugs and Triad crews. Nicholas and Dom wanted the head of the snake, not the body.

"There's a boat approaching the marina. It's moving slowly. They have their lights on. I wonder why? Oh, because sailing around in the dark would look suspicious."

Even though Vivian couldn't see him, Nicholas nodded.

"The boat is pulling in two rows over from you. It's a good-sized yacht."

Dom interrupted Vivian's play-by-play with two terse words: "No joy."

No leader had shown up at the warehouse.

A minute later, Dom keyed his mic again. "They're making a big show of unloading pallets here. Moving very slowly and looking around more than they should be. At least twenty guys, all armed."

"Trap?" Nicholas, still crouched in the shadows, had to whisper the question.

"Looks like. Watch his back, Vivian," Dom said.

Sounding slightly peeved, she replied "I am. Speaking of... that yacht's riding pretty high in the water. Nicholas, I don't think..."

He tensed as her voice trailed off. Just as he was about to break his silence, she came back on the channel.

"A man just climbed out of a car. He's walking toward where the yacht is tying up. It's two rows over and three slips to the left from where you are. There are four men walking around the first man. Nicholas! They all have guns drawn."

The yacht was also a trap. Unlike the truck at the warehouse in Shoreline, though, this trap was baited with a high-ranking officer of the Triad.

Nicholas rolled off the far side of the *Witchy Lady*, sinking up to his waist in the freezing waters of the marina. Dangling from a cleat, he waited until a wave rocked all the boats against the docks. With one fluid swing he transferred to the edge of the dock. Fingers clenched so hard that he felt the wet wood give slightly, he worked his way, hand-over-hand until he felt safe enough to pull up onto the walkway itself.

"They haven't seen you. They are on the boat now, but they're all looking outward."

Tense minutes passed. Nicholas knew he couldn't take on the men while they were in such a tight space. Someone, likely one of his team, would get shot. He waited. His team was stationed in the parking lot and on two boats closer to the entrances of the marina. Taking the leader when he exited, when the Triad thought their trap had failed and they let their guard down, would be easier.

"Returning to base," Dom said over the channel. "Overwatch team left in place to monitor the location until DEA can hit it."

"Nicholas, they're all moving now. Wait. The man, the one they're all protecting. He stopped."

Nicholas didn't need her to relay that information. He could see the man in question. The fine hairs at his nape rose as he felt the Triad leader's gaze settle on him. *He can't see me. Not in this gloom.* Despite the reassuring thought, some instinct told Nicholas that he *had* been seen.

The leader turned to his men and said something. Three trotted off, leaving just one man to guard the boss. It was clearly a move meant to tempt Nicholas into attacking.

Logic and training told him to ignore it.

How did he see me?

He clicked his mic three times—the signal to move in.

Kekoa jumped from the nearest boat, rolled once, and immediately launched himself at the boss's bodyguard. The bodyguard turned toward his attacker at the first hint of movement. Nicholas remained in the shadows, watching.

The boss didn't even look over his shoulder as Kekoa and his guard rolled across the dock. He remained staring at the shadows where Nicholas crouched. Then he raised his hand and crooked a finger.

Even as shock rolled over him, Nicholas leapt from his hiding spot. A knife flew by his head, just missing his ear. He landed in the spot where the Triad leader should've been, but the man nimbly avoided the still-tousling Kekoa and guard. He ran down the dock far quicker than most men moved.

Nicholas gave chase. Both men reached the end of the row, turned, and sprinted toward the exit. Wanting to avoid shooting the fleeing leader, Nicholas didn't draw his gun. So, he could not fire back when his quarry turned and shot three times in quick succession. Only Nicholas's enhanced reflexes saved him from taking at least one of those rounds in the center of his forehead.

Weapon now drawn, Nicholas dropped to a knee. He waited until the Triad boss jumped from the dock onto an already-moving boat. Adjusting his aim a fraction higher, he squeezed the trigger. Blood sprayed across the white sides of the boat. The leader came down on the ankle Nicholas's shot had just shattered. A scream of pain echoed across the water.

Kekoa, one side of his face already swelling and bruised, walked up beside his boss. "You good, sir?"

"Yeah. Got a piece of him. The one you took down?"

"He's back there trussed up like a hog ready to be roasted. Doubt he talks, though."

"Probably right, but let's get him out to the freighter ASAP."

Kekoa nodded once. "Copy that. Freighter's getting awfully crowded, sir."

Looking out at the running-lights of the retreating boat, Nicholas growled, "Not as crowded as it should be."

CHAPTER FORTY-ONE

Nicholas and Dom descended the workshop stairs without speaking. Their boots barely made a sound. Every movement used the least amount of energy as they stripped out of their gear. Dom laid out guns to be cleaned. Nicholas hung their vests and helmets on the correct racks. Then, he whipped his shirt over his head, walked to the exam table, and started attaching cardiac leads.

Vivian looked from one to the other. When her boss stretched out on the table, head cradled by his folded arms, and stared at the ceiling, she started to rise.

Dom stepped into her peripheral vision, halting her. He placed a black briefcase at her feet.

"Drone was important. You did great."

"Thanks. I'd like to spend more time with it."

"We'll arrange that. Make sure it's charged up, please."

She nodded. Looking around him to where Nicholas lay, she dropped her voice to a whisper. "Everyone's OK?"

The security chief nodded. "He's coming down off the stims. Give him a few. I'm going to shower."

After removing the drone from its case, Vivian pulled the video back-up card and the battery. She checked all the rotors and camera connections. Once the battery was charging and the drone's footage was uploaded to their server, she walked across the room.

Nicholas's scars rippled with each deep breath. He turned his face into Vivian's left hand as she flexed her fingers through his hair. "That feels nice."

"What's wrong?"

He opened his eyes to look up at her. Nimble fingers ripped the EKG leads from his chest. He sat up, swung his legs over the edge, and cupped her face with both hands. "Right this second? Not a thing."

Even as he kissed her, Nicholas knew his words were a lie. Every brush of her splinted hand against his body reminded him of her pain. The differences in their height reminded him of her fragility. Every sensation reinforced his feeling of failure.

"Come home with me," she murmured. "My place is closer. You can shower and rest there. We'll re-group in the morning."

"So perceptive." He played with the Velcro strap of her splint. Head bent to watch his thumb work back and forth over it, he could avoid meeting her eyes. "No. I need to go home."

He leaned forward to kiss her forehead. "Good night."

Vivian watched him grab a jacket and walk away.

"Nothing? Not even a name?"

Dom shook his head. "Cheyenne guys don't have his prints on file. There's no pictures of him in any of our databases. He's not talking. Just sits there, waiting."

"So, a ghost." Nicholas rolled his head, feeling his re-built vertebrae shift. "No way a Chinese national is sent to guard anyone less than a Red Pole."

"You know we're not sure they even use those titles any longer," Dom interjected.

Nicholas dragged one hand over his hair. Frustrated, he spat his next words. "So close. We were so close."

"DEA rolled up on the warehouse two hours ago. I got a text from Agent Giles. He said, 'Thanks for the promotion'."

Despite his foul mood, the comment made Nicholas chuckle. "Well, there's that at least."

"Yup." Dom leaned forward in his chair. "You've been running up a pretty big tab with Cheyenne. They *will* collect."

"I know. I just need to get these guys. They hurt Vivian... and Lee."

While he noted the precedence of the names, the security chief did not comment. "Maybe it's time to pull back, wait and see what the fallout from the raid is. We've pulled at least ten mid-level dealers off the streets, shut down two gambling dens, and crippled the Triad's heroin supply network. And we did catch the guys directly responsible for attacking Vivian and Jessie."

"But not the guy who paid them."

"I know that, man. I'm saying, take the wins. Lee's safe, Vivian's safe, Jessie is... ok Jessie is still Jessie. You *do* have businesses to run."

His friend's words made perfect sense, but Nicholas found himself obsessed. "I can't think about her getting hurt again." He looked across the desk, misery etched on his features as deeply as his scars. "It makes me want to rip things apart with my hands. That's not healthy."

"You know my policy: as long as she's not a threat, I don't care about your love life."

"But she *is* a threat. To my mental well-being, if nothing else."

Dom rose, pulled his suit jacket from the chair, and slid into it. "I meant a security threat. That stuff you're talking about is one hundred percent not my problem."

"Liar."

"As you say, Mister Reed."

Vivian sat in a cozy leather chair in Father John's office. Evan, stretched out on the floor, carried on a one-sided conversation about the wonders of the robot he'd assembled. She listened half-heartedly while typing on her laptop. Though, if she was being perfectly honest, she wasn't really paying attention to her schoolwork either.

"Viv?"

She jumped and could feel her stupid skin warm from embarrassment. "Sorry, what?"

Evan crossed his legs and sat up straight. "Are you OK?"

"What? Yes! Of course. I'm sorry. I was distracted by my coursework."

The teenager shook his head. "That's not what I meant. You remember our chat earlier this year? Well, now you have a broken hand to add to the list."

She felt tears well in her eyes. Here was a kid who'd watched his battered mother turn to addiction and then OD. He'd bounced around foster and group homes since the age of nine. With everything he'd seen, and everything he continued to deal with on a daily basis, he was worried about *her*. "Oh Evan. I wasn't lying to you. Mister Reed is not hurting me. No one at work is. I just had some bad luck with your average Seattle low-life."

He still looked dubious. "But you are dating Nicholas Reed?"

"Uh... I guess? It's weirdly complicated. To be honest, I don't know what we're doing." She held up her splinted hand and wiggled her fingers. "This thing comes off tomorrow. It will be so nice to have full use of my hand again. Now, stop your worrying and show me again what this robot can do."

CHAPTER FORTY-TWO

The text from Vivian said only "Need you here ASAP." Nicholas bolted from his office, mumbling an incoherent (and highly improbable) excuse to the lawyer he'd been speaking with. His bike was in the garage. He barely paused to fasten his helmet before leaving. At her building, he took the stairs two at a time.

All of which explained why, when he pounded on her apartment door, her name was less of a frantic bellow and more of a gasp. That he gasped again when she jerked the door open and stood there glaring at him had nothing to do with physical exertion, though.

"Nicholas? What did you do, run all the way here? Get in here." Vivian reached out, grabbed his wrist and pulled him past the threshold. "I said ASAP, not 'OMG the building is on fire!'"

"You... You're... What are you wearing?"

With her weight on one foot, one hip cocked to the side, Vivian smirked at him. "This—" She ran a hand from her collarbone to her waist. "—is called a robe, Nicholas. It's what women wear when they get out of the shower. You may have seen one before?"

He swallowed, still mentally off-balance. "I thought something was wrong."

"You weren't wrong."

"Huh?" He couldn't stop staring at the patch of pale skin showing at the v of her robe's neckline. Her still-damp hair curled in tendrils around her ears. Her feet were bare. Her hands were on her...

"Hey! You got your splint off."

"I told you that was today." She held up both hands and wiggled her fingers. "Good as new. That's why I called."

Nicholas rubbed the back of his neck. "Vivian..."

She stepped closer and twined her fingers behind his neck. "Hi." She had to stretch a little bit to kiss him. Her tongue teased at his lips, but Nicholas was still too distracted by the thought that she might have been in trouble.

"Vivian, hey. I thought you were in trouble or hurt. I was scared." He rested his hands on her shoulders and gently, but firmly, pushed her away.

Her blue eyes flashed. The instant before she opened her mouth, he realized she was about to use what Dom referred to as her "loud voice". He was already wincing by the time her first verbal salvo hit him. "Go ahead, Nicholas. Tell me what's stopping you this time. Give me some wonderfully noble excuse about how you're trying to protect me, or about how I'm too fragile. There's no splint on my hand for you to look guiltily at, though. Should I break the other hand, so you have another excuse?" She pivoted—Nicholas noted how the silky green robe clung to her thighs and hips—and stalked a few feet away before turning around again. "I should have known! How could I be stupid enough to believe that you were really interested in me? How could I have been stupid enough to let you pity me and coddle me? Do I look like a child, Nicholas? I don't need your—"

"Vivian!" Nicholas stripped out of his suit jacket and tossed it across the back of her couch. He yanked his tie loose but left it hanging around his shirt collar. He stalked to where she stood, still muttering under her breath. "Hey. What's going on?" One calloused hand slid down her arm from shoulder to wrist. His thumb stroked over the sensitive skin there while he smiled softly at her.

She glared back, not feeling charitable enough to be easily soothed. "How long have we been together, Nicholas?"

"Together? Do you mean since we first met or when you started working with me—"

"This," she hissed, gesturing between them with her free hand. "You kissing me. Me kissing you. Whatever this is. How long?"

Nicholas counted in his head even as he realized that she wasn't really interested in the precise amount of time they'd been together. He wasn't quite sure what had brought on this rather violent fit of insecurity. "A little more than three weeks."

"Exactly." She snatched her hand from his grasp, tucked a damp strand of hair behind her ear and crossed her arms over her chest. "Nearly a month, Nicholas. I know most of that has been spent trying to find the assholes who attacked me, but it's about time you made up your mind."

"I have! What's wrong? What happened today to make you—"

"Today? *Every* day Nicholas. Every day I'm reminded how I'm not your type or out of your league. Too unsophisticated, too blonde, too smart—"

"Hey!" He looked and sounded annoyed. "I want you to stop talking about yourself this way. You know how much I value your skills. You know how much I adore you."

"Then why won't you sleep with me?"

The words hung in the air between them. Vivian blushed. Nicholas blinked several times, too stunned to reply.

"Ah." He felt like a particularly slow-witted teenager. "That's what's bothering you? You thought I didn't really want you?"

She nodded, obviously trying not to cry. He swallowed, hard, feeling like an ass for hurting her, even unwittingly. Not sure if he wanted to pick her up and cradle her to his chest or shake some sense into her, Nicholas jammed his hands into his pockets.

"You thought your hand being in a splint was a turn-off?" He didn't wait for her to answer. "It was, but not in the way you might be thinking. Every time I saw you, Vivian, I was reminded of what a blind idiot I'd been. I was reminded how brave you've been—you've always been—and how much danger I've put you in. You were hurt, Vivian, and it was my fault. It just felt... wrong... somehow... to sleep with you while you were still injured."

Nicholas sucked in a deep breath before continuing. "I think the first time in years I laughed, truly laughed, was in your office. You make me feel joy. You give me hope. You exasperate the hell out of me, too. You're amazing, Vivian Richards, and I want to be able to tell you that every day for the rest of my life. You think you aren't good enough for me? I *know* I'm not good enough for you."

They stood facing each other, not moving or speaking for more than a minute. Then Vivian choked back a sob and flung herself at his chest. He rested one hand at her waist and cupped the back of her head with the other.

"For the record, I want you in every way imaginable." Nicholas kissed her, taking his time. "And in some ways that you probably haven't imagined... yet."

"Promise?"

He pulled her waist flush with his. Eyelids half closed, he murmured, "Promise."

She grinned, but an errant hiccup ruined whatever seductive undertone she was attempting. That made Nicholas smile and Vivian giggle.

"Did you really just rush over here? You left a meeting just because I texted you?"

"Well, they were also very boring." He kissed the tip of her nose. Before she could react, he lifted her off the floor and swung around.

"Nicholas! Put me down!"

He lowered his head to kiss the skin just behind her earlobe but continued to spin her around. "Mm, no. We're celebrating."

"I'm getting lightheaded."

"That usually happens during celebrations." He was laughing now. He didn't set her down, but strode to the couch and flopped onto it, pulling her down with him. She sprawled half on his lap and half on the seat beside him. Her robe bunched at the top of her thighs. He stroked the pads of his fingers over her soft skin.

Vivian leaned her head against his shoulder. She hummed softly while he stroked her leg. She delighted in having full range of motion in all her fingers, twisting them in Nicholas's hair and toying with his shirt buttons. When he leaned his head over to brush his lips across her hairline, she sighed.

"What do you want?"

She looked up at him. "You."

"Now?"

"Please."

Nicholas lurched sideways, depositing her on the couch in an undignified heap. She blew a strand of hair out of her face and glared up at him. He tugged his cell phone from the pocket of his trousers and turned it off. When he noticed her aggrieved expression, he smirked. "No interruptions." He reached out a hand to pull her to her feet. Before she could get her balance, he'd scooped her off the floor again.

"Always with the swooping and the carrying," she muttered.

Nicholas's green eyes traced over her face, and lower. In a deep whisper he noted, "Your pulse jumps every time I do this. Afraid I'll drop you?"

"Usually, I'm just afraid I'll say something ridiculous."

"What are you afraid of today?"

"That you'll put me down."

Nicholas stopped in the middle of the hallway. He shifted her easily in his arms, pushing her back against the wall while guiding her legs and arms to wrap around him. His hands cupped her face. There was only a brief moment of soft teasing at her lips before his tongue invaded her mouth. He sucked her breath from her body, tilted her head for a deeper angle, and pushed against her until the hard wall and his hard muscle caged her. Only when he felt her grip on his shoulders start to flutter did Nicholas pull back.

He'd meant to say something clever or seductive, but this was Vivian. He didn't need words. The brush of his thumbs under her eyes made her look up at him. They stared at each other, every ragged breath a paragraph of unspoken emotion.

She was significantly shorter than him. He'd noticed before, but not as clearly as he did at that moment. He could feel her pressed against his waistline, just high enough to apply downward pressure where he wanted it, but not enough to provide tactile relief. Grasping her upper thighs to hold her close, he continued toward her bedroom. It hadn't escaped his notice that she was nude beneath her tiny robe.

When he laid her back on the bed and looked down at her exposed body, he growled. "What if Dom had answered the door?"

Her eyes sparked with mischievous intent. "He's seen me in my PJs before."

That made his voice drop another octave. "We'll talk."

Vivian hooked her foot behind his thigh and pulled. "Later." She knew she didn't have the strength to pull him off balance. That he fell forward anyway she took as a sign of his enthusiasm. She pushed on his shoulder while he tried to devour her with another kiss. Finally managing to push him onto his back, she attacked his shirt buttons. His tie she flung over her shoulder with delighted abandon. She kissed her way from his collarbone, past his innumerable scars, to his navel. She reached for the clasp of his suit trousers, but he pulled her hands away and flipped her on her back.

Nicholas stood to remove his shirt completely and toe off his shoes. He looked down at Vivian. She was sprawled upon the bed, her flushed skin contrasting with the emerald silk of her opened robe. He dropped to his knees. Lips quirking into a grin when she squeaked in surprise, he bent and kissed her inner thigh. He let his breath coast over the sparse curls between her thighs.

"Vivian," he murmured. He entwined his fingers with hers. "Look at me."

She opened her eyes and focused on his face. His breath and tongue brushed across her sensitive flesh. Vivian moaned. Her eyelids drooped. He squeezed her fingers and laved her once more. She understood his unspoken request and stared down at him. Her whole body shuddered. When her hands clenched on his and her back arched, Nicholas adjusted his hold, moving his hands to her hips and dragging her farther toward the edge of the bed.

Vivian made a soft keening sound. Then her whole body jerked.

Nicholas waited until he felt her muscles cease contracting. He rose, pulled a condom from his wallet, and shed his pants and underwear. Picking up a seemingly boneless Vivian with one arm, he shucked her robe from under her and pulled the sheets back.

"Pink sheets? Really?" He sounded annoyed, but his features were teasing.

"I happen to like pink, thank-you-very-much." She garbled the words together. Her brain was still starved of oxygen.

He pulled her against his chest, letting her rest in the curve of his arm and hip. "You OK?"

"Mm. Jus' gimme a sec, k?"

Nicholas was perfectly happy to lie there the rest of the night feeling her warm body safe and sound beside him. He needed to find a way to have her in his bed every night. The thought almost sobered him enough to cool his ardor. Fortunately, Vivian chose that moment to slide beneath the sheet.

"I thought you were recovering?"

"Shaddup Nicholas," came the muffled command from beneath the sheets. Just in case he was thinking of disobeying, Vivian robbed him of the ability to form coherent thoughts.

Nicholas's eyes nearly crossed. She seemed to be experimenting, trying different speeds and tongue motions to see what he liked. Truth be told, he liked it all and feared for both his control and his sanity. She hadn't used her hands at all.

"Vivian."

She hummed. *Dear God*, he thought, *she actually hummed.*

"Vi-vi-an." Each syllable was jerked from his strangled throat. He briefly wished her hair was up in its usual ponytail just so he'd have a lifeline.

"Yes?"

"You trying to kill me?"

The look of pure empowered delight that spread across her face was equal parts beautiful and terrifying. "I've been wanting to do that for a long time."

He refused to delve into the significance of that statement. Not right then, anyway. Later, when he had full control of his brain, maybe. "I'm happy I could oblige."

She fell onto her back. Her head turned toward him, she smiled and tugged at his fingers. Nicholas swung over her, moved her legs to either side of his hips and pulled on her hands until she sat up. He kept one hand on her hip, guiding her, while the other nudged her chin up.

When she slid down onto him, Nicholas sucked on her tongue. The hand at her face moved to cup her left breast. He rolled her nipple between his thumb and forefinger while she rode him. It only took a minute to bring her to another screaming orgasm.

He laid her on her back, wrapped his hand behind her knee and brought one leg up to her shoulder. Vivian moaned in delirious pleasure. Nicholas thrust slowly, enjoying the spasms that clenched around him every time he moved. It felt so good, so right, that he didn't want to stop.

Then she opened her eyes all the way and smiled at him. "Nicholas. Kiss me."

He was undone by the warmth of her look, the trust in her eyes, and the simple truth of her need. When he surged forward to capture her mouth, she came suddenly. The jerking of her body took him right over the edge.

The next few minutes were very hazy. Nicholas felt incredibly alive and wearily sated at the same time. He briefly noted Vivian rolling from beneath him. He turned his head on the pillow to watch her. Before she slid into shorts and a tank top, her nimble fingers jerked her hair into a ponytail. He must have grunted an inquiry, although he didn't really remember forming the question in his mind.

"I'm going to order Chinese for dinner. I can't very well answer the door with post-coital hair." She grinned and dodged the pillow he half-heartedly threw at her. "Get up, Nicholas. You're not eating in my bed."

Every neuron in his brain fired with the memory of kneeling between her spread thighs. "Pretty sure I just did," he murmured.

"You say something?" She poked her head back around the door frame.

Nicholas stood and stretched. He knew she stopped to watch. The fact of it made him smile. "I'm up. No Chinese, though. Let's go out and celebrate."

"I thought we celebrated already?"

"It's a multiple celebration sort of evening." He took delight in the blush that shot up her cheeks.

"Do I have time to do my hair?"

He shook his head. "You look beautiful as you are. Besides, I like your post-coital ponytail."

CHAPTER FORTY-THREE

Curled against Vivian's back, Nicholas slept soundly. They'd had a glorious dinner in a private dining room then returned to her apartment. He'd shown her again how much he wanted her. She'd fallen asleep on his shoulder. Seeing her dream-induced smile, having her safely beside him, Nicholas truly relaxed. So, it took several rings before he heard his phone.

Vivian, wearing only a T-shirt, shifted against him and murmured something. Nicholas rolled onto his back, pulling her around to rest her head on his chest. He blinked at his phone display. The number showed as "Unknown". Very few people had his phone number.

"Hello?"

"Good morning, Mr. Reed." The voice on the other end spoke with just a trace of a Mandarin accent.

Nicholas tensed. "Who is this?"

"I'm called Shen Jun. I'm the man you shot."

"You'll have to be more specific; I've shot many men."

The chuckle on the other end of the phone was mirthless. "No, you haven't. If you were that bloodthirsty, I would not have eluded you at the marina."

Feeling Vivian come awake, Nicholas shifted his arm so he could brush his free hand over her lips. She remained silent but alert.

"How's the ankle?"

"Shattered. I'm disappointed to say that our next meeting will be delayed by several months."

"Don't be silly. I have the means to come to you. Tell me where you're hiding. I'll be on the next flight."

The Triad leader's tone turned snappish. "I, unlike your cowardly brother, am not hiding, Mr. Reed."

"Bold talk from the same man who ordered the rape and kidnapping of an innocent woman."

"That happens to be the reason for my call. I did not order the attacks on Miss Richards."

Nicholas's chest jumped when he snorted. "Because you're above such things?"

"She owes me no debt and there's no profit in accosting her. It seems, in fact, that there is significant *risk* to troubling that particular young woman."

"And?"

"I ordered... one of our organization's associates... to cease his activities against her. He chose to disobey me. There is a penalty for such things. His connection to your Miss Richards predates your entry into her life."

"Give me a name."

This time the laugh on the other side of the phone did sound amused. "Now where is the fun in that? There's an opportunity for me in keeping you busy chasing this man."

"I think you'll find I can simultaneously destroy your organization *and* find your former associate," growled Nicholas.

"Entire empires have tried, Mr. Reed. Why do you think you'll succeed where they have failed?"

"I'm stubborn."

Shen Jun laughed again. "Happy hunting, Nicholas. Give my regards to Vivian."

The line went quiet. Nicholas glanced at the phone screen, then set it aside. Vivian sat up and stretched her arms over her head. That did interesting things to the T-shirt she wore. Nicholas watched, intrigued. She smirked.

"So... coffee?"

He glanced at the still-dark sky. "Or, we could stay in bed for a few more hours."

"Neither one of us is sleeping after that phone call."

"I wasn't suggesting sleep."

Vivian stuck her tongue out at him. "Come on. I'll get the coffee started while you tell me exactly what he said."

Hours later, in the privacy of Nicholas's office at Reed Investments, Dom listened as he recounted the phone conversation.

"Well, that's a new one."

Vivian, who'd been summoned upstairs *to fix Mr. Reed's network connection* said, "Oh?"

"They don't usually admit that we've hurt them."

"Or give us their names," Nicholas added.

"If that is his name." Seeing Vivian's quizzical look, Dom explained. "Shen Jun means either king, talented, or handsome, depending on the context. It's likely a nom de guerre."

"Ah. I don't understand why the Triad won't just send a replacement leader. Or do they already have more than one leader here?"

"It's possible. From his accent, I'm fairly certain Shen is American-born, though. Or, at least, he's been in the US for a good percentage of his life. That makes him unpredictable. Americans rarely rise to high positions within Triad branches. He's almost certainly stepped over bodies to get to where he is."

"He'll have lieutenants here that will run what's left of the gang until he returns."

"Is he in China?"

Nicholas answered her. "It's possible he's on the mainland. He could also be hiding in Hong Kong,

London, or even Bali. We'll look, but I don't have much confidence that we'll find him." He shrugged. "The world's a big place with a lot of people."

"The immediate problem is that he's cut off this *associate* who disobeyed him."

"Yeah," Vivian groused. "The man who has a serious grudge. A long-lasting grudge, apparently."

"*That* man is our primary concern, now. He's burned with the Triads—all of them around the world. They may not be centralized, but they do talk to each other. He's going to be desperate—*more* desperate— and looking for revenge."

"Great." To both men's consternation, Vivian rose and started pacing. "We looked at Detective Kwon's personnel record. It was clean. Maybe too clean?"

"You think it's been scrubbed?"

"No." When she shook her head, her ponytail danced. "I mean too clean in the sense that someone who's never been in trouble with Internal Affairs may well be—"

"—working for Internal Affairs." Nicholas nodded as he finished her sentence. "That tracks."

"So, he might be an ally. He's probably trying to find dirty cops on the Seattle force. I think we should call him and compare notes. We've always suspected that local law enforcement was involved in my parents' deaths."

Nicholas exhaled through his mouth while shaking his head. "I think you're forgetting that Kwon is convinced I've stepped into my father's shoes. He's not going to share."

"Well fine. *I'll* call him. I also want to read Suisse's file. Can you get that?" She directed her question to Dom.

"You can probably do it on your own, but yes, I'll get it. If you do arrange a meeting with the detectives, I have a bit of jewelry I'd like you to wear."

Giving Nicholas a teasing wink, she said, "Why Mr. Fehr, I had no idea we'd progressed to the gift-giving stage of our relationship."

Dom rolled his eyes. "I'll leave it on your workstation in the shop. It's a locket with a recording device, camera, and transmitter."

Her tone serious once again, Vivian replied, "Thank you." She glanced at her watch. "I need to get back. The staff secretaries are already whispering about us after the paparazzi incident. They probably think I'm up here fixing something other than your network connection."

"Hm." Nicholas, somber as a judge, glanced at his head of security. "Mr. Fehr, don't you need to take a long lunch?"

Dom crossed his arms and leaned back in his chair. "Flee now, Miss Richards, while I inform Mr. Reed of his company's policy on sexual harassment."

Vivian sighed. "You two are hilarious."

After the door shut behind her, Nicholas focused on Dom. "What is it you wanted to discuss?"

"I'm worried about Jessie. Vivian's stalker is the primary concern, but I need you to keep your sister's behavior in mind for the future." Dom pulled a flash drive from his pocket and handed it across the desk.

CHAPTER FORTY-FOUR

Vivian stood to relieve the pins and needles in her left foot. She'd been sitting with that leg tucked underneath her, scrolling through various news articles from both San Juan Island and Seattle. While she ran a simple Google search for the name *Suisse*, another program probed at the Seattle Police Department's personnel records. She walked to the mini-fridge in the medical area and grabbed a water bottle. Just as she started back across the floor, the computer beeped.

The Google search returned three results.

San Juan County Sheriff's Office Makes Major Drug Bust

Local Deputy Moves to Seattle

Stalking Charges Dismissed by King County DA

Vivian stared at the first entry. San Juan County only had around fifteen thousand residents. The sheriff's department employed twenty or so deputies and a dozen civilian employees. How was it possible Suisse was from the islands, and she'd never met him? She opened the link, dated eight months after her parents' deaths. It discussed a large heroin trafficking ring busted by the sheriff, the Washington state patrol, and the DEA. The drugs were tied to a Chinese Triad and had been transported on Washington state ferries...

Bile rose in her throat. Tears flooded her eyes.

She took several gulping breaths and tried to focus on the words of the article. There, buried in the ninth paragraph—helpfully highlighted by Google—was the name of Deputy Adam Suisse. He was listed in the litany of officers and agencies involved in the bust, but with the notation that his investigation had brought about the ring's downfall.

The second article turned out to be a quick blurb on the sheriff's webpage congratulating Suisse on accepting a position with Seattle PD. The third hit made Vivian's stomach churn again.

The King County District Attorney declined to present to the grand jury the case of an SPD detective accused of stalking a woman. Wilson Dewey said there was insufficient evidence of the charge against Detective Adam Suisse. The detective was also cleared by an IAB investigation and reinstated with back-pay. Joy Dunning disappeared three months ago. Her former boyfriend, the prime suspect in her disappearance, has stated that Detective Suisse was harassing and stalking Ms. Dunning.

Joy Dunning's name was the first on their list of missing women.

The walls of the workshop felt like they were closing in on Vivian. She pushed her chair away from the table so forcefully that the monitors shook. Surrounded by high-tech security, the emptiness of the space left her feeling vulnerable.

She needed someone nearby.

She needed physical locks to turn.

A whimper escaped her throat as she stumbled up the stairs.

Dave Kaskoy saw her emerge from the workshop, hug the wall as she walked to the IT department, and fumble with the locks. When the security system notified him that the deadbolts engaged within that room, he rose from his chair.

He found her retching into the wastebasket beside her desk.

"Vivian?"

She jerked, startled. She'd turned on every light in the room, but even in the blinding brightness, her pupils were dilated.

Dave's hand dropped to his gun. He turned around to check behind him. His eyes scanned the space. "What's happened?"

"Suisse." The blonde woman shook her head after choking out the one word. She hugged her arms to her chest.

"The detective? What about him?"

"He's the one. The one who's after me. He's been after me this whole time."

The security tech noted her pale skin, wide eyes, shivering, and frantic glances. He pulled out his phone. "I'm calling Mr. Reed."

"No!"

"I *have* to report this."

"Please, I can't... I need to process this without Nicholas taking over."

"Vivian, this isn't something you can go through alone." Dave noted some color returning to her cheeks.

"You're here. I'm not alone."

A hint of a smile tugged at his lips. "Fair enough." He held out a hand. "Let's go back to the security office."

As he locked the doors and re-set the motion sensors for the IT department, Dave glanced at Vivian. "You realize that Mr. Fehr's phone alerts every time these doors lock. He's going to wonder what's up."

She shrugged. "I'll call him in a few minutes. I need to think right now."

Once he had her ensconced in a chair within his office, Dave re-checked all the building's sensors and video feeds.

"Right then. All's quiet. Now, tell me what has you so spooked."

She shot him a harassed look. "I said I needed time to process."

"Yup. So, process out loud and I'll just sit here. No comments unless asked for."

Not quite believing him, Vivian stared into space for over a minute before she started talking.

"The summer between my sophomore and junior years at U-dub, I worked on the Anacortes to Friday Harbor ferry line. I grew up there—Friday Harbor. I kept noticing the same cars coming back and forth two or three times a week, but with different plates. Same car, right down to the scratches and dents but with different plates. I made a list. My dad..." She swallowed and blinked back tears. "He knew the San Juan County Sheriff. I asked him if I should tell the sheriff. Dad didn't want me to be involved, so he took the list to the sheriff. I don't know what he told him to keep my name out of it. A week later, I came home from work and our house was on fire. I got my little brother out. My parents were killed. The house was a complete loss."

She twisted her fingers together, still not making eye contact with Dave. Given the number of times she'd recounted the details of that night, it should've been easier. It wasn't.

"The sheriff's office refused to listen to anything Simon or I told them. I gave up trying to convince anyone. I was too busy just..."

Dave said, gently, "Surviving. You survived, Vivian. Is this the same smuggling operation Nicholas Reed stumbled upon?"

She widened her eyes in surprise.

He nodded once. "All of us who came over from Cheyenne know about Mr. Reed's past. Tell me what part Detective Suisse plays in this."

"I didn't know him back them. It's an unusual name. I'd have remembered it. Maybe he worked on Lopez or Orcas."

"Vivian?"

"Sorry, he was with the sheriff's department."

"OK, but why do you think—"

She pointed to his computer. "Do a Google search for his name."

Dave read the articles. He turned back around to face Vivian. "That son of a bitch. So, he responded to the break-in here, probably knowing the Triad involvement, and discovered you were still around?"

"I think he had to know I was alive this whole time, but probably thought I didn't represent any real threat. Until I started working for the man taking down Triad operations in Seattle, that is. Even then, he might have thought I was just caught up in everything."

"Until you were there when Lee was shot. He'd have to be an idiot to think you a mere employee after that."

She went back to staring at the wall. When she finally spoke again, it was a simple question. "Why?"

"Why do you scare him so much? Because you were eventually going to make the connection between his time with the San Juan sheriff and your parents' murders. And then you were—are—going to tell Mr. Reed."

Her eyes narrowed in confusion.

"Vivian, you have to understand, when we came back from... rehab... with Mr. Reed, he hit the ground running. He was, um, well, he lacked the control he has now. The guys—both Reed employees and Triad guys—

running what remained of that ring, he hunted down without mercy. One of them has a broken back and will spend what remains of his life in a federal prison ward. Two of them were *disappeared*."

She blanched, then frowned again. "But wouldn't that be a reason to *not* piss off Nicholas? Why would Suisse risk coming after me directly? Keep in mind, too, that he is credited with taking down that drug ring. Why would he help break-up the operation he worked for?"

Dave shook his head. "That bust was a set-up designed to get him attention and a job with Seattle PD. The Triad's always looking to get more law enforcement sources. They, Triad, took a momentary hit for a longer-term gain. As for why he'd risk Mr. Reed's anger... I have no idea."

He waited a beat before asking, "Now can I call Mr. Fehr?" He saw her pull her phone from her purse. "Or are you going to?"

Vivian smiled. "Oh, you go ahead. I have a trap to set."

Alarmed, Dave pointed at the door. "I do *not* want to know what you're doing!"

CHAPTER FORTY-FIVE

Her text to Detective Suisse's cell phone simply read:

I know what you've done. I'll tell Kwon.

Then she texted Detective Kwon and asked him to meet her at the Seattle cruise ship terminal. By the time of their scheduled 2 a.m. meeting, the terminal parking lot would be deserted. She stopped in the workshop to grab her coat and the locket Dom had left for her.

Vivian walked across the empty parking lot. Detective Kwon had parked in the far corner, under one of the bright security pole-lights. He stood next to his car, watching her and peering into the shadows.

"Stop there!" He yelled the instruction when Vivian was still several yards away. "Take off your coat. Now, hold your arms out to the side and turn around, slowly."

Vivian did as he asked, then said, "Honestly, Detective, are you that afraid of a twenty-four-year-old systems administrator?"

"Come closer. And, yes, you scare me more than the average crook."

She cocked her head. The end of her ponytail fell onto her shoulder. "Why?"

"Cell phone in here please." He held out a Faraday bag.

At that, she balked. "No. I understand you're nervous about eaves-dropping. Of the two of us, though, I'm the one most recently threatened with abduction. My cell phone will remain on and in my purse. Those are my terms."

He stared at her for almost a minute. "Fine. I suppose if your boyfriend wants to frame me, a recording isn't going to matter."

"What? Why would you think he—"

"Is your boyfriend? Come on, Ms. Richards. You've been staying at his house. You've been seen together at his sister's club and at his family's Christmas party. I don't need nearly thirty years as a detective to figure that one out."

"That," she snapped, "is not what I was going to say. Why would Nicholas need to frame you?"

"That's what he does. He had those two men who assaulted you and his sister so neatly sewn up that they turned themselves in and entered guilty pleas immediately. Isn't that how *the* Reed takes care of those that cross him?"

"One, he's not *the* anything. That was his father. Two, those guys were actual criminals. Are you a criminal, Detective? Would I have really come alone if I thought you were a threat to me?"

The detective snorted. "You're clearly not the best judge of threats. Nicholas Reed is a crook, just like his father. I came here to help *you*. Do you even know that his men are the ones who killed your family?"

Vivian paled. "I know his father's men were responsible, yes. He told that me himself. Do *you* know that your partner worked for the San Juan County sheriff's office four years ago?"

"Yes. I had myself assigned as his partner because of it. I'm going to bring down Reed and his dirty money. That includes any SPD officers on his payroll."

"You knew Suisse was behind the attacks on me and you didn't try to warn me?"

It was the Detective's turn to pale. "He... what? I thought... No. It was Reed, not Suisse."

"Detective, Nicholas is a complicated man, but one thing I know for certain. He would not hurt me. There is no reason, no ulterior motive, for him to be behind these attacks. Nicholas Reed is a good man."

People, Vivian had observed, didn't give up on their worldviews easily. Detective Kwon was no different. "He doesn't feel threatened by you? Isn't tired of you?"

"Not in the way you mean. I told you, he's the one who confirmed for me that my parents were murdered. He's the one who presented the evidence and told me what he... had done... to the men responsible. He might be tired of me romantically, I guess, but I'm telling you, he would never hurt me." Vivian noticed movement behind the detective. She frowned and stared into the darkness. Unable to see anything, she decided it was a flicker from the light. "One more thing, Detective Suisse is definitely *not* working with Nicholas. He may also be directly responsible for each of the missing women we've been searching for. If you truly suspect he's dirty, then we need to compare notes."

"Yes, Joel, let's compare notes," said Detective Suisse as he stood from behind the trunk of Kwon's car. He had his service weapon pointed at his partner. "Hello again, Vivian. Thank you for meeting with us and for that illuminating exposition on just exactly what you know. I'm afraid I'm going to have to insist on that phone, though. Just take it out and throw it over here."

"You fucking worm," snapped Kwon. "I knew you were dirty."

Suisse responded to his partner's slur by pistol-whipping him. Kwon crumpled to the ground. The younger detective looked at the body at his feet, then raised the gun and pointed it at Vivian.

"The phone, Vivian."

"No."

"No more play-time, girl. Tom and his stupid partner might have let you escape. I won't. Toss the phone and walk to me."

What is taking Nicholas and Dom so long? She knew Dave had called them. She also knew they were tracking her every move. She had to stall.

Suisse raised his gun a little higher. "Even if you're wearing body armor over those cute little tits, it won't stop a bullet to the brain. Toss. The. Phone."

Wincing at the damage that was sure to occur to her brand-new phone, Vivian knelt to place it on the ground. She kicked it so that it slid across the pavement.

"You have to know he'll kill you if you hurt me."

"Exactly. You're my insurance policy. Reed coughs up five million and allows me to disappear, I might return you in one piece."

Vivian tossed her head as she laughed. "You idiot. He'll pay the five million and still hunt you down. Give up now and I'll let Detective Kwon take you in without involving Nicholas or his associates."

Suisse nudged his partner with one booted foot. "Eh, he won't be going anywhere for hours yet. You and I are taking a little ride." He motioned his free hand, indicating the nearby unmarked police sedan. "In you go, blondie."

Still trying to stall, Vivian took one small step around the front of the car.

"No! You're driving." He pointed at the driver's side door even as he kept the gun trained on her forehead.

This time, Vivian knew that the shadows behind the detective moved. She saw Dom slide, wraith-like, from behind an outbuilding. That he was there meant Nicholas was closer. Confidence straightened her spine.

Something with a matte finish but bright edges flashed between them. Suisse screamed. The gun in his hand jerked but did not fire. As he tried to juggle it to his left hand, Dom stepped up behind him and slid a wicked-looking blade against the detective's throat.

"You should've taken her offer." Nicholas strode into the light from Vivian's right. He brought his hand down in a chopping motion onto the policeman's wrist. Suisse screamed and fell to his knees, cradling his right arm from the elbow down. Vivian saw a small throwing knife protruding from the area just beneath his palm.

Nicholas knelt and checked Detective Kwon's pulse. "He's got a pulse and is breathing. Might be a skull fracture. Ambulance?"

Dom crouched over Suisse. "For Kwon, yes. We'll have to patch this asshole up before we fly him out, though. I think you hit an artery."

Pivoting, then standing, Nicholas walked to Vivian. She hadn't moved, or said anything, in several minutes. The latter fact terrified him. "Hey you." He reached out and pulled her into a tight hug. A shudder ran from her shoulders to her knees. The breath she took was fractured. "Shh. You're safe. Brave, and ridiculous, and beautiful, and safe."

She bent her head back, blue eyes alight with fury. "Ridiculous?"

"There's my girl."

She poked him in the side just below his protective vest. "Not your property."

Nicholas dropped his head to nuzzle her neck. "Property, no. *My* love, yes."

"I don't understand. Why didn't he shoot?"

"I severed his radial nerve." Seeing her still-questioning expression, he explained further. "He has the worst case of carpal tunnel ever."

"Oh. What are we going to do with him?"

"Well, I could rearrange his skeletal system, if you like."

Snuggled against his chest, Vivian shook her head. "I don't want him on your conscience. Or mine. Can't we call the FBI? Have them arrest him?"

"What do you say we leave that up to Detective Kwon? If he fails to handle it to your satisfaction, then you can tell me what hole you want me to drop *Mister* Suisse down."

CHAPTER FORTY-SIX

"Dom's taking Suisse out to the ship?" Vivian kicked her shoes off and slid into her chair in the workshop.

"For now. Kwon's badly concussed. We'll have to wait on his decision. I don't feel comfortable leaving Suisse in regular SPD custody."

"What if Kwon wants to bring Suisse up on charges?"

Nicholas paused in the process of putting away the weapons he and Dom had carried that night. "We'll show him the recording we have from your locket and all the evidence we've managed to gather. Hopefully, he'll have evidence that will hold up in court. But I think even if Seattle PD doesn't want any part of this, the Justice Department will. Some of those women were definitely transported across state lines."

"Are we going to find them? Alive?"

"I promise we'll try. It will be our only focus. I'll even add yet another debt to my tab with Cheyenne."

Vivian traced errant circles on the tabletop with her finger. "So, you're not mad?"

He turned, crossed his right leg over his left so that some of the weight was off his bad hip, and considered her. "Mad?"

"About my going off alone. I mean, it's not like you couldn't find me. I took the locket!" Defiant, she continued, "You heard every word, didn't you?"

"We did. Speaking of..." He stalked across the open space between them. She had to crane her head all the way back to see his face. He leaned over, one hand on each chair arm. The position brought her lips tantalizingly close. "There's something I've been meaning to tell you."

"Yes?"

Nicholas spanned the last few inches between their lips. He stroked her bottom lip with his tongue until her mouth opened beneath his. His kiss was slow, measured, testing. When she whimpered as he pulled away, his lips quirked in a quick smile. "What you said to Kwon was true. I *am* getting tired of you, romantically."

He managed to keep a straight face right up until she surged out of the chair. Laughing at her frustrated outburst, Nicholas caught her about the waist and spun her around. His callused hands slid up her sides, barely brushed the sides of her breasts and cupped her face. "I can't decide if you're more beautiful when you're angry with me or right after I've kissed you."

"So you're trying to combine the two?"

"Research purposes."

For several minutes their usual banter was replaced by warring tongues and wandering hands. Once again, it was Nicholas who pulled back first. He rested his forehead against hers. "Not here."

"Ever?" Her leg wrapped against his hip. She rose onto her tip toes, pressing against him from the chest down.

"Not." He kissed her lips. "While." He dragged his tongue across her collarbone. "I have." Hot breath puffed against the spot just behind her earlobe. "Self-control." His hand slid from the knee beside his hip all the way up the back of her thigh to the edge of her lace panties.

"Since when have you had self-control?" Her toes were barely on the floor now. He was holding her meshed against him.

"Since I met you." He toyed with her ponytail. "I have an extensive wine cellar and a gallon of mint chocolate chip waiting at home. Ready to celebrate?"

Vivian sobered. The man who'd destroyed her life—then tried to kill her—couldn't harm her ever again. But they'd only partially decapitated the Triad branch in Seattle. Shen Jun wouldn't stay away forever. He'd be back and looking for vengeance. She took a shuddering breath.

"Hey." Nicholas pulled her into a tight hug. "You're safe. I promise."

Her eyes brimmed with sudden tears. "I know I am, silly. It's you I'm worried about."

"Stop," he whispered. "I'm safer—I'm *better*—with you in my life."

Her smile lit up the basement. He held out his hand. "Come home with me?"

Eyes sparkling, she said, "But I thought you were tired of me?"

Nicholas nodded, every feature arranged to appear serious. "Well, we're still friends, of course."

"Do you kiss all of your friends like that?"

"Sure. Have fun comparing notes with Dom." Scooping to retrieve her shoes, he squeezed her hand. "Now, as my *very* good friend, will you please come home with me, Miss Richards?"

When they reached the Reed mansion, Nicholas raided the wine cellar after directing Vivian toward the freezer. Tiptoeing and giggling like teenagers, they made their way to Nicholas's bedroom. While she retreated to the bathroom to change one of his old hockey jerseys, he poured the wine. He left the glasses, spoons, and the opened container on a small table positioned next to the wide window seat. She took the hint. When he emerged from his own trip to the restroom, he found her curled on the cushions and looking out at the rainy remains of the night.

Nicholas placed his back against the wall before pulling Vivian back between his splayed legs. She turned her head to lay her cheek on his shoulder. Her wine glass was mostly empty, but the ice cream had barely been touched.

"Lightweight."

She grumbled under her breath. "Too late, or early, for ice cream."

"Do you want to go to sleep?"

"Mm hm. Right like this." She jerked a bit after realizing what she'd said. "If that's OK, I mean."

"It will be." He pushed her to a sitting position and gently pulled the rubber band from her hair. He ran both hands, fingers spread, into the thick mass of blond curls. "Your ponytail was attacking my nose." Adjustment made to his satisfaction, he pulled her back into the cage of his arms and legs. She snuggled down, making a soft mew of contentment.

When the first red arrows of dawn shot across the sky, they illuminated two heads resting against each other in peaceful sleep.

ABOUT THE AUTHOR

Cassandra Davis (Amy to her friends and family) was raised an army brat: constantly traveling, making new friends every four years, and surrounded by a unique military culture. In the seventh grade, she complained to her English teacher that she'd read every fiction book in the library. The teacher handed Cassandra a blank notebook and told her to write her own stories.

After working as a US Senate aide for four years, Mrs. Davis became a homeschooling mom and author. Her first novel, *Dremiks,* was p ublished in 2012. She now lives outside Austin with her husband, sons, and her Australian Shepherd. When not creating alien civilizations or superhero stories, Cassandra spends her time playing on-line games, baking tasty dairy-free recipes, and cheering for her University of Kentucky Wildcats.

You can follow her on:
Twitter: (@aCassandraDavis)

Facebook: (www.facebook.com/CassandraDavis.author)

Web: www.cassandradavis-author.com